Copyright © 2024 by N.O. One

One Love

No portion of this book may be reproduced in any form without written permission from the publisher or author, except as permitted by U.S. copyright law.

All Rights Reserved ©

This is a work of fiction. Names, characters, places, brands, media and incidents are either the product of the author's imagination or are used fictitiously. The author acknowledges the trademark status and trademark owners of various products referred to in this work of fiction, which have been used without permission. The publication/use of these trademarks is not authorized, associated with, or sponsored by the trademark owners.

Cover Design – The Pretty Little Design Co

Editing – Encompass Press Ltd

Cover Photography – Chris Brudenell

Cover Model – Sabrina Marzano

Published by Hudson Indie Ink

www.hudsonindieink.com

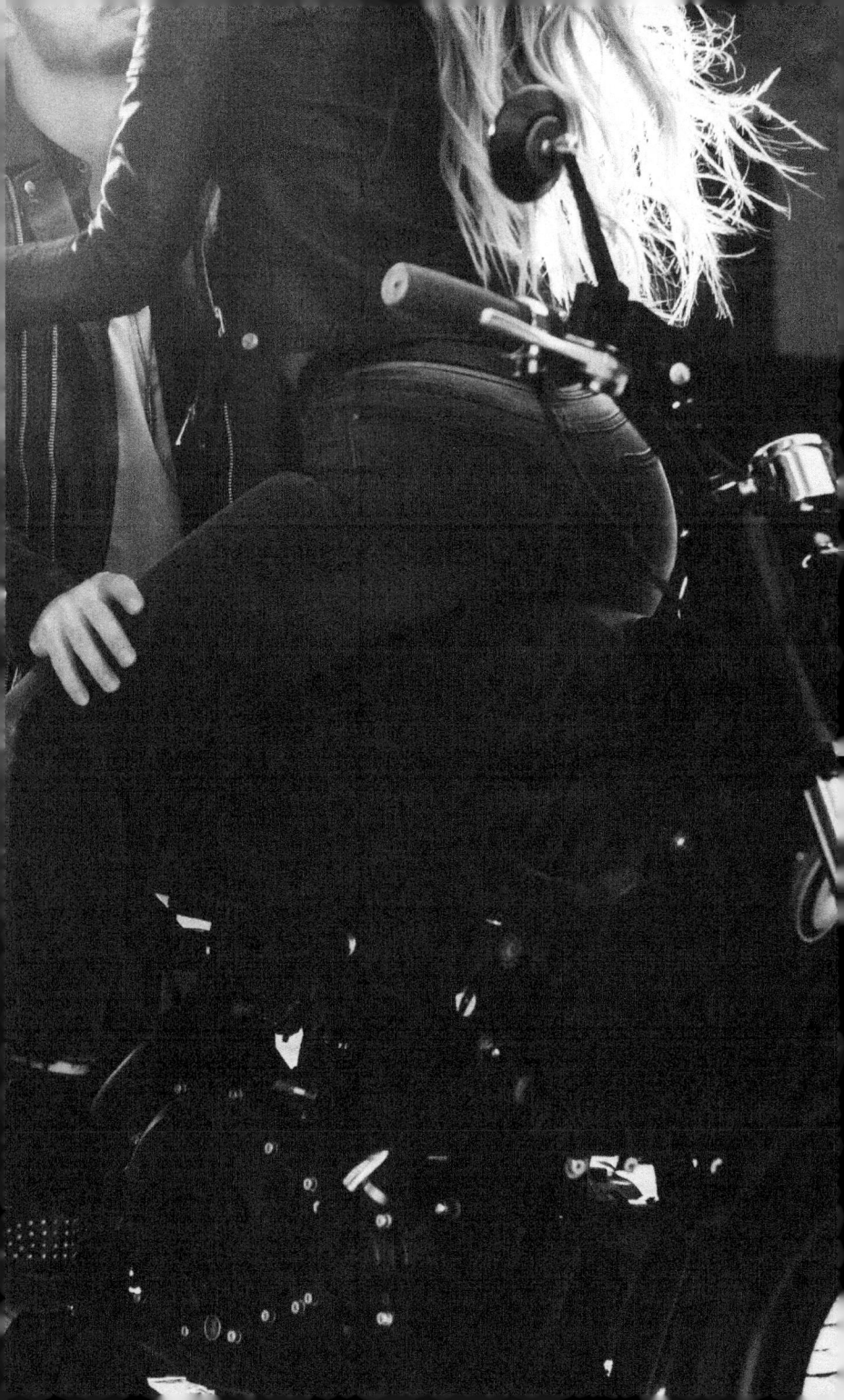

NEW YORK MAFIA
heirarchy

THE DON
Marco Mancini
↓
UNDERBOSS
Ray 'The Stinger' Martini
↓
CAPOS
J - Shadow

Tommy - Babyface

George - The Butcher

Eddie - Snake Eyes
↓
SOLDIERS & CREWS

on and on about the pain. Fucking hell, where did they get this guy?

"Gotta bolt!" Crank calls out as the chair he was occupying screeches back from his weight.

"Time's up." I'm about to stab him completely through his eye socket when he cries out.

"He's hiding out in his bunker. No one knows where it is. He's there with his family."

I nod, the information barely helpful, making me feel like I've wasted my fucking time.

Again.

"Night night." I stab the knife into his brain matter, over and over again, relieving my frustration in the process.

It's not his fault, he's just a soldier and didn't play a part in Murphy's death not even two weeks ago, but he works for the Irish mob and they will all pay for the blood on their hands.

After slaughtering every piece of shit who had a hand in killing Murphy, putting my daughter and me through Hell, at this point, I'm just picking off Irish mob lackeys, one by one. If I don't get the answers I want, they die. Also, even if they do give me answers…they die.

To this day, I still can't bring myself to go to Murph's house where it all went down. It's too much. Too soon. Too painful.

"Clean it up." My order isn't aimed at anyone in particular but I know my Reapers will take care of this problem. George or Jimmy or whatever the fuck this guy's name is...was, slumps down on the concrete floor as a pool of blood and internal juices surround his head like an evil halo. I look down at him, the permanent scowl I've sported on my face the last couple of weeks not wavering an iota as I wipe the blade of my knife and put it away.

"Let's go."

Marco Mancini has called a meeting of his capos. As the only female leader in any mafia I've ever heard of, I have the privilege of sitting at the table where important decisions are made. He may be my boss, but he's also one of the only people in this world that I trust.

I trusted Murphy, too. But they took him away from me.

I'm not the last to show up since I wasn't too far from his Upper East Side residence but I'm not the first either.

In fact, the house is like a fucking circus with kids running around all over the place. Like...a fucking boatload of them. One of them, I can't remember its name, comes up to me and hands me a drawing. I look down and frown.

"It's a bird." His words are all nasally like he's got a cold, which is confirmed when he sneezes all over my boots. It doesn't take much to make me scowl but I try really fucking hard not to scare away this...what? Four or five or six year old?

From the homemade clothes to the beads on his wrist and around his neck, I know this is one of Petal and Everest's kids. And judging by the noise, they're all here. Hell, I can't remember how many they've got now since she just keeps popping them out like a gumball machine.

"It doesn't look like a bird." I'm being honest but I'm not sure if that's the right thing to say to a kid.

"Phoenix!" I hear Petal's sweet voice calling out to her kid but I'm a little entranced by his deep green eyes. I'm betting he'll be scarred for life after seeing my beat-up face and the limp I'm sporting.

"Don't be sad, it'll be okay." I jolt back at his words like he's physically hit me. I don't have the chance to ask him what he means before his mother scoops him up and cuddles him tight against her chest while another kid presses against her back like a little monkey. I have no idea how that piece of cloth is holding his chubby ass in place.

"Sorry about that, he's very shy but once he finds a soul that speaks to him, he can't stay away."

I blink up at her and frown.

It's like we don't speak the same language.

"J, let's go!" Marco's voice brings me back to reality. Taking a step back I nod at the kid and give Petal what I hope is a smile.

"Have fun." I pass the drawing back to the kid but he shakes his head and walks away with his mother, hand in hand.

My stomach does a little flip as thoughts of Hallie crash into my mind. I never got a chance to see her grow up, and now I can't even be with her as she goes through the hardest years of her life.

Not that I could help her with that. I'm the story mothers tell their daughters to keep them from turning out like me.

Shaking off the emotions, I get my head back in the game and walk over to Marco's office where he meets with his capos.

I've been here a hundred times, at the very least, yet I'm always amazed by the soothing scent of the fireplace mixed with the spice of the whiskey he pours into his glass. One finger and two ice cubes.

"Take a seat, we've got a situation on our hands." Marco pauses and looks over at me, his eyes turning soft for the briefest of seconds like he wants to make all the rage and pain go away, but I give him a slight shake of my head. I can't do this right now. I can't linger on the events of these past ten days. I have a job to do and a man to hunt down and I can't do that if I'm all up in my feelings.

I'm sure I'll break down at one point, the mind and body physically need it to continue a balanced life, but right now is not that time. Then again, balance has never been an option for me so what the fuck do I know?

And Marco gets that, so he just continues like nothing happened.

"Eddie, what's the status?" I shift in my seat, my current position shooting electric shocks into the muscles of my side. Luckily, my ribs aren't broken but they *are* bruised all to hell, which means the only thing I can do is wait for them to heal.

The bullet to my leg? Well, it was a through-and-through so I had the doc patch me up and give me pain meds. I'd rather feel the pain every day than lie down for a week and lose my ever-loving mind.

"So far, we've lost three soldiers, Boss." Marco's head is down, his deadly gray eyes like daggers aimed straight at Eddie as if this is his fault. "You know the Pellerino kid?"

"Yes, he joined us last year." Marco's voice is even when he speaks. Too even for comfort.

"Right, well, we found him last night on the above-ground tracks at Yankee Stadium. Cops got there before us, though. Had to pay a fuckload of money to switch bodies with some guy who offed himself in Queens somewhere." I grit my teeth at Eddie's status update. Three of our men gone in such a short time happens. Three of our men killed in the exact same way? That's not weird, that's a pattern.

"What do you think, J? The Irish?" I wince when I try to move too quickly but do my best to downplay the pain. "And for fuck's sake, take a few days off and let your body heal. We need you."

Right, as if I could downplay anything in front of eagle-eyed Marco. I swear the man has the gift of telepathy.

"Will do, Boss," I lie, and he fucking knows it, but says nothing more, just waits for my thoughts. "I don't think it's the Irish here. Found out today that Ronan is hiding out in a bunker." Everyone around me chuckles and I can't help the small curl of my mouth, then grit my teeth again as it splits my bottom lip. When I get my hands on the guys who beat the fuck out of me, I'll split their lips too...from ear to fucking ear.

"The Shadow has him pissin' in his pants is what I heard last night. Fucking right," George says, a toothpick dangling from the corner of his mouth and pride in his eyes when he winks at me. It's not a condescending thing he does because I'm a woman. I think he has a tick. Fucker winks at his car most days.

"Find him." Although Marco's wrath isn't aimed at me, the determination in his glare tells me he wants the head of whoever is fucking with us on a platter.

"On it," is all I need to say to convince him the problem will be solved.

"What about Mr. Wright at the Galanos casino? Find anything on that guy?" Ah, mister misogynist prick who doesn't like to lose to women? Yeah, I need to follow up on that asshole, too. We may not know what his deal is but something's not right. Ergo, we're watching him closely. So many people to kill, so little time to plan.

"Yeah, I'm going on Thursday. Galanos said he's there like clockwork." Considering it's Sunday, it'll give me some time to heal my face and body before showing up at a casino looking like death fucked me over.

"Good."

Twenty minutes later, we're dismissed but I don't make it more than three feet outside his office door before I hear the click-clacking of River's heels along the marble floors, the pitter patter of four tiny paws trying to keep pace with her.

"J! Holy shit! Who did this? I'll fucking have them chopped up in tiny pieces!" I almost laugh at her indignation on my behalf, then remember that laughing would hurt like a bitch so I force a frown to stay in place. Not that it's any better, but at least it's a familiar expression for me.

"Calm down, *Tesoro*. Your days of stabbing people with your heels are over."

"Not if I can help it." She mumbles her words as Marco plants an open-mouthed kiss on her lips that lasts only a second. "And don't distract me, I'm pissed off." She turns to Marco and grabs him by the shirt collar, pulling him in close enough for their lips to touch as she speaks. "You fix this. Okay? You fix this."

Fuck, the emotions in her voice make my ribs hurt all over again. River was there when Murphy died, she held my daughter in her arms, comforting her as best she could while I said my goodbyes. She cried for me, for Hallie. But beneath the huge heart, this woman is fierce and deadly in her own right. A true queen standing next to a king.

"*Te lo prometto*, Tesoro."

I've been around long enough to know he'll keep that promise, no matter the consequences, because disappointing his wife is nothing less than impossible.

"*Bene.*" River's Italian is heavily accented but nobody cares. I feel like a voyeur, but just when I'm about to turn around and walk away, River turns her green eyes on me and fuck...I feel a demand coming on. "Come on, you deserve to relax!"

Just as she speaks, an uproar of children's voices cry out like they've just seen a ghost and I cringe. How in the living fuck is this supposed to be relaxing?

I'm ushered to the rooftop, an excited River pulling me by the wrist like I'm five, and the overwhelming urge to shake her off is real. I tamp that shit down because hurting her feelings feels worse than beating up someone's pet. Everyone has a line they won't cross...mine is kids and animals. Everything else is fair game.

"Petal and Everest are here and they brought their babies! I don't know how they deal with so many at a time but they're organized and everyone has a role. It's fascinating." I'm pretty sure River's a little high on estrogen because I've never heard her speak this quickly before.

As long as I've known River, she's had no desire to have children. I'm guessing it has something to do with the fact that she basically raised her brother, Everest, all on her own when their parents died; River was only seventeen then.

But she's pregnant now so I'm guessing the idea is growing on her. Literally.

"I don't want to intrude." Translation, I don't want to be up here.

"Please," she scoffs. "Petal doesn't understand the word intrude. Everyone is always welcome everywhere."

Not sure everyone can appreciate that kind of viewpoint. If someone came to my place without an invitation, they'd get the barrel of my gun as a welcome mat.

As soon as my face hits the cool air of the Manhattan sky, I take a breath, but it's instantly cut short when I feel tiny hands pulling at my jeans. Looking down, I see a munchkin with curly blond hair and big blue eyes looking up at me, arms and legs pumping up and down like he wants to jump.

I just stare at him, unsure what I'm supposed to do here.

"He wants you to take him in your arms." Phoenix is back, one hand on the top of his brother's head like he's trying to calm him.

"I don't think that's a good idea." My eyes dart from Phoenix to his little brother. Fuck, I forgot their names.

It's only when I lock eyes with the little one that I remember. Deep blue eyes so big it's almost a caricature.

"Ocean," I whisper, and Phoenix's smile is immediate, like my remembering his brother's name is a gift.

"Yes!"

"I can't pick him up, my body is a little hurt."

Phoenix nods, smiles, then takes his brother's wrist and pulls him back. "See ya!"

I smile at that and wave my hand when River calls me to sit with her and Petal.

Fucking hell, I hope I don't have to bond.

Immediately, I'm transported back to a couple of months ago when Hallie, my beautiful, kind, heartbroken Hallie, begged me to go get a manicure with her. Although it was the most excruciating experience of my life—I say this without exaggeration—it is also the most precious memory I have of me and my daughter.

Fuck, I miss her.

Her grandparents called me only a few hours after literally ripping her from my arms after her father's funeral, telling me that she was safe and better off with them in Florida.

Here's the thing. In the eyes of the law, I don't exist. And with the work I do, I cannot exist. Therefore, a legal custody battle is impossible. So, for right now, I'm going to wait it out, choose the right time before I get my daughter back.

Only when the head of the Irish mob is hanging from the proverbial tree will I bring her into my world. Until then, I'll allow her to stay with her grandparents where I know they'll keep her safe.

Compromise.

"Oh, J, come sit with us." Everything in me screams to run as Petal reaches her hand out and motions for me to sit on their outdoor sofas, heat lamps all around. The youngest of her kids is fast asleep against her shoulder, his tiny body wrapped up tight in the cloth that envelops Petal's entire back and torso.

"Stefano is taking the kids to watch a documentary about bees and honey." I frown at Petal's words and their choice of movies. Don't kids like cartoons? Video games? At least this explains the sudden relative silence falling over us. Honking horns in New York is just background white nose. "Briggs chose it and Everest is all too happy to join them." Briggs is their first born, probably eight years old by now. Fuck, his birth was like a breath of fresh air for River and Everest. Petal too, obviously, but that's a story for another time.

N.O. ONE

"So, I wanted to have you here for Kai's birthday. You know how important it is for me to keep his memory alive, but also to give you this." March eleventh...River's words and her solemn tone make sense. The festivities, the big crowd. River always makes a big deal of today like it's her way to ask for forgiveness. She hands a small brown box to Petal, a satin green bow on top, and grins from ear to ear.

There's almost a smile on my own face. I'm curious about what River's going to announce but I have a feeling I already know. I ignore the warmth in my chest at having been told before Petal, but mostly, I'm honored to be here in this intimate moment between us three women. It's strange how different we are, how worlds apart our stories began, yet here we are, together, sharing important moments in our lives.

"Oh, you made the box out of wine corks! It's amazing, I love it so much." Petal is more engrossed with the rows of corks aligned perfectly to make a box than she is with the actual gift inside. I'm two seconds away from ripping the bow off so we can get on with it and I can go home. "J, that reminds me. You should use witch hazel on your bruises, it helps the blood flow, makes them heal faster. Or Epsom salt in the bath. My mother used to do that all the time, but she only had me so it was easy. With five boys, it's easier to dab some witch hazel and continue on my way." She speaks as she pulls the bow free, glancing at me once in a while, her smile perpetually on her lips.

"Will do." My nod is like a full stop to this entire conversation.

Once the cardboard is pulled back, it takes Petal a second to understand what she's looking at. But once she does, her squeal is genuine, her happiness palpable.

"Oh my goddess! You're pregnant?" Tears are immediate between the two women, their arms wrapped around each other wholly in support of one another. It's some witchy magic that the kid is still asleep. Then again, with the sheer amount of pot Everest smokes, I'm thinking his little swimmers have built-in sleeping pills in their DNA.

"I guess we'll be going through our pregnancies together." There's a brief moment of silence and it takes me a second to realize what Petal is saying.

Holy shit, they're both pregnant? Six kids? In eight...well, nine years?

My vagina takes this moment to close the door, lock it, and swallow up the key. Definitely not a life for me. For Petal and Everest though, it seems kind of perfect.

"Congratulations to you both. I have to go, need some rest." Both women look up at me and Petal stands, all barely five feet of her, and places her hands on my cheeks, her eyes mesmerizing and impossible to ignore.

"You'll find happiness, J. You will, I promise. Grief comes in stages. Breathe them in, take stock in each of those feelings, do not ignore them. The bruises on your body will fade but if you ignore the bruise in your heart, it won't be able to heal."

I nod, my jaw tight to avoid any leakage from my eyes. It's a bad time to be crying. Plus, the salt hurts my cuts.

"I'll do my best. Thank you." Attempting a smile, I nod and walk away as the women cuddle up and start talking about babies and clothes. By the time I reach the stairs, I hear blissful silence.

I'm happy for them. Truly, I am. But it all just makes me miss my baby girl.

I say my goodbyes to Stefano, who's busy caring for the kids and all their foody needs—although I'm sure Everest is eating for four—and head out to my truck when my phone buzzes in my back pocket.

> **Unknown:** How did you survive all those kids?

This motherfucker's stalker tendencies are starting to piss me off. More concerning than this weird flirting he's trying to pull off is the fact that he somehow knows what's going on inside the Mancini mansion. I mean, sure, he did try to help when Murphy and Hallie were kidnapped by giving me their address. And yeah, he gifted me Riley all trussed up and ready to die, but this shit needs to stop.

As always, I forward the message to Glitch without the faintest hope of getting a hit of where or who this guy could possibly be, adding a job for him to do while I'm at it.

> **Me**: Do a security check on the Mancini house for any breaches and fix that shit.

> **Glitch**: On it.

I ignore my stalker at first, jumping in my truck and turning on the engine.

> **Unknown**: You'll find me when I'm ready to be found.

> **Me**: Fuck off.

Chapter Two
J

Being a semi-regular in Galanos's casino means I no longer feel the need to wear the stupid cocktail dresses to fit in. My black pants, tank top, and blazer will do just fine. They know me there now. It would seem my reputation precedes me, especially after my little show in that first meeting. A meeting that seems like it was a lifetime ago.

So much has changed in such a short space of time, and while I'm all about taking what comes and dealing with it, I think I'm close to my limit.

That being said, the casino is actually a welcome change of pace. My bruises aren't fully healed and I still have a limp if I'm not concentrating like fuck on keeping it hidden, but despite initially not wanting to come here looking like this, I've decided I no longer give a shit.

"All in." This guy's got a major tell when he's bluffing, and as he clears his throat and sits up straighter, I know I'm gonna call this fucknut.

With a smile—that no longer cracks my lips open, thank God—I take a deep breath, as if I'm really debating what to do. It's just the two of us left and I'd hoped this would last a little longer, but his predictability is boring me.

"Call." I push my chips into the center of the table and watch as he smugly places his cards down, face up, to show the ace of hearts and the king of spades.

It's a good hand to have pre-flop, but those first three cards have come and gone and we've already had the turn, with only the river card to come. Basically, it's his last play and he's got fuck all but a hope and a prayer.

The cocky grin on his face quickly disappears, replaced by a little anger as I show that I have two-pair. Threes and fives. At this point, even if he hit an Ace on the river, he'd still lose.

The dealer places the final card down, declares me the winner by pushing all the chips over to me, and begins clearing the cards from the table while the guy just looks lost, as though he might cry. I don't wait around for his commentary, preferring to say nothing more as I stack my chips before picking them up and walking away.

Well, that was unsatisfactory to say the least. Mr. Wright hasn't been here all night, so I've spent the last two hours occupying myself at the tables hoping Zavier will make an appearance. I have some questions for him, but I want him to come to me. If he thinks he's important enough for me to continuously chase down, he's severely mistaken.

I scan the dimly-lit room as I make my way over to the cashier. There are way more men here than women, which fucks me off a little, but I have to give it to Galanos, he has employed just as many male servers as he has women. His croupiers are a healthy mix too. Speaking of croupiers, it's been a while since I've seen the one I'm sure was on the take. Maybe the casino's security finally picked up on it and fired his ass, or left him dead by the side of the road. Either way, not my circus.

"What a vision in black you are." Zavier, who had the idiotic idea of opening up a casino in Marco's territory without giving him a heads up, is lucky he's not standing any closer. The tip of the blade now hidden in my palm comes close to his ball sack as I turn around to face him.

He has a wide, toothy grin on his annoyingly handsome face, his dark brows rising in surprise as he looks down to see how close he came to being castrated.

"Didn't realize you were so desperate to get in my pants, Shadow. But I'm a behind-closed-doors kinda guy." He smirks, raising his hands and stepping back with a small chuckle.

"Shame. I'm an out-in-the-open kinda gal. We'd never work." I shrug, sliding my dagger back up under my cuff, and he laughs louder this time. I ignore it, opting to get to my point because I need to get out of this stuffy environment. "I have some questions, Galanos."

"What happened to calling me Z? I kinda liked that, you know. Our own little nicknames for each other." He feigns offense, widening his eyes and shaking his head. I continue to stare at him, not needing to respond to his bullshit right now. "Ah, okay. We've got our serious work face on tonight. Do you wanna come to my office?" He tilts his head toward the door leading off the main floor, that cocky grin still gracing his lips.

"Not really, but I can't threaten you properly for answers out here. Too many witnesses." It's my turn to smirk, but it doesn't faze him. He just rolls his eyes dramatically and gestures for me to follow.

Frustrating man.

Most men like him would be quivering in their polished shoes, but there's something different about him. I don't think I like it.

Closing the office door behind me, I watch Zavier head toward his desk and perch on the edge to face me, palms on the surface as he crosses his legs in front of him. The picture of cool, calm, and collected.

"You had questions?"

I had expected him to beat around the bush a little more, but him being straightforward makes this easier.

"There have been bodies piling up around town, with a similar M.O. to your cousin, Yiannis. What do you know?" I could try and use seduction to make him answer me, or torture, both get the job done, but I get the impression neither would work with Zavier. He's smarter than he lets on.

The look of genuine shock that briefly crosses his usually cocky features tells me all I need to know before he even speaks.

"Isn't my cousin dead? Killed by his own brother years ago?"

"Yeah, but it's pretty suspicious that you rock up to the city and now we're finding bodies with a connection to your family history." It is suspicious, but I don't for one second think it's him, he doesn't seem like the type to get his hands dirty and his reactions aren't that of a guilty man right now.

I'm fucking great at my job and reading people and sensing lies come as naturally to me as breathing. This is the only reason Zavier is still standing, because I draw the line at killing innocents. Well...semi-innocents; Zavier isn't exactly an angel, but he's not done anything worthy of me bleeding him dry as of yet.

"Of all the things you could find me suspicious of, murder isn't one of them, Shadow. But I think you already know that, don't you?" He raises an eyebrow and smirks again.

Deciding to drop this line of questioning, because if he has nothing to do with it, he doesn't need any more information than I've already dropped, I take a seat on the leather armchair directly in front of him. This puts me at a lower level than him while still basically standing, showing him my guard has dropped.

It hasn't, but impressions are everything.

"Okay. What's the deal with Mr. Wright then? I know you're not telling me everything there."

His booming laugh fills the small space as he shakes his head. "You're something else, woman." He pushes off from the desk and crouches down in front of me so we're at eye-level again and rests his palms on my thighs. "Why don't you tell me a few things? Like why I haven't seen you riding that sexy ass bike of yours lately."

My eyes are drawn to his hands, lying perfectly still, unmoving, but causing a bubbling anger to rise from the pit of my stomach. He begins to slide his hands close to my pelvis, so slowly, pausing when I answer him. "It was stolen."

"Shame." Hands still on my thighs, he stands, leaning over me, his face moving closer to mine like he's about to kiss me. More like he's trying to distract me.

Just as I'm about to show his nether regions the tip of my dagger, the fire alarms start blaring and Zavier jumps back, glaring at the camera in the corner of the room. The sprinklers burst open next, spraying us and everything in the room, and no doubt inside the casino.

"Dick move. Come on, Shadow. Fire exit's just out there."

I know exactly where the fire exits in this place are, but whatever. Saved by the bell and all that. Well, Zavier's ball sack was saved.

Now soaking wet, I walk out through the office door to see the sprinklers haven't gone off anywhere other than Zavier's office, but the alarm is still blaring and everyone is casually making their way outside the building. I don't want to be here when the fire department and police turn up, so without a goodbye, I leave Zavier behind, making my way through the small crowd of people toward my truck.

Some greasy-haired fucknut with a death wish knocks into me without an apology, and I've just about had enough of being touched by anyone tonight. The bruises on my face are a lot less prominent now, but the hole in my leg still fucking hurts and I don't appreciate inconsiderate people.

The dagger at my wrist is getting a lot of near-use this evening, and for the third time tonight, I let it free from the binding and it slides into my palm. *I can just stab this man a little bit and walk away.* I'm following him, getting closer to where he has now stopped to talk to one of the servers from the casino, and he's complaining about his belongings or some shit. As I move to stab him in the ribs, another fucker with a death wish nudges me out of the way.

"Fuckers!" My outburst makes greaseball turn around and roll his eyes at me before he continues his complaint.

I'm done with tonight. Where's the other fucker who bumped me? I'm more angry at being stopped from stabbing someone than I was at being knocked a little by the greasy fuck.

Taking a calming breath, my eyes scan the small crowd of people...nothing gives any of them away as the stab-blocker. Fuck it. I do notice Zavier talking to someone I haven't seen around here before though, and if I'm being honest with myself, the new dude's got a fine-ass profile. A sleeve of dark, swirling tattoos over his forearm, the black T-shirt he's wearing hugs his figure perfectly...

Then guilt punches me in the gut for thinking of someone else other than Murphy like this. I should be able to appreciate a fine man, but no. My second chance with Murphy had barely begun before it was all ripped away and now I just don't think that kind of thing is in the cards for me anymore.

Shaking my head and calling it a night, I head back toward my truck, sitting behind the wheel and staring into the dark sky as soon as I'm inside. I turn the heater on because it's fucking cold, especially after being drenched by the sprinklers in Zavier's office. The engine rumbles to life and I begin my drive home, going over what I've learned tonight.

Which is absolutely fuck all.

I do need to stay away from Zavier though, because he seems to think he has a right to touch me and I'm trying real hard not to stab him in the ass for it.

Once I'm parked outside my apartment building, the drive home almost a blur, my phone buzzes in my pocket.

> **Stalker:** You look good wet.

> **Me:** Fuck off.

> **Stalker:** Smelled good too.

> **Me:** Fuck off.

> **Stalker:** I love your witty responses. So unique and imaginative.

> **Me:** Fuck off.

I could just not respond, completely ignore whoever this person is, but they're just so persistent, I kinda admire it. Kinda. I forward the chain of messages to Glitch again, knowing he's going to find a grand total of nothing, like every other time before this, but I need to do something.

I'm totally helpless against this person and haven't got a clue who it could be. They've been useful, but also super creepy with their knowledge, and I'm not sure if I want to stab them or hug them when I finally find them. Probably stab them.

An hour later, after I've showered and climbed into bed, another message comes through.

> **Stalker:** Goodnight, Stabby Queen.

> **Me:** Fuck off.

Chapter Three

J

"I miss him." Hallie's confession breaks another wilted piece of my heart, especially when her voice breaks on her last word.

"Me too, Hals." It's a different type of loss for Hallie and me. I mourn the what-could-have-been while she's mourning everything she had and will never be able to experience again. His sweet morning smiles, his soul-healing hugs, his wit and his unwavering ability to love without conditions. Mostly, she'll miss being the center of his existence. One day, I'd like to be that for her. At least one thing is for certain, I will do everything in my power to fulfill that for her.

"Are you going to see him today?" The background noise on her end stops as she speaks, a shrill bell going off somewhere in the distance. "Shoot, I have to get to class."

"Yeah, I'll tell him you miss him. Go to class and text me when you can." I want to add a million words before we hang up but each and every one of them is choking me, unable to escape the tightness of my throat.

Today marks exactly one month since we lost Murphy. No, not lost. He was ripped away. Ripped away by savage monsters who thrive on the pain of the innocent.

Marco's organization may have a shit ton of blood on its hands but we do our best to uphold the rule of not killing the innocent. We certainly don't kidnap good people to make bad people come out of their hiding holes. Although, the longer Ronan Callaghan stays buried in his safehouse, the more difficult it's going to be for me to hold up my end of that particular rule.

When Hallie was taken from me at Murphy's funeral three weeks ago, all I saw for days was red. A veil of hatred and violence flowing freely through my mind. Then, slowly, I began to think about the options. Did I really want her exposed to my life and my job on the daily? No. But I also did not want her to be far away from me. Certainly not fucking Florida, on the opposite end of the fucking coastline. Yet, here we are, having brief conversations when her grandparents aren't watching her. She texts me late at night and sometimes calls me during the day when she's in school, like right now—minutes before her first class.

It helps that we're in the same time zone but it's just not enough for me.

I need to figure out another way to have her near me but also safe. It's a fucking conundrum.

Padding over to the kitchen for my second cup of coffee, I sigh at the warmer weather making its appearance. April is touch and go in this area but it's usually a time where we start shedding our winter clothes. So much so, I slept in just my underwear and a cotton tank top. I drop a pod into the machine and lean against the counter just as the buzzer goes off on the intercom. Who the fuck is that? Nobody knows where I live outside of the Reapers and they would text me before showing up.

Out of habit, I grab a gun from the miscellaneous drawer—which isn't all that miscellaneous to be honest—and swipe my sweatpants off the chair.

Standing to the side of the door, I pick up the receiver to the intercom and wait a beat before speaking.

"Yeah?" I know, I know, original.

"Delivery." A deep, slightly accented voice murmurs over the line before hanging up.

I didn't order anything, for obvious digital footprint reasons, so this early Monday morning disturbance is making all the hairs on my body stand up straighter than a virgin cock at a whorehouse.

After placing the receiver back on its holder, I slip on my sweats then push my feet into the old Vans I only wear to go to the mailbox and look out the peephole before opening my door, gun at the ready.

My hallway is empty but for the security cameras that I know store the recent footage somewhere in the basement. I once had Glitch access the footage after a couple of neighbors complained about "hoodlums walking the halls." Their words, not mine. Turned out it was a bunch of teens hanging out with a friend who lives on the second floor. I swear to fuck, some people are paranoid to the core. Needless to say, no one knows I checked and they never will.

With my keys and phone in my pocket, I close the door behind me, making sure it's locked and secure before going downstairs. Actually down the stairs, not the elevator. If something is happening right now, I don't want to be stuck in a metal box and at a disadvantage.

Once I reach the first floor, my senses are on high alert, aware of Mrs. Perry exiting her apartment just across from the main entrance. Turning my body just in time to shove my gun behind the elastic of my sweats at the small of my back, I give her a neutral smile. In all the years I've lived here, I haven't spoken more than ten words to any of the other residents. This woman? Well, she clearly has zero fucks to give about what I do or do not want. In fact, I'm pretty sure she sees me as some kind of kindred spirit, but not in a Petal love-and-rainbows kind of way. Oh, hell no. She's one vicious broad, and of all the people in the world, she's one of my favorites. Not that I'd ever tell her that or she might just invite me in to play Bridge with all her other bitchy seniors. Did I mention Mrs. Perry is pushing eighty-five? She's a widow and, to be honest, I'm not a hundred percent sure she didn't put him in the grave herself with that viper tongue of hers.

It's her love language and, clearly, it's become our own special brand of banter.

"Well, don't you look like a whore out of business?" What does that even mean? I blink twice at her as she makes her way to the mailboxes, her thick New York accent punctuating every syllable. For her age, she's surprisingly alert, her cat-eyed glasses—circa nineteen sixty-three—giving her glare an extra punch as she eyes me up and down.

Sure, I'm not exactly dressed to the nines, but sheesh, a whore? Out of business, at that.

"Well, at least I can remember what a cock looks like." I give her a pointed look, all the while following her walking progression so that my back stays hidden from her.

Mrs. Perry chuckles, one corner of her mouth ticking up. "You're not the only one."

I outright grin at her words, not in the least bit surprised that she's still getting her big *O* on at her age. Way to go, grandma. Way to fucking go. But I don't say that, it would disrupt our regular routine.

Just as she places her hand on the buzzer to unlock the glass doors, she points her chin to the mailboxes, looking over her right shoulder. "A young man that looked like he'd spent the better half of his life in prison dropped something off in your mailbox." Christ, who needed cameras with Mrs. Perry around?

"Nosy much?" Reaching into my pocket for my keys, I punch one into the keyhole and smirk.

"Someone has to be." Her retort has me shaking my head. This building has every angle covered in cameras, it's the reason my small apartment costs significantly more than other buildings around here.

There's always the chance of someone watching.

Before the doors completely close, she throws out her last remark. "White looks good on you."

I grin, knowing full well she's never seen me in anything but black and probably never will again.

Watching her leave, I survey the grounds as she steps into a car she's probably hired for the morning. Either her husband left her a fortune or she's making bank at her weekly Bridge games. Both options are possible.

Once the car pulls around the circular drive to the building, my attention returns to the mailbox where a set of keys rests on top of a plain piece of paper. I don't touch it, looking around again as if someone is going to jump out of the corners somewhere and knock me out. I step back so all the shadowy parts of the floor are visible before returning my attention to the keys.

They look familiar but that's impossible. What the actual fuck?

My hand flies in and out of the box, quickly grabbing the keys like a snake is there waiting for me.

Holy fuck, it can't be. How?

Gritting my teeth, I snap up the paper and read it three times before it makes any kind of sense.

NOT BROKEN JUST BRUISED.
FIXED HER UP FOR YOU

N.O. ONE

My eyes dart from the note to the keys and back to the note, trying to make sense of this crazy as fuck situation. Is the Irish mob playing with me? Teasing me? Or maybe it's a trap. Kill myself on the bike...problem—aka me—solved. It's not like they haven't tried before when they ran me off the road last month, destroying my bike in the process. I'd had to run off to safety, but when I came back to the scene, the bike was gone. I'd always assumed it was the Irish who took it...was I wrong?

Stepping closer to the doors, I look outside as I make sure my tank top is pulled over my gun and hiding the obvious bulge. I look left, then right, then left again before craning my neck to the right. That's when I see her.

From this distance, my baby looks as new as the day I bought it, and although I'm weary as fuck, I can't ignore my accelerating heartbeat as I see her there, shiny and blood red, waiting for me to ride her.

Pressing the same buzzer Mrs. Perry punched earlier, I take a tentative step outside. My gaze scans my surroundings, looking for anyone who could be responsible for this but only seeing the street lined with a few cars and the occasional van.

My hand digs into my pocket for my phone, thinking Crank needs to go over every inch of her to make it's not some kind of death trap.

"Yeah, Boss." Crank's voice booms in my ear after the first ring.

"Get a crew over here with a van." My voice is low, my words clear.

"Your place?" It's barely eight-thirty, we usually don't have anything going on until around ten. Flexible hours are the shit.

"Yeah."

"On it, Boss." We hang up and I just keep staring at her, shocked that she looks almost brand new. There's a weird scratch just under the cap on the gas tank, a triangle of sorts that wasn't there before the crash. Yet, I know for a fact this is my bike.

Someone's fucking with me and I will figure out who it is, but first, I need to change into something worthy of my slick bitch on wheels.

Thirty minutes later, the bike is pushed up into the van, secured with ratchet straps hooked onto four different lashing points and taken straight back to our garage where Crank immediately begins to look her over. I followed with my truck, my mind whirling a mile a minute trying to figure out who the fuck is doing this.

All I know is that the voice on the intercom didn't ring any bells and that Mrs. Perry saw some tough guy putting something in my mailbox. I'm assuming he had tattoos all over his body and face for her to automatically think he'd been in prison, but I'm not eighty-five, we don't have the same social norms.

Wait...

The keys weren't just dropped in there, they were carefully placed. And how the fuck did he get into the building?

Goddammit. As if I didn't have enough shit going on with my life.

Could it be the very real pain in my ass who keeps texting me? I know, I know, he's helped me in the past, but holy fuck, this whole stalker game is driving me insane. If he wants my attention, he's going to get it and it won't be pretty.

Unless it's the Irish, but for some reason my gut tells me otherwise. Why would they go to the trouble of this whole charade if a bullet to the brain could be just as effective?

"So, it was just there?" Fizz is eyeing the bike like it's a caged animal infected with rabies.

"Yeah, with this note." I hand her the paper I found, never removing my eyes from Crank as he checks the fuel line for any holes.

"Got something?" I mean, a fuel leak could blow me to pieces if the tank is full and creates some kind of spark, right?

"Nah, all clear so far." At his words, I stop, my hands on my hips and my eyes narrowed, staring into space as I try to put the pieces of this bizarre puzzle together.

"Sounds like your stalker, to be honest." I nod at Fizz's words.

"Yeah, it's crossed my mind." More than that, I'm pretty fucking sure this dude's fucking with me. Although, there are worse things than gifting me my bike back.

"How much longer, Crank? It's not like you're building her up all over again." Yeah, yeah, I'm a little short but fuck, I still haven't had my coffee and I shouldn't be allowed to people without a proper dose of caffeine.

Crank's head looks over the seat of the bike as he crouches on the other side, his brow going up as if telling me to calm my tits but knowing better than to give me lip.

"I'll grab some coffee." I mutter my words and just as I'm about to turn away, I throw over my shoulder. "Hurry the fuck up."

"Yeah, Boss."

Fucker.

"You're crankier than usual." Fizz chuckles, and when I frown at her she holds her hands up in surrender, trying her best not to laugh. "Crankier…like Crank? Get it?"

I have to fight the urge to roll my eyes because I'm not a thirteen-year-old teen and immediately, the familiar pang in my chest immobilizes me for a second before I reach the coffee station and fill my bloodstream with caffeine.

"Where's Glitch?"

Fizz shrugs as she sips her coffee. "Probably in his nerd cave."

I snort. We used to call it the bat cave but he insists that he's a self-proclaimed nerd and very fucking proud of it. Who am I to burst his bubble? He's a lot hotter than any nerd I've ever met with his black-rimmed glasses, disheveled brown hair, and colorful inked sleeves on both arms.

"Do you know if he's got anything on Mr. Wright?" May as well kill two birds with one stone.

"Not sure. I heard Glitch got a home address so Shoo and Tab staked out his house last night. The car looked like an army feasted on fast food this morning. Fucking gross." Her black curls swing back and forth as she vehemently shakes her head at her words. "They said something about following him out to the turnpike then losing him shortly after that."

"How the fuck did they lose him again?" Fucking Christ, who is this guy, Houdini?

"No idea, you'll have to ask them."

I glare at Fizz but I'm not really looking at her. My mind is trying to make sense of all of this shit.

"Boss!" Crank's booming voice gets all of my attention as he calls out for me.

"Find something?"

"Nah, she's clean except for that chicken scratch. It's the same bike, I checked the serial number we created for her. Only the body on the right side has changed, I'm guessing it was replaced when they fixed her up." Wiping the tank off with his rag, he rubs a little harder just below the gas cap. "What's this?" I know what he's asking but I want his take on it first.

"What do you think it is?" I watch his brow furrow as his head turns this way and that.

"Looks like a triangle." I nod at his words, agreeing.

"That's what I thought, too." I step away, still confused when his next words get my attention again.

"Could be the letter D."

My phone buzzes in my hand with an incoming text. Motherfucker.

> **Stalker**: You like my gift?

> **Me**: I don't take handouts.

> **Stalker**: It's a gift, not the same thing.

What is this guy's deal? If he thinks he's impressing me with his stealth stalker vibes, he's...well, not completely wrong but I'd burn in the depths of Hell before giving him that satisfaction.

> **Me**: If you want me to take it, give it to me in person.

> **Stalker**: I did.

I frown at my screen. What the fuck is he talking about?

> **Stalker**: You should be more careful with your surroundings.

Racking my brain, I try to remember anything I could have missed out there this morning.

The street, the cars...the van. Was he in there the whole time? How did I miss that?

> **Me**: Stop your fucking games and tell me who you are.

Out of frustration, I do the most useless thing possible in this situation but at least it makes me feel just a little bit more in control. I change his fucking name—again—in my phone because Pain In My Fucking Ass is much more fitting than a plain old stalker.

> **PIMFA**: When the time is just right.

Chapter Four

J

This isn't where I expected to be when Murphy and Hallie found me in Alma's diner two months ago. To be honest, I don't usually plan that far ahead, but I was beginning to see a life forming with them. I could have made it work. Somehow.

"I suppose this is the universe telling me I was stupid to even think I could have some kind of normality with you, Murph. Whatever that is." I huff a low laugh as I stare at Murphy's headstone. Fuck, I sound like River's sister-in-law with all the hippie universe shit.

Sighing heavily, I pull the petals from one of the dead roses sitting across his grave. I need to compartmentalize this whole thing because, in my line of work, stewing over this kind of tragedy will only fuck me up. Make me lose focus. And this is why I allow myself to mourn my parents once a year, so I don't combust from trying to hold it all in. Guess I'll be adding another to that list.

Thankfully though, I can remove one name from that list. I no longer have to mourn the loss of my baby girl. I finally get to celebrate her life. But to do that, I need to fix everything first. I may have missed her beginning, but I vow to be there for everything else. Her own personal shadow to keep her safe.

"I swear I'll get our girl back, Murph. I won't allow her to lose both of us."

The only members of the Irish mob my Reapers and I have been able to locate recently are Riley's sister and his daughter. It's a fucking shame women and children are off limits because threatening Ronan with them would for sure have him crawling out of his hole—or maybe not. People like him don't generally give a shit about anyone but themselves.

We're stretched thinner than usual with the Mr. Wright job on top of the string of dead mafia soldiers to clean up, plus the whole trying to figure out my mystery texter and hunting down the Irish bastards who managed to flee. Meaning nothing seems to be getting our sole attention right now, which isn't how we usually work.

"Why couldn't you have just stayed away from me, huh? You'd still be alive, safe..."

Cold droplets of rain begin splashing against the bare skin at the back of my neck, slowly at first, before it starts to get heavier, and I look to the sky. I allow the rain to fall onto my face, washing away the few tears I allowed to escape.

"Okay, I get it, Murph." I close my eyes and just sit for a few minutes, getting wetter by the second and not giving a shit. "I'll stop feeling sorry for myself, okay?" As if by some kind of fucked up magic, the rain slows, the quick burst leaving behind a few mud puddles in the surrounding grass, and I shake my head. I don't believe in any higher power or fate or whatever, but I know for a fact that my boss's wife would tell me otherwise. And maybe, just this once, I'll allow myself to believe it was a sign.

My phone vibrates against my chest and I'm thankful it was in my inside pocket where it could stay dry from the quick shower. I pull it out and want to shoot the fucking thing when I see a message from Mr. Stalker.

> **PIMFA:** Mr. W is at the casino if you need a distraction.

Mother fucker.

What is this guy's deal? Assuming, of course, that it's even a guy. At this point, I don't care who it is, I just need them to leave me the hell alone. All they're doing is raising more questions when what I need are answers.

"Work calls. Catch ya on the other side, Murphy Gallagher." I kiss the leftover stem of the dead, now petal-less rose and drop it back on top of his grave before walking away with a heavy heart and heading for my bike.

It may seem heartless to some, the way I can close off my emotions, but it's gotten me this far and I'm not about to stop now.

The cool night air whips past me as I ride to the casino. Fuck, I've missed my bike. The truck wasn't the worst thing in the world, but my bike is like a slice of peace at my fingertips. I'd give her a name, but that would be too sentimental if I lost her again.

Time moves too quickly and I'm already arriving at the casino. I'll need to make some time to take a longer ride later in the week. One of the hostesses greets me as I walk in, the usual cheery smile that they all share on her face, and I head straight for the poker table, spotting Mr. Wright immediately. His thinning hair and scrawny complexion are a dead giveaway, no matter how much he tries to dress himself up in designer suits.

My trademark leather pants and black tank-top don't look too out of place this evening. The weekends are usually when the high-rollers play, wearing their suits or cocktail dresses, but for a Tuesday, it's pretty casual. Except for the douches like Mr. Wright, of course.

As soon as I sit down, Mr. Douche himself glances up from the cards in his hand and actually snarls at me before throwing them down, gathering his chips, and moving to stand. He doesn't spare me another look as he grumbles to himself and walks toward one of the Blackjack tables.

I can't help the small grin that forms on my lips, knowing that just my presence has annoyed him so much.

He's still close enough for me to keep an eye on him, although my plan is to catch him on his way out rather than trying to tail the sly fucknut—because that shit just ain't working.

We still don't know his deal, his importance, but he's sneaky enough to have gained my interest.

"Excuse me, ma'am."

I turn to the hostess now standing beside me, a tray on her palm holding a glass of what appears to be whiskey on the rocks. Just how I like it.

Instead of answering her, I raise a brow, encouraging her to say what she needs to say.

She clears her throat before lifting the glass and trying to hand it to me. "This is for you."

"I didn't order a drink." I never do, because I can't trust a soul in this place and I'm not dumb enough to put myself in that kind of vulnerable position.

"Apologies, ma'am. I just do as I'm told." She smiles and continues to hold the glass out toward me.

Firstly, I am not old enough to be a ma'am. And secondly, why is my glare not making her fuck right off?

"Take it back. Thank you." I try to remember that she's just doing her job, and aside from calling me ma'am, she hasn't done anything to deserve my rudeness. I can respect a woman who stands in front of me for this long without wilting like a dead flower.

She finally turns and walks away, placing the glass back on the tray. I watch to see if she speaks to anyone, but she just heads toward the bar. The only person in this building who could possibly know my drink of choice is Zavier, though I can't recall telling him at any point, so much has happened since I began this job. I've allowed too much to slide.

My phone buzzes, and as much as I would like it to be one of my Reapers, I have a feeling it's my stalker with a death wish.

> **PIMFA:** Could've sworn you were a whiskey girl.

Okay, so this means he's here now. Watching me. But where?

I scan the room, my senses on high alert as I'm still trying to keep an eye on Mr. Wright too. I don't need this kind of distraction. Although, my stalker told me Mr. Wright was here. Have I walked into some kind of fucked up trap? I mean, I'm armed, so good luck to them if I have.

Zavier has just walked into the casino through the door that leads to the back offices and I decide to test my current theory on the mystery texter.

> **Me:** I'm not.

I watch him as I wait for a response. He's talking to the security guard and checking his watch.

> **PIMFA:** Liar

If he's got one of those smart watches, then it's got to be him.

> **Me:** No. I'm a whiskey woman. No girls here.

> **PIMFA:** Touché.

This time, Zavier's hands are in his pockets the whole time, so unless he's mastered the art of reading and replying to a text without even looking, then my theory is fucked up the ass.

> **Me:** Who the hell are you?

> **PIMFA:** You look disappointed.

How the hell does this person know...?

> **Me:** Fuck off.

I find myself actually growling under my breath, shoving my cell back into my pocket and focusing on Mr. Wright. Not being ten steps ahead of this fucking stalker is really getting to me.

The poker game is over now, a guy with an eighties porn 'stache scraping up all the chips, so it's time for me to move on or they'll expect me to play the next game.

Hoping to move things along and make my current target leave, I decide to join him at the Blackjack table. My being near him is clearly a trigger if his earlier response is anything to go by. I just want to know why.

There are a few other people at the table, with only one seat left for me to take next to a couple at the edge of the half moon. They're acting like newlyweds and an ache bubbles in my chest at how happy they are together. I'm happy for them, it's sweet, but the realization that this kind of normal isn't it for me makes me feel guilty for allowing myself to fall for Murphy again.

Sweet and normal are two words that perfectly describe the father of my child, but they're not words I'd ever associate with myself. And I don't want to, either.

There are a couple of women with short gray perms who look to be in their seventies laughing and joking together to my left, a bearded guy with a scar over his right eye next to them, and Mr. Wright on the opposite end.

The dealer hands out the first two cards to everyone before we all place our first bets or tap out. I use some of the chips I always have on me when visiting this place, because there's no point cashing them all in every time. Saves trips to the cashier. All the players are invested as the dealer lays the third card for Mr. Wright first. He takes another hit, asking for a fourth card, which is where he stops, refusing any more cards. He hasn't busted, but he also doesn't move his eyes from the table, so I'm guessing he's around the nineteen or twenty mark with his cards.

The bearded man is next. He takes one hit before he stands, and when he looks up across the table, his eyes captivate me. They're unlike anything I've seen before; a green so pale they're almost white, but there are flecks of gold dancing like a fire within them. I feel like he's digging inside my mind for all my dirty little secrets before a dangerous smirk crosses his face, making the scar on his cheek lift a little. The harshness of the line over his eye just adds to the danger he's emitting.

I should be on high alert. This is the kind of man that is unpredictable, but he doesn't evoke the same kind of curiosity Mr. Wright did when I first met him. It's different somehow.

The two women to the right of him both busted and now it's my turn. I tap on the table to indicate a hit, swiping my hand out flat as soon as it's placed down to indicate I'm done. Pulling my eyes to my cards, I see the queen of clubs is my third card, which gives me twenty-one when added to my three of diamonds and eight of spades.

I look back up and the scarred guy is on his phone, the attention he gave me gone as quickly as it came. I'll need Glitch to look into him.

The young couple who are playing separately both bust, as does the dealer, leaving just three of us with a hand. We all show our cards and, as suspected, Mr. Wright only has nineteen. The scarred guy has twenty-one, just like me, and the dealer hands out the winnings before scooping up the cards and dealing another round.

It goes like this for about fifteen minutes before Mr. Wright finally speaks up.

"Why won't you just go away? Stop following me, vermin."

Rude. But I don't react with anger. Instead, I ignore his jibe. Technically, he could be talking to anyone at this table.

"Why are you even here? You're cheating again. I know it." He's louder this time, but I continue to starve him of a reaction, my eyes focused on the cards in front of me.

I win again, but Mr. Wright busts this time.

"Argh. Stop cheating, vermin!"

"Excuse me, sir, but you need to calm down or you'll be asked to leave." The dealer tries to reason with him, but he's riled up now. I can see it bubbling under the surface of his skin, like he wants to crawl out of it and fuck me up.

Good luck trying, cunt.

"No! I won't fucking calm down. This thing is following me. She's cheating time and time again and she can't be allowed to get away with it. I will take my business somewhere else, then we'll see how happy your boss is, won't we?" His rant causes the table to go quiet and the dealer scoops up the last round of cards before pressing the security button below his side of the table.

"Sir, please calm down—"

"I won't!" Mr. Wright stands from his stool and moves to come around the table at me.

I'm ready, as usual.

But the scarred guy stands at the same time and stops him in his tracks, his fingers circling his wrist like a noose.

"I wouldn't do that if I were you." His deep voice sounds vaguely familiar, but I can't place it, too busy containing my anger at Mr. Wright, who is practically foaming at the mouth to get to me.

The words coming from his mouth are a garbled, angry mess, the veins in his head about to burst from his bright-red face. The scarred guy holds on to him with ease, beginning to lead him over to one of the security guards by the main entrance.

Time to go, I guess.

I follow a few feet behind until I'm stopped in my tracks when Zavier approaches them. He looks to instruct the guard to take Mr. Wright out, then turns to the scarred guy, a frown on his face.

Assuming I'll get some answers as to who this guy is, I send a text to Shoo—who I asked to wait outside with the van in case I needed him—letting him know Mr. Wright is on the way out before joining Zavier and this mystery dude.

"...said you'd never come onto the floor." I only hear the end of whatever Zavier is saying.

"Things changed." The scarred guy's response is accompanied by a shrug, making Zavier chuckle as he glances at me now standing with them.

"Good evening, Shadow. Everything okay?" Zavier is all charm and attempted grace, but he knows damn well what just happened.

"Aside from Mr. Wright being a fucking douche again, yeah. Who's this?" I nod to the new guy.

That dangerous grin is back on his lips as he answers for Zavier. "You could ask me yourself. I'm right here, in person." He holds out his arms, the long-sleeved black shirt he's wearing tightening across his chest.

"Shadow, this is Dmitry Novák. Dmitry, Shadow." Zavier gestures to each of us in turn, introducing us in the most awkward way ever, and I raise an unimpressed brow.

"Is that Russian?" My question is purely for professional purposes, I always need to know who I'm dealing with in my world.

The guy scoffs, rolling his eyes like my question is ridiculous. "Czech, and I already know who you are."

Dmitry's confession isn't exactly music to my ears. Having people I know nothing about know who I am? Yeah, not cool.

Before I can form a response, Dmitry winks and walks a-fucking-way. He goes into one of the staff doors and disappears. I don't like it.

"How does he know me, Z?"

"Ooh, nicknames are back." He grins.

"How?" My tone is harsher this time.

He rolls his eyes, a smile still firmly etched in place. "He's head of security. He knows the names and faces of every person that comes and goes from this place."

I don't like it, but I also can't be mad about that. Z's doing what he should do with security and I've gotta admire that.

Tonight has been a royal clusterfuck, my initial mission fucked up the ass because of a pretty, albeit imperfect, face distracting me. I should've left it alone for the night, carried out what I planned to do and asked these questions another time.

Now I'm left feeling frustrated, pissed off, and a little hot under the collar.

I pull out my cell and message Tab, knowing he'll still be awake at this time of night. We always are.

Me: Get your gloves, I need to punch something.

Chapter Five
J

"This reeks of the Greeks!" We all groan at Shoo's ridiculous rhyme. Of us all, he's the least affected by the clean-ups, no matter how gruesome or disturbing. Granted, being a little fucked up in the head is a necessity if we want to do our jobs correctly, but he's at least one step beyond that. "Come on! It's a good one."

"It's really not," Tab deadpans as we roll the newest casualty in the tarp before we load him up into the plastic-protected interior of the van. Two days later and Tab is still sporting an angry bruise on his cheek, failing to avoid my right hook. I mean, I warned him that I needed to punch something. So I did. His face. "I'm fucking gutted, man. These guys are all newbies. Can't be older than, what? Twenty-two?"

He's right. Whoever is doing this has our young blood in his sights, which I know is a clue, but I don't know the meaning behind it.

"It's not the Greeks. At least, it's not Zavier." My words get stuck in my throat as I help lift the body. Holy fuck, he may have been young, but he was a big boy.

"What about his...what is he, his cousin or something? The one who killed his brother then disappeared," Tab calls out as he pushes the body deeper into the van before closing the double doors and turning to face me.

"Aleko Kastellanos. I thought the same thing but Glitch put out feelers and with triangulation and satellites or whatever the fuck he does to get us answers, he confirmed that the guy is down south living his best life." Glitch spent way too much time digging into this guy, a little excited about his new life as a quickly-rising-in-the-ranks member of the Sons of Khaos. Apparently, the new and revised version where, instead of riding Harleys, they're straddling sport bikes, and instead of running guns or drugs, they're making bank betting on street races.

"His brother was one deranged, fucked up dude." Shoo's right, the older Kastellanos was devious and impossible to trust, but when Aleko found out his brother was dipping his toes into sex trafficking and liking the feel of it, he put a bullet in his head right in front of Marco Mancini.

"Yeah, Aleko ain't but a step up, man. I can't imagine killing my own brother without even a second thought,"

Tab pipes in as we clean up the site as best we can, on our knees scoping out the scene for any traces that could tie this crime to the Mancinis. We can't have the police sniffing up our asses. We'll take care of our own.

"I dunno, if said brother is a threat, yeah, I'd do it." Shoo's answer earns him a groan from Tab.

"You're an only child, man. You can't understand the bond between brothers." Looking at Tab, I notice a twinge of sadness in his tone but, as always, we don't ask questions in our group. We welcome the information but we don't seek it out. What makes us work well together is that we allow space and we talk when we're ready.

"'The blood of the covenant is thicker than the water of the womb.'" We all stop when Shoo speaks again, a little taken aback by his serious tone. "You're my covenant, I choose you. My blood family can all go fuck themselves."

We're silent for a while after that. I mean, what the fuck are we supposed to say? Nothing. That's what. He'll open up when it's the right time for him.

We work in silence for the rest of the job and right before we leave, Tab slaps Shoo on the shoulder and grins. "Same, brother. Same."

A small smile quirks up at the corners of my mouth knowing they've bonded just a little bit more.

"Hey, Boss, do we have an update on that Wright guy? Any weak links in his inner circle?" Tab breaks the silence as I use tweezers to pick up a hair. May not be ours at all but you can never be too careful.

"Not really. All I've got is his age, fifty-four, wife left him, probably because he's a sniveling little prick, and his son was killed a few years ago, age twenty-six. Wright's a loner but, for some reason, he's become some kind of fucking Houdini with our tails so we're gonna need to get a little inventive when we follow him. Glitch can't find anything in his name. No house, the plates are a dead end, and I've never seen him with a smart phone on him." Taking a baggie, I stand, surveying the area as I finish my update. "Thing is, apart from our suspicions of...something, this guy doesn't have any red flags out there. Can't kill him because he sucks at Poker." And Blackjack, but who's counting?

"We'll figure it out," Shoo calls out as he and Tab wrap things up and give one last sweep of the UV light before heading to the front of the van where my bike is parked. "We always do."

"All right, take him to the cold chamber so we can get him ready for the wake. Have Fizz pick up a nice suit or whatever Eddie and his wife want him to wear," I call out before pushing my helmet on and watching them drive away. One more body to bury in a world where death is the norm. Except this one hits closer to home since it's a capo's son.

Murphy's genuine smile flashes across my mind and before I push it away, I let the warmth of it seep into my heart, making sure my humanity is still there.

Shoo is right. We'll figure this shit out, and when we do, it'll be one last fucking puzzle to solve before I get my girl back.

My next stop is the precinct to meet Detective Redding, our very well-paid public servant who makes sure our body count stays out of the media and under the law's radar.

When I roll up, Ford Redding is standing in the shadows of the grand staircase smoking a cigarette and watching for me. In another world and another time, I could have found his sharp eyes and quick smile attractive but I'm too jaded for normal men. Good men. Despite appearances, Ford is protecting and serving all while getting a bonus from us.

Sadly, our resources are much greater than that of the police, and since we never target the innocent, he decided that getting into bed with us was a guaranteed orgasm for every participant. Couldn't say the same about the Irish, could we?

"Hey," he murmurs around a cigarette hanging from between his lips. "Where's the scene?"

We never talk about specifics over the phone. I don't trust technology more than I need to.

"The docks, East River." He knows exactly where I'm talking about since multiple calls were diverted by one of our dispatch call handlers.

"Right." His eyes dart to my hand where a thick envelope awaits him. "You gonna make this right?" It's the same question he always asks, making sure no crime goes unpunished.

"Gonna do our best." That's my go-to answer. I don't like to be called a liar in case we fail. Although, we never fail. Eventually, we'll get this asshole. "Any dirt on Wright?"

"Squeaky clean. No outstanding warrants, no unpaid tickets, no child support or unpaid alimony. First name John, no middle name. Works as an accountant from home, which, by the way, is completely paid off. As is his car." He shrugs as he takes another drag of the cigarette. "Got nothing."

I think about what he's just told me and wonder where Wright gets all the money he so easily loses on the regular at the casino. Fuck, I need more. This is just chump change.

"Lemme know if you need anything else." Ford drops his cigarette to the sidewalk and stomps it out before tipping up his chin in a goodbye gesture.

"Sure thing." I look down at the filter and growl, "Pick that shit up, it's disgusting."

Watching him freeze then look over his shoulder at me, I smile when he turns back around and does exactly what I tell him.

Satisfied, I walk away.

As I sit on my bike, Ford trotting up the stairs to the precinct, I realize I'm a little jacked up. It's still relatively early, barely midnight, but for some reason, driving aimlessly seems pointless.

Taking out my phone, I call Flower, who answers on the first ring.

"Hey, Boss!" There's noise in the background, glasses clinking and guffaws sounding loud enough to be right in front of me.

"How'd it go tonight?" Flower, who prefers to work alone, had Wright duty tonight until about eleven. Then it was Binx's turn.

"I'm at Sonic's for a drink. Wanna join?" Out of all of us, Flower seems the least broken. Except I know different. Flower is just great at pretending.

I let her invitation swirl in my mind. Sonic's is only about a five-minute ride from here. Before I can talk myself out of it, I tell her to wait there.

The cool air of early April is almost chilling this time of night but my leather get-up shields me enough to enjoy the ride to the bar, with little to no traffic on the way. By the time I arrive, the parking lot is beginning to clear out. It's a popular bar with people my age; trendy beers and decked out with televisions for constant sports updates. The parking lot is usually packed on any night of the week.

Inside, it's impossible to miss Flower as she slams back a shot—probably tequila—then howls at the ceiling while three men stare at her with hungry eyes and mouths practically salivating.

Poor bastards. They have no idea what they're coveting. She looks like a sheep but her canines are sharper than a wolf's.

When I take the empty stool next to her, no doubt freed up by her just for me, her face lights up like a five-year-old staring at the Christmas tree. I don't often go out. This is an exception, and I can tell it means something deep for her.

"There she is!" Flower calls out as I gesture to the bartender.

"What can I get ya?" The pretty blonde leans in, bright eyes darting all around as she surveys the patrons at the bar.

"Lemon tonic, ice, no alcohol." I add that last bit in to avoid any surprises. A few months ago, I bought a few ready-made cans, not paying attention to the gin that was already mixed in. The steep price should've clued me in but then it seems like prices at the liquor store are all skyrocketing.

"Sure thing." She walks away and I turn my attention back to Flower, throwing a glare at the salivating guys who quickly recoil then look away. At least they aren't too stupid.

"So what happened?" I ask, getting down to business. Sure, I'm here to have fun, but I want information first.

"Nothing. He stayed home all evening. Boring as fuck." Her elbow on the bar, she rests her chin on her palm and pouts. Like this, she seems so young, her ginger hair a thick, unmanageable mess on the top of her head that somehow still looks on point, and her big blue eyes reminding me of the anime that Hallie likes to watch, she doesn't look a day older than eighteen.

Yet she's my age, almost ten years older than she seems.

"So, you came here instead of going home to your girlfriend?" The bartender brings me my drink and I pay her before she walks away.

"We had a spat. But it's fine. I'll go home, grovel, then eat her pussy until she comes all over my face. She'll forgive me."

Jesus, okay, that's more information than I was expecting.

I'm about to take another sip of my tonic water when familiar pale green eyes lock onto mine over Flower's shoulder, making my entire body freeze and my jaw clamp down.

What the fuck?

My eyes narrow and my grip tightens on my glass, so much so I'm afraid I'll shatter the thing. What the fuck is he doing here? Is he following me? Is Zavier having me followed?

This is not a chance meeting and there is absolutely zero surprise anywhere on his face. In fact, the tiny smirk at the corner of his mouth is all the proof I need that this little encounter is planned. By him, not by me.

Flower is giving me the lowdown on Wright, but I can't register a damn thing she's saying because all of my focus is on the tatted guy walking to the bathroom on the opposite side of the bar.

"I'll be right back." I cut off whatever Flower was going on about and without giving her the chance to ask anything or even protest, I jump off the stool and stalk over to the door marked 'restroom' before he has a chance to close it in my face.

My knife is in my palm and my hand is at his throat in the second it takes me to push him against the now-closed door.

"What the fuck are you doing here?" My growl is low and deadly, my glare a living, breathing monster filled with hate.

Dmitry doesn't even flinch or recoil or show a single hint of fear in those golden-flecked eyes. In fact, it's only when his smile, firm lips imprisoning a row of straight white teeth, distracts me from his eyes that I realize he's got a knife at my throat too.

When the fuck did that happen?

"Having a drink." His tongue slides out of his mouth, slow and teasing, before the top row of his teeth bites down on his plump, bottom lip. As his eyes trail a fury blaze of heat down from my eyes until finally landing on my throat, I become all too aware of his raging fucking hard on. Well, this is interesting.

I scoff, my eye twitching at his nonchalance. "Am I supposed to believe this is a chance meeting?" My glare drops to his lips again and I can't control the watering of my mouth at the sight.

"Coincidence is the nightlight we use when truth is the monster under the bed." His voice drops to a whisper as every hair on my body stands on end. "Never pegged you for someone afraid of a little darkness."

"How did you know where to find me?"

My body presses harder against his, my forearm at the base of his neck and my blade poised right above his carotid artery. One nip and I could have him bleed out.

"Hmmm, I love that we play with the same toys." His knife isn't threatening any vital areas as he digs the blade a little too deep and breaks the skin. I don't flinch but I'm not going to lie, it stings.

Worse, I like it and it's all the distraction he needs to bring his free hand up to my jaw and turn our positions so that my back is now against the door. Behind me, the music and loud voices in the bar drown out the sounds of our panting.

It's just him and me in a shitty bathroom playing with knives and I can't help the thrill that sings throughout my bloodstream. I'm fully aware that being turned on by violence probably means there's something wrong with me. Wrong and without hope of repair. In this moment though, I couldn't give any less of a fuck.

"Tell me," I start, my voice even and low. "Do you have a death wish?"

Dmitry brings his dagger to my cut and scrapes up just a little before he holds the metal up to his mouth, the tip smeared with my blood. I watch, rapt attention focused on his bold moves, as he slowly drags his tongue along the blade and closes his eyes like he's tasting a fine wine.

I roll my eyes at his overly dramatic antics, almost smiling but pushing that shit down fast.

"What the fuck do you want, Dmitry?" I grit out, tired of playing games.

"This." One word is all he says as his eyes linger on my mouth then drag up to my eyes. "You and me, alone, in a compromising position. But more than anything, I want to hear you say my name again." I narrow my eyes at him, searching his face for any malice, any clue that might indicate he's a danger to me.

I grin when a slow groan drags out of his mouth, his body going completely still.

"Now, by my calculations," I begin, narrowing my eyes but speaking slowly, like I'm giving instructions to a two-year-old. "I'm willing to bet a big—no, a huge—sum of money on the fact that one awkward move on my part and you'll never be able to father children." My head cocked to the side, I press my knife to his balls just enough to accentuate my words.

Dmitry tsks once, twice, his mouth closing in on mine, his breath fanning out across my face as he murmurs just loud enough for me to hear him clearly. "What am I going to do with you, *můj ďáblíku?*" At this point, I have no idea what he's saying, his words suddenly turning foreign with hard syllables and dominant vowels. For all I know, he's calling me a cunt.

"It's okay, though. You'll soon learn that your threats don't scare me. They turn me the fuck on." I narrow my eyes again, this time to search his face. Calm confidence oozes from him. He isn't buff from the gym but he is definitely solid, probably nothing more than good genes. The scar that travels from just above his eyebrow to land in the middle of his cheekbone doesn't take away from his features. If anything, it brings more attention to the chilling green of his eyes, the sharp edges of his jaw and the prominent, straight Roman nose that is currently breathing me in from my collar bone right up to my temple.

My personal space doesn't exist anymore. Every inch of me is covered by every inch of him as his fingers press just a little harder around my neck and his lips brush across my own. The moment is brief, the electricity traveling through me lasting only a second, but I feel it. The sting, the slight burn, the tantalizing ignition of every one of my nerve endings, is real. It awakens something in me that I lost with Murphy and that thought just pisses me the fuck off.

I don't know this guy and I'm not in the business of getting into the proverbial bed with someone I met five seconds ago.

My knife presses against his balls, his sharp intake of breath telling me I'm in the right place, before I tell him a few truths of my own.

"Look, you delusional fuck. I'm not some naïve, sheltered college kid looking for a good time. My weapons aren't props." With how close he is to me, there's no need for me to speak loudly. Hell, I could whisper and he'd hear me perfectly. I do, apparently, need to speak clearly. "I'm in a good mood." I'm not anymore but I'll take one for the team. "And you're Zavier's little tech guy so I'm just going to say this once then I expect you to walk away." My blade pierces the thick denim of his jeans as I make sure it's not too close to his baby makers. I'm generous like that.

"Fuck," he breathes out, zero fear or willingness to back away clear in the way his pupils dilate and his nostrils flare. "You're so fucking hot when you lay down the law." Instead of pulling away to avoid permanent damage, this fucking sociopath leans in closer, like he's searching out the pain.

And that? It is a small clue that pain and probably violence has the same effect on him as it does on me. For a fraction of a second, everything around me disappears. No more music thumping, no more stuffy smell from the bathroom, no more cool feel of the closed door.

This blissful moment holds us in a bubble where I can let my body dictate what it wants.

"It doesn't matter what you believe right now, Little Demon. All that matters is that you and me..." His nose returns to my cheek where he inhales me like a wolf sizing up its prey. "We're the same. There isn't a single soul out there in the world that can understand us and, baby, I'm okay with that."

When his mouth captures mine, I'm so lost in this weird twilight zone where I'm getting hypnotized by a stranger who thinks he knows me, that I allow the kiss. No, that's not right. I don't allow it, I fucking welcome it like a breath of fresh air after a lifetime in a coal mine.

Our mouths are deadly as he takes what he wants with every lashing of his tongue against mine, every hard bite from his teeth when I try to take control. This only fuels me on, knowing that I can't scare him with my violent needs. That I can't hurt him with my rage.

My free hand curls into a fist, rearing back before pushing against his shoulder, not because I want him gone but because I want to know how far I can take this. How far he's willing to let this crazed moment go before he walks away.

Fingers tightening right under my jaw, it's becoming clear that he's cutting off my air supply just enough to get my brain to kick into survival mode.

Adrenaline releases in my bloodstream and my body freezes. My entire body, that is, except for my mouth. The same mouth that, instead of stopping this ridiculous kiss, ups the stakes, trapping his bottom lip between my teeth and biting, hard, until skin breaks and blood coats my tongue.

We both moan, the coppery taste like a burst of vivid colors in an otherwise black and white television show.

I'm so fucking turned on, I don't realize my knife is still threatening his groin, or that the thumping outside is no longer from the music, but someone banging for us to get the fuck out of here. We just can't be bothered to care as we fuck each other using only our mouths, letting our bodies predict what this could feel like if we were flesh to flesh and he fucked every hole I had.

Hell, maybe I'd find a way to fuck a couple of his, too.

Just as quickly as it begins, Dmitry pulls away without ever taking his eyes off me. Lips swollen and smeared with blood, he lets a smile spread across his mouth.

"I can't wait to make you mine."

And just like that, the moment is gone and my senses come rushing right back.

My knee jerks up without a second thought, making unapologetic contact with his balls before I push him off me and step to the side.

Putting my knife away, I snarl at him as he hunches over, gripping his crotch and chuckling the whole time, eyes—always, always, always—on me.

Not quite knowing what to say that wouldn't sound like I'm justifying myself to him, I reach out for the lock, turn the knob, and open the door just as a woman, nearly twenty years older than me, has her fist raised and ready to bang on the door again.

I stop, look over my shoulder, then smirk.

"He's all yours."

Chapter Six

J

"Three in one night so soon after Eddie's kid tells me one of two things. The killer's either getting close to their end game, or something made them mad enough to take risks." With my arms folded across my chest as I stand like a bouncer outside the church, I sigh.

Fizz chews the inside of her cheek and nods in agreement. "But what's the end game?"

"Fuck knows. Maybe an all-out war between us and the Greeks. The thing is, whoever it is clearly has no idea that since Aleko shot his brother Yiannis dead and all that business with the Ambrosios, the Greeks haven't really been a problem. They're basically extinct here in New York. Pinning all these deaths on them feels too suspicious to me. Too meticulous. Yiannis and his crew were never neat about the way they gouged out their victims' eyes, keeping them, apparently, since they've never been found."

Fizz shudders, and I don't blame her. Seeing that for the first time all those years ago almost made me lose the contents of my stomach.

"Whatever happens, I don't want you going anywhere on your own until we catch this fucker." My words are soft but the message is firm. This killer is working his way through the soldiers under Marco and his capos, and while my Reapers haven't been hit yet, at this rate, it's only a matter of time before he tries.

"Yeah, yeah, Crank's already given me that speech." We both turn in his direction and pride warms my chest at how well our Reapers work together. "It hits a little too close to home, huh? Losing Eddie's kid like that?" I nod, still watching Crank, wondering if there was anything we could have done to prevent it. "Anyway, he insisted on staying outside with us instead of joining the service in the church." She tilts her head over to Crank, who's leaning against his truck behind Marco's Aston Martin on the side of the road.

"You could've gone in, ya know?" I gesture toward the entrance.

"Oh no. Nah-ah. Nope. No churches for me, thank you." She shakes her head vehemently and purses her lips, her brows furrowed. "Had enough of them when I was a kid. My mom forced me to go every Sunday. Said it was the only way to be close to my dad after he died." She sighs deeply, as if lost in thought, and I don't push her or try to fill the silence. "I was in the church choir, attended Sunday school, until I realized it was all about appearances. I was the perfect little daughter with a wild imagination and she was the perfect little wife…to the biggest monster I've ever laid eyes on. If God could allow him to…to…well, then that's not a God I want to put my faith in." She goes silent then, determination on her face before she turns to me. "I guess it's been a while since I've been this close to a church." She laughs lightly, almost a scoff, and I get it.

These subjects aren't off limits for us, but this is new information to me. If I were anyone else, I'd wrap her in a warm hug, tell her everything is going to be okay, but I don't think that's what she needs. Besides, I don't do hugs unless I'm being ambushed by River. Fizz didn't just open up to me for sympathy. To be honest, I'm not sure she meant to tell me any of that at all. I understand that this place could be a trigger for her though.

"Wanna go home or you good?"

She smiles in response, her brown eyes glittering in the late afternoon sun. The weather's starting to turn as the evening draws in, but it's fine for now.

"I'm good, J. Thanks. Sorry." Fizz is a strong woman, but like all of us, she has her demons. This is one that I could slay for her. Or with her.

"Don't you dare apologize for telling me about your past. Or anything, really, unless you fuck up on a job. Then...ya know..." I wink, and she laughs properly this time. "You can always talk to me, Fizz. Hell, you all know enough about my past since this Irish shit storm rolled in. Maybe we should have a mass share sesh." I'm only half joking. If we knew more about each other's pasts, maybe we'd be better prepared for what may come at us.

"We'd all have to get fucked off our faces for anything like that to happen and you know it." We both laugh this time.

A few more minutes pass in a comfortable silence before I notice Fizz fidgeting beside me.

"So, how are you doing with the Hallie situation?" Her words are almost tentative, and while I'm happy to listen, I'm not so much about the talking.

"Yeah, fine."

She nods once and replies with a smile. "Okay, cool."

Ten minutes later, the church doors are opened up behind us and Fizz immediately heads toward Crank by the side of the road. "Later, J." She turns to wave before jumping into the passenger seat of his truck as people begin exiting the church.

Eddie and his wife, Leanne, are first out. Leanne's hands are covering her face, tissue dabbing at her wet cheeks and eyes puffy as she clings to her husband's arm. Eddie's face is the complete opposite, determination etched on every line of his face, giving me a single nod in acknowledgement as he walks past me. Their pain is palpable, heavy in the air, and though I may have survived—barely—what I thought was the death of my child once, I know I wouldn't be able to do it again.

She's the only reason I haven't already burned the world down to rid the Earth of every single member of the Irish mob that has ever existed. Her safety is the only reason I'm allowing her grandparents to believe they have some iota of control in this situation. I'm the snake they can't see, coiled and biding my time, waiting to strike once all the rats are in my sight.

Marco is next through the doors, and he pauses to show his respects to his capo, Eddie, and Leanne. As soon as he's done, he looks up, and I know he's searching me out so I go straight to him as he begins to walk toward the cars.

"We need to find this motherfucker, J." His words are gritted out, deep and low, for my ears only.

"Yeah we do. We think there's a pattern to where the killer is hitting us, but I wanna test the theory."

"Of course you do." Marco chuckles.

"What I know is that it isn't Zavier. He's not squeaky, but he's also not responsible for what's happening. My Reapers and I will come up with a plan to try and get a step ahead of this fucknut."

We stop beside his Aston and he turns to me. "Do what you've got to do, J. I've got a guy looking out for Ronan, by the way. He thinks he's close but I'll call you in when I know more."

Rounding the car, Marco opens the driver door and slides in before starting up the engine. I stand and watch as he drives off, relaxing a little now that most of our soldiers are on the road and not all in one place. While everyone can handle themselves just fine, and together we're a force to be reckoned with, we really have no idea what this killer's gonna do next.

When my phone vibrates in my pocket, I can't help rolling my eyes because I have my suspicions as to who it's from. Hallie will be having her evening meal around this time so it can't be her. The grandparents are strict on their schedule and there's still a 'no contact with your mother' rule in place—one she ignores whenever she gets the opportunity. And my Reapers have all gone home with the masses after the funeral service.

> **PIMFA:** Afraid you'd catch fire if you went into the church?

What a dick.

> **Me:** Fuck off

Restless and unable to catch any sleep after getting back from the funeral, I jump on my bike and head for the casino. There's something bugging me about that Dmitry guy and I'm itching to confront him. I may have walked away the other night, but that was more to preserve my own sanity and stop myself from doing something stupid. It felt wrong to have those kinds of thoughts only a month after losing what could have been my happily ever after.

Wow, a month. Over a month if I'm being accurate. Which is more time than we actually spent together. Fucking surreal to think about how much my world has changed since then.

I have so many balls in the air right now, if I could just get to the bottom of this one simple thing with Dmitry, then I can put more energy into everything else.

Parking my bike, I climb off and head to the casino entrance as I remove my helmet. The weather has taken the cold turn I expected earlier in the day and I'm glad for my leathers.

"Where's Dmitry?"

The pretty hostess with long black hair widens her eyes at my question. "Er, please, give me a second."

She knows who I am, at this point all of the staff know me, and within seconds she's on the phone.

"Sir, she has asked for Dmitry…Yes…Okay." Placing the phone down on her welcome desk, she raises her eyes to me. But she's not looking me directly in the eye. Instead, she seems to be concentrating on my forehead. "Wait here a moment, please. He's on the way."

Not listening to a word she said, I head further into the casino and to the door leading to the back offices. I can't get through without a keycard or pin code, so for now, this is as far as I can go. The door opens and I see him. Zavier. Not Dmitry. And I see red.

I'm not playing these games.

"Shadow, so ni—"

Without waiting for Zavier to finish, I push past him and to the first door on my right. It's some kind of kitchen, not what I'm after.

"What are you doing? This area is restricted, even to you." Zavier is trying his best to sound firm, but his tone is also a little resigned as he follows me down the hall.

I pause my search and turn to snarl at him. "Nothing is restricted to me, Z. Now where the fuck is he?"

"I don't know. I'm not his keeper." He shrugs, but I'm not buying it.

Before I can say anything else, that deep tone shoots straight to the center of my bones. "Are you stalking me?"

Slowly turning, I see him heading toward me down the corridor. I can't help the scowl on my face when I hear Zavier chuckle as he says, "I'll leave you to it."

"Am *I* stalking *you*? You've got some nerve."

"Yes, I do." He wags his brows, approaching me with purpose clear in his pale gaze. The scar cutting through his eye seems more prevalent in the harsh lighting of the corridor, but no less captivating.

For some reason, I want to know the reason behind it, what he had to endure to get it.

I don't give him the chance to cage me against the wall—which is clearly his intent—stalking toward him with my eyes glued to his. Most men cower under my glare, but he just grins and moves into the position I was almost in, his back against the wall.

There's a severe height difference between us, and size for that matter, but I've put bigger and badder men on their ass before now.

"What's your story and how do you know me?" Questions I could've asked the other night if I hadn't been so turned on by the violence oozing from him.

My chest is about an inch from his, and we're so close that the scent of mint and lavender fills my nostrils.

"No knife this time?"

I want to smack the smile off his face. Instead, I pull the knife from my waistband and hold it against his balls.

"Better?" I barely recognize my own voice with the way I'm snarling at him.

"Like a walk down memory lane." He continues to avoid my original question and my anger grows. Or frustration. Fucking annoyance.

That's not the only thing that grows, because this fucker's dick is pressing against the denim of his jeans.

"Why the fuck are you hard right now?"

"I like a woman who constantly threatens my balls." He narrows his eyes, grin still firmly in place, eagerly waiting for my next move.

"Fuck you."

"Yes, please."

I don't think I've ever snarled before, but here we are.

"You're cute when you growl like that. Like a tiger." He snaps his teeth close to my face, but I remain still, unflinching.

"You know what? Maybe I'm not just threatening your balls. Maybe I should just do it and ask questions later." I raise a brow, fully aware I'm not about to cut his balls off because A, he hasn't actually done anything wrong that I know of and B, I'm not a monster—unless they deserve it.

"You can always try, baby. I'm right here." He winks, holding his arms out by his sides, completely open to attack.

The noise I make is more of a guttural cry of frustration at this man, knowing I'm getting no answers out of him like this. Turning him on? Yes. Putting the fear of God into him? Not even a little.

"Fuck. You." I slide my knife back into my waistband and step away, backing up toward the exit because there's no way I'm turning my back on this unpredictable sociopath.

I mean, I kinda admire it, but mostly not. Breaking him is taking valuable time from everything else going on.

"I love the way you say fuck when you're pissed. Your cheeks puff out like a little chipmunk."

Narrowing my gaze on him, I don't grace him with a reply, pulling on the door handle slamming it behind me as I step back into the casino.

When it comes to this guy, I need a new plan, but I'm too worked up to figure any of that out right now. I make my way through the casino and back to my bike before heading home. It doesn't take long, traffic being minimal at this time of night. It's my favorite time to ride.

Cutting the engine, I climb off and pull my phone out of its holder, seeing the other pain in my ass has sent me a text. What a surprise. I'm beginning to expect them at this point.

> **PIMFA:** In case you were serious…
> *Pin drop*

The pin drop is a location by our loading docks, one of the warehouses, if my memory serves me right. *What in the actual fuck?*

Serious about what?

Chapter Seven

J

An hour ago, I was feeling the weight of the day on my shoulders but as soon as that text hit my phone, it was like getting a shot of adrenaline straight to the brain.

Game on, you fucking stalker. Game fucking on.

The chill of the April night whips around my body like a breathing, living thing, slapping every inch of me as I ride my bike to the pinned location, my GPS guiding me down the streets of New York. I recognize the destination but I can't trust that it's safe. When I sent the pin to Glitch, I told him he had twenty minutes, thirty tops, to get me answers before I reached my target.

I'm excited but I'm not a fucking idiot. My logical brain reminds me of the times this guy has been on my side, but what if he's playing the long game? What if he's the cat and he truly believes I'm a mouse frozen in his orbit?

I may be going alone but the Reapers now know exactly where I am and if I know Crank, and I fucking do, he's already getting the crew together to drive out here and wait for any signal I give.

My gut, though, tells me I'm safe. Mostly, it tells me I'm about to get some much-needed answers.

Pulling up to a warehouse in the Bronx, I stop the bike, taking in my surroundings. Rows and rows of containers line the premises, all waiting to be sent out on the docked cargo ship. The place is organized, signs at every corner, for better worker efficiency. When my gaze returns to the warehouse, I see the crack in one of the sliding doors, a faint light splashing out into the night.

As I swing my leg around the back of the bike, I pull my helmet off and shake away the strands sticking to my forehead. The rest of my hair is in twin braids on either side of my head. That too, is more efficient.

Unlike in the movies, wearing a helmet with loose hair beneath it only results in a nest of knots and hours spent trying to untangle the mess. Pulling off a helmet to then shake your hair out like a sexy vixen is the greatest myth Hollywood ever told.

My phone vibrates in my hand.

> **Glitch**: Location belongs to Zavier Galanos. Legit shipping company,

> primarily used for import/export of Greek trade products.

Zavier? But he wasn't the guy texting me, though. I'd watched him that night at the casino. Unless he has some Houdini skills, I'm being punked right now.

Fuck it, I need answers and, to be honest, knowing this is linked to Zavier has a calming effect. I don't know why but I almost—almost—trust him. At the very least, he has caused me to chuckle, albeit despite myself, a few times, which is more than I can say for the rest of the human population.

Wiping the sweat from my forehead, I carefully rest my helmet on the back footrest and whip out both my gun and my blade.

Trust or no trust, a girl can't be too careful.

The door easily slides open, only needing a one-footed push to give myself enough space to slink inside. Where the exterior seemed nice and neat, organized, inside it's just a mess of shit strung around all over the place. Dirty tarps hanging like sheets on a laundry line, ropes stacked high enough to block the view beyond them, and I frown at the clutter creating a sort of labyrinth.

"I'm here, fucker. Show your face." It's not like I'm trying to be discreet, I'm here so I can leave a little wiser than when I arrived.

No answer.

Christ, this guy likes playing games, doesn't he?

That's when I notice the lone table, completely out of place among the clusterfuck of shit lying around. It's clean, no dust, and devoid of anything on top except for a sheet of paper held down by a vase with one black long-stem rose.

I roll my eyes. What the fuck is that supposed to mean?

As I get closer, I look down at the paper and scoff.

TWO CHOICES:
☐ *YOU PLAY*
OR
☐ *YOU WALK AWAY*

Do I feel like playing at all hours of the night? No.
But do I want to walk away? Fuck no.
So, I decide to answer with my own choice.

Scribbling my words on the bottom of the paper, I'm about to fold it up and put it in my pocket when something grabs my attention.

It's signed. It's just one letter, but that's not what's niggling at my brain. Searching out my memories, I try to remember where I saw that letter like that before.

A contract? A letter when I was a kid?

Fuck.

A letter. A fucking letter.

When I got my bike back, there was a triangle scratched on the tank except, it wasn't a triangle, was it?

D.

"You motherfucker." I scream out those two words and, in the distance, I hear the faint sound of a chuckle that makes my entire body buzz with excitement. It could be sexual but, also, it's probably just the anticipation of violence.

Folding the paper in two and sliding it inside the back pocket of my leathers, I walk around the table and begin his game.

"Dmitry, Dmitry, Dmitry. Did you have fun stalking me?"

With one finger, I peek around a piece of red tarp, noticing the area behind it is lined with intermittent candles giving me enough light to see where I'm going. How fucking gentlemanly of him.

"Does Zavier know how much time you spend not working?" As I speak, I use the barrel of my gun to pull away the sailcloth, ready to stab him if I have to.

A creak sounds just to the right of me and instead of turning toward the noise, I crouch, making myself smaller, less visible. Although, I have a feeling this entire space is set up to his advantage, and despite this little game of hide and go seek, none of the hairs on my body are freaking out and telling me to run.

Just below one of the tarps, I don't miss the quick come and go of a shadow, making me grin like a dog on a full belly. I could taunt him again, see if I can get him to move, but as I take a step back to look under the crinkly barrier, I feel the presence behind me.

I don't hesitate, moving on instinct alone. My arm swings around, ready for impact as I hit something solid with the back of my elbow. The grunt that *hmphs* out of him is like a fresh shower after a good kill.

With both of my hands occupied with the gun and the knife, I'm not quick enough to push myself off the floor to a standing position before he's caught me by the back of the hair, pulling me to the nearest wall.

I don't fight him, that would only waste my energy. I just let him drag me up to standing as he reaches for my knife.

We both know I'm not going to shoot him, he's not an enemy...yet.

But I might see how far I can bury my blade in him...somewhere less important so he's maimed but not dead.

Just as he thinks he's got me where he wants me, I drop the gun, drop to my knees, and flip around until his hold on me is ripped away.

We're standing mere feet away, the large space echoing our loud breaths as we size each other up.

"Has anyone ever told you that you're sexy when you're stabby?" Jesus, who is this guy?

"I recall someone calling me a Stabby Queen. Maybe you know him? Six feet what...four inches? No balls, big on stalking. Likes to hide in the shadows and..." I look up at the ceiling like I'm trying to find the words. "Oh yeah, cut himself shaving so...no hand-eye coordination." I raise my brow at the scar that runs down from his brow to the top of his cheek, flashing him a fake smile, teeth and all.

Dmitry doesn't even flinch, bringing two fingers to his eye and tapping his index twice. "You forgot the green eyes." Leaning a few inches toward me, he stage-whispers.

"They got me laid on more occasions than I'd like to admit. Especially when I'm wearing my black-rimmed glasses." His cocky grin says otherwise; he loves to admit it.

I shrug. "Pity fucks don't count."

My eyes catch on my gun, still lying on the floor, as my breaths begin to calm. Bending at the knees, I take my eyes off him to pick it up. I realize my mistake as soon as the gun is at my fingertips.

Never take your eyes off your opponent. Devon Quinn taught me that and if he were here, he'd kick my ass for such a rookie move.

I don't even fight the hold Dmitry gets on me as he slams me against the wall again, but this time, his entire body is pressed tightly against mine. Hard cock and all.

"You know, we need to stop meeting like this," I say, tone bored, even if my body is nothing less than on fire from the heat of him. "I'm going to start thinking you're a sex fiend. Might have to report you to the appropriate authorities."

"Hmmm." Dmitry's nose runs up along my exposed neck then across my clenched jaw and I feel every one of his breaths like I feel my pussy throbbing for something. Anything. "You could call me out for so much worse than just a hard dick anytime you're within a mile of me. So.

Much. More." He accentuates his last three words with a nip of his teeth on my heated skin. "Yet, you choose to focus on that. On the part that's most interesting to you." I scoff at his words but the air gets stuck in my throat as his leg fights its way between mine, rubbing at my pussy and creating a desire that I'm going to need to alleviate.

Guilt assaults me but I push it down. This isn't about love or about forgetting Murphy. This is business. And, well…I work better after a good orgasm.

"Less talking, more rubbing." My intention is to sound unaffected but really…my ache is real and the things I want him to do to me are multiplying in my mind like horny rabbits on a rampage.

Dmitry's fingers wrap around my wrist, pressing on my nerves at the base of my palm until my hold on my knife disappears. The next thing I know, he's got the tip of the blade at my neck and his mouth is slowly sliding across my lips, whispering, tempting, teasing me.

"The first time I saw you was weeks before you sauntered into our casino and threatened a bunch of stuffy old men jacking themselves off at the prospect of making more money." I'm listening to his words, putting pieces of the puzzle together, but also enjoying the sting at my neck as I push into him instead of away.

Riding his thigh, I'm aware of my pussy getting wetter and wetter as I get what I want from him.

"I wish I could say it was a chance encounter." Fuck. He's talking and, little by little, he's piercing my skin with the tip of my own knife. My skin tickles under the light tear of blood I can feel dripping down the side of my neck. "But, my little demon, when you walked in dressed like vengeance and murder with fire burning in your eyes, that's when I fell for you." He's talking about that night at the casino when I'd worn my red dress and pretended to be a high-rolling airhead.

"Got a lot of cameras on me?" My voice is barely recognizable as I fist his button-down shirt with my free hand and bring him close to me so I'm speaking into his mouth.

"All of them. Every piece of technology I can control swings in your direction." His mouth drops on mine and we assault each other like this kiss is the only way to survive. I'm pulling and he's pushing, I'm rubbing myself as he pops open my leathers, my zipper practically disintegrating under his blazing touch. "I watch you. I consume you." His hand now in my pants, he groans. Guess he can feel the lack of panties on my end.

"I could kill you for invading my privacy." My threat would be a hundred times more convincing if there was any bite to it. There isn't, though. I sound like I'm two strokes away from completely coming apart. It's fucking embarrassing but I'm just going to chalk it up to stress and needing relief.

"You could." Lips and mouths and tongues are at war as his fingers find my clit before they push into me and curl like he's telling me to follow him. I bite the meaty part of his shoulder, making sure I leave a mark as my chest heaves, breathing hard and fast, the familiar fog of pleasure making me dizzy with anticipation.

His hand fucks my cunt with the same desperation with which his lips own my mouth. It's raw and uncalculated, filled with rage that isn't aimed at me but channeled through me nonetheless. My tongue searches his out, my teeth needing to sink into something again as my orgasm builds and builds, my whole body shaking like an earthquake taking complete control and ravaging every inch of the city.

Dmitry pulls back from the kiss and I'm barely able to hold back a whimper at the loss of him.

A fucking whimper? But goddammit, I want to feel good. I want to escape the pain and the loss and the worry and fucking rage that boils inside me every second of every day.

I want to forget, even if it's for a minute. One blissful minute of pure nothingness.

One blissful minute of being someone else's priority for once.

Holding me prisoner with his stare, his scar only making his eye more prominent, more hypnotizing, he speaks words I can barely register as his fingers go deep enough for his entire palm to press against my clit. "The moment you winked at the camera of the casino, you became mine." Taking the knife away from my throat, he scrapes up my blood and brings it to my lips, spreading it from left to right and barely trying to avoid cutting me. Then he hands me the blade, his hand closing around mine at the hilt, and brings it to his neck, giving himself a twin cut and repeating the action on my lips.

"I may not be yours yet, Little Demon, but I'm a patient man. I'm a giving man." He curls his fingers one last time, and as my orgasm explodes from my pussy to the very nerve endings on my scalp, he shares our blood. Devouring my mouth, he licks and bites my tongue as I convulse in his hand, fucking it hard until the force of it leaves me breathless and spent.

Until the calm of nothingness appeases my mind for that perfect moment in time.

Taking his hand out of my pants, he brings his fingers to his mouth and sucks on them as his eyes bore into mine, telling me a million things without speaking a single word. He dares me to...what? Be offended?

I'd be offended if he didn't lick my cum after fingering me. Eating my pussy is a privilege and my cum should never go to waste.

"I will bring your enemies to you on a silver platter and I'll gladly give you the tools to make them suffer." I blink at his confession, my brows furrowing in confusion. Now that my senses aren't being sabotaged by my libido, I remember that I don't fucking know him. And this? It's just a means to a very satisfying end.

"I appreciate your declaration of...whatever that was, but let me tell you something..." I bring my blade to his shirt and wipe it off. "I don't need you, or any man, to bring my enemies to me. I'll grab those motherfuckers myself and I'll watch them die slowly, at my hands." My mouth lands on his once more because, well, he tastes like me and I'm fucking delicious. "But if you like watching so much, make sure you tune in for the show."

Dmitry's face is priceless. Eyes bright with lust and a perfect mouth wide with amusement. I'm not trying to make him laugh, my aim is to make him let go of this infatuation.

It's not happening.

Zipping up my pants, I look down at his raging hard-on then take the paper out of my back pocket before slapping it on his chest, a full-on grin on my face.

"Thanks for the orgasm and I'm sorry I can't return the favor." I wink and walk out, grabbing my gun on the way, whistling and imagining his face when he looks at the paper I gave him.

Because, bitch, I have my own rules.

TWO CHOICES:
☐ *YOU PLAY*
OR
☐ *YOU WALK AWAY*
☒ I choose both motherfucker.

"Duly noted, Little Demon. Duly fucking noted."

Chapter Eight

D

Some fucker's keeping my little demon busy with dead bodies to clean up and I don't like it. Going a whole week without seeing her in the flesh after finally experiencing what can only be described as pure fucking bliss is excruciating. Yeah, I could just turn up on her doorstep, but she's not quite ready for that yet.

Soon.

I'm the tortoise, slow and steady, enjoying every single moment of build up to the win. Because she's worth all of it; the pain, the longing, the time and effort I put into watching her each and every day.

Admittedly, the whole Murphy thing put a wrench in my plans. He was a good man, a great dad, but he just wasn't right for Jordyn—even her name slides off my tongue like butter. For a while, I was happy with just observing, and I didn't wish death on Murphy, but the more I see, the more I learn…she's mine.

Following her through the street cameras is easy enough since the great city of New York makes them available to the public through the Department of Transportation website. Hopping from one private camera to the next, well, that takes talent, which I have in spades. It's all worth it because watching her is like binging my favorite show. Her rounded ass looks fucking amazing in the black coveralls she wears on a cleaning job. Her dark-blonde hair shines under the light of the moon and I want to pull it so hard she screams with pleasure onto my cock.

"Did you get all that, Dima?" Zavier rushes into my office, my lusty daydream vanishing along with my growing boner. "Oh, for fuck's sake. Really? Again? Why aren't you watching the casino?" He slams the door closed behind him.

"It's recording everything at all times. Don't piss your pants." I down the rest of my Redbull before crushing the can and throwing it into my overflowing wastebasket.

"You were supposed to be watching that poker table. I need you to send one of your security guys out there to get those cheaters the fuck out. With evidence…which you would know we finally have if you were fucking watching!" Zavier gets louder as he speaks, and I get it.

There's been a youngish couple in regularly who have been winning big, and I was technically supposed to be keeping an eye on them for when they fucked up. But after going a week without my demon fix, I'm fucking jonesing. Watching her is all I can do. That, and sending her the occasional text message, just so she knows.

Putting a tracker on her bike was a fucking genius idea. Makes it easier to know which cameras to pop or hack into and when so I can see her beautiful, scowling face. The fact that her mechanic didn't find it disappointed me a little, because I thought they were better than that, but it's a nice learning curve for him.

"Dude, I have Serena watching the casino cameras in the main security room too. You know, the one that isn't my office. Hang on." I hold my finger up to him and lean back in my swivel chair, putting my feet up on the desk as I pick up the walkie talkie beside me. "Rena, you catch the cheaters?"

It crackles before she replies, "Yeah, Boss. Sean's on the case. We won't be seeing them in here again."

Waving the walkie talkie at Zavier, I raise my eyebrows. "See? All sorted. Untwist your panties and go do what you do best, Mr. Face." I'm aware phones and intercom systems are probably easier than what I use to communicate with my security team, but fuck it, walkie talkies are fucking cool.

Being a silent partner in this casino affords me most of the privileges and not even half the shit, but I do still enjoy giving Zavier a hard time about how uptight he is. He likes to come across all calm and collected out on the casino floor, in front of clients, but I know that he's poured everything he has into this. It's important that it continues to do well.

Zavier rolls his eyes at my dramatics, shaking his head, but there's a smirk there too. Fucker should know better than to think I'd fuck this up for us in any way. He sits himself against the edge of one of my three desks full of monitors, crossing his feet at the ankle and helping himself to a Twizzler from the package by my keyboard.

"How do you know where she is anyway?" He speaks around his chewing, curiously glaring at the screen in front of me.

Jordyn's carrying a black body bag with the help of Shoo, her mountainous crew member, and they're loading it into the back of their black van. The woman with tiny ringlets in her hair is standing by the driver's door waiting for them to finish loading it up. They've been there for about two hours now, so she'll be hopping back on her bike soon.

"Just watch." I smile at the screen, watching as they finish the job, shut the front door of the small house, and she does exactly as predicted. A tilt of her head goodbye to her crew before she slides on her helmet and straddles her blood-red machine.

"What am I supposed to be watching?" Zavier's confusion is sweet. He's the angel on your shoulder, whereas I'm the devil. Well, if the angel was a horny bastard who tries to sleep with your woman before you've even had a chance to meet her properly because he wants to fuck with you.

"Wait for it." My grin remains in place as she rides off, going off screen. As soon as she does, one of my other screens lights up, a map of the city across it, with a little black dot following her exact location.

"You didn't! You sick fuck." Zavier laughs and pats me on the back, moving to get a closer look at the moving dot. "How the fuck did you manage that?"

"That would be telling. And I love you like a brother, but no."

"Ha. It was great knowing you, man, 'cause when she finds out what you did, she's going to cut off your balls and make you bleed out while she finishes her lunch. Make sure you update your will so I get your shares of the casino." He sighs, shaking his head, and moves over to the small sofa-bed by the back wall, sitting like a king with his arms spanning the back and his legs open wide.

The screen flashing the little black dot tells me that my little demon is headed home, so I switch one of the screens over to the camera in front of her apartment before turning to face my partner, best friend, and brother in all ways but blood. He gets me, knows I like to stay behind the scenes, to watch, to be his technical shadow, and I love that he's not afraid to be who he is. Being the main face and name of our casino excites him, he loves this shit.

If I hadn't spent a few years in jail after being caught in college trying to hack into an international bank then my name would be on the documents too, but we wanted to be as legit as possible. After Zavier's cousin, Yiannis, fucked shit up, here, years ago, we wanted fuck all to do with that.

The mafia turning up on opening night was unexpected. We honestly hadn't thought they'd be interested in what we were doing, but I won't lie and say I wish they'd never turned up. Seeing Jordyn for the first time was like an electric shock to my system, and when she fucked those dudes up in Zavier's meeting, well, my dick has been hard for her ever since.

Jordyn O'Neil is my drug, my obsession, my fucking demon queen, and I will worship her like the goddess she is for all time. Not with flowers and chocolates though, but with death and destruction. It's where she thrives, and fuck do I love to see her thrive.

"Something on your mind, Z?" When I heard Jordyn using the nickname I gave Zavier when we were kids, it cemented that she's meant for me. I'm meant for her. It may take a while before she sees it, but I'm a patient man. Kind of.

"I think I'm gonna have to give up that land we wanted for a second location." He sighs.

"Ah yeah, figured. There's something off about that Mr. Wright dude. It's been impossible to find anything on him, but that's only half the problem." I spin from side to side on my chair and crack open the Redbull I have on my desk, taking a huge gulp and feeling zero relief. I know I'll continue to feel none until I can touch her again.

"Why didn't you say something sooner?" Zavier sits forward, an eyebrow raised in question.

I shrug. "Wanted to see how far he'd take it. I think he's got a gambling problem. I'm not even sure he actually owns that land. It says Mr. Wright on the documentation from The Office of the City Register, but with what we know about this guy, it's not quite matching up."

"Fuck's sake, Dima. I told you to keep me in the loop with these things." He's not angry, but annoyance is clear in his tone.

"Yeah, well, you're a shit liar. Needed you to be all in on the deal for as long as he tried to drag it out." One of my monitors beeps and I twist my head to see she's almost home before turning back to Zavier.

He's chuckling. "I *am* a shit liar. But you know I can handle what needs to be done. You should've told me your suspicions." He's right, he can handle himself real well. Where I excelled in all things technology, his special skill has always been adapting to any situation.

"Okay. Next time. Promise." I wink and he laughs again, shaking his head.

"I believe you. Thousands wouldn't. Anyway, I've been off the main floor for long enough. Time to get back to work." He pointedly glares at me, as if to tell me to get back to work too, but that's what I have a security team for.

The door clicks closed behind him as he leaves and I immediately turn back toward my monitors. My alert that she's nearly home was on point and I can now see her pulling up outside her apartment building. I have the view from the street camera as well as her building cameras. Whoever set it up was a fucking amateur, and I've fixed that shit so I'm the only one who can watch her now.

If anyone has noticed they're locked out of their systems, nothing's been said. I bet they're shitting themselves and trying to keep it quiet so they don't get sued.

I flick the main screen over to the one just outside her apartment door, watching her pull out those braids and run her fingers through that thick, dark-blonde hair as she unlocks her door. Once she steps inside, I relax, knowing she's getting some much-needed rest.

My little demon's busy, always on the move, working a job or looking out for someone, and I've made it my responsibility to do that for her.

Picking up my walkie talkie, I push the button to speak. "Rena, I'm headed home. Hold down the fort."

The crackle precedes her words. "You got it, Boss."

I pull up my security app on my phone, selecting the camera I managed to get into her apartment a few weeks ago, and watch her start the coffee machine. Then she pulls off her black tank top and slides off those black pants, leaving her in just her underwear as she grabs a mug. Picking up her phone from the table, she appears to be reading a message before a small smile graces her beautiful, pouty lips and she begins tapping something in response.

Only one person makes her smile like that. Her daughter, Hallie.

She needs to accept me too, but I'll work on Jordyn first. Hallie is a part of the Jordyn O'Neil package, and while I didn't know that when my obsession first began, it doesn't change how I feel.

I'm all in with this woman, just waiting on the day she calls me on it because I know, without a doubt, we'll both win.

Chapter Nine

J

"Ugh, I have a math test in ten minutes." Like clockwork, I've got Hallie on the phone just before her classes start for the day. It's always short but at least I can hear her voice every morning and soothe the ever-present ache in my chest. Little by little, I'm putting my ducks in a row, and when the time comes, I'll be on the first plane to Florida and bringing my daughter back to New York where she belongs.

"Did you study?" I know she did, she's got her eye on the prize and it's called Columbia University.

"Duh, but my teacher's math tests are juvenile. I've been doing fractions my entire life and I feel like I'm just getting dumber here. I'll never get into Columbia at this rate and I'll disappoint dad because it was our dream. Dang it, I have to go, the bell just rang. Love you, bye."

The line goes dead as I mutter an, "I love you, goodbye," to exactly nobody on the other end.

I looked into the stats at Columbia and holy shit. It's over sixty-five thousand a year with a four percent acceptance rate. Hallie may only be thirteen but if she wants to make her dreams come true, she'll have to be motivated for the next five years.

That being said, I'll gladly do whatever needs to be done to make sure she gets in. I'm not above threatening a dean's career to make sure my daughter is happy.

It's barely eight o'clock when I slip out of my bed and pad my way to the kitchen for my second coffee of the day. Spring is in the air as the sun's rays land on the tiles of my kitchen floor, making them nice and warm for my bare feet. The advantage to this apartment complex is that no matter where I stand, no other building can see inside my unit, which means I can walk around in my panties and tank top without having to gouge out some creeper's eyes for checking me out with his binoculars.

Been there, done that. Do not recommend.

Leaning against the counter in my tiny one bedroom, I fiddle with my phone, getting updates from the crew and reading their quick responses as they come in.

We're cleaning up dead bodies as fast as they're coming in, and with each young soldier we bury our anger grows into a living, palpable mountain of untapped rage. I have so much hatred festering inside me. Between losing Murphy days before Hallie was ripped from my arms and the barely-adult members of the Mancini organization getting popped off one by one like sitting ducks, I'm surprised I'm not out there slashing throats like it's an Olympic sport.

I'm smarter than that, though, and self-control is my superpower. Although, I'm kind of enjoying the chink in my armor when Dmitry comes around. Those minutes in the warehouse reduced the pressure of my cooker enough to allow me a soothing breath.

Of course, as I read Crank's message that yet another body was found this morning, I'm suddenly stabby all over again.

As I'm reaching for my coffee, another text message comes in. This is from Shoo. I ignore it for a second while grabbing a banana from the fridge but the phone dings again. I roll my eyes because Shoo doesn't know how to write an entire message in one text. No, this guy has mastered the art of text cliffies. Each line is a cliffhanger, making you hold your breath until he gives you another crumb on the next line. Fuck that...I wait for the entire message to be there, the pings coming in every five seconds until silence alerts me that he's done.

Crossing my legs at the ankle, I take a bite of my banana, my eyes scanning the increasingly excited messages on my screen.

> **Shoo**: We got him.
>
> **Shoo**: Sitting cozy at the warehouse.
>
> **Shoo**: Like a Christmas present.
>
> **Shoo**: Doesn't seem eager to talk.

Who the fuck is he talking about? There are at least three "hims" I'm looking for at this time.

My eyes skip to the end of the thread to land on a name I haven't seen in a while.

> **Shoo**: By the way, it's Shane Brennan.
>
> **Me**: I'll be there in an hour, keep him nice and warm for me.

I grin as I press send on my response. And by "warm", he knows I mean scalding hot.

By the time I shower and head out the door, I'm jacked up with excitement. This dude ran me off my bike last month and, for some reason Glitch can't explain, he was like a ghost. We had a name and that's it. Hell, I was ready to cross out his name and move on, thinking the trail was cold. Well, like I told Shoo, he's in hot water now.

There is only one other vehicle at the warehouse when I roll in and park my bike just behind the blacked out F150. Shoo has an apparent problem with brand names so he asked Crank to work on his truck and make all mention of them go away. I mean, to each his own and I don't ask questions.

Looking around the large, empty lot, I make sure we're alone without stragglers roaming around looking for scraps or their next hit. Even if they tend to be unreliable witnesses for the cops, I don't like having eyes on us, no matter who it is.

"Oh, shit, you're in trouble now, Shay-Shay." I send a glare in Shoo's direction, effectively shutting him up. How many fucking coffees has he had this morning?

"Don't fucking call me that, you freak." At Shane's loud, albeit somewhat shaky, words, I turn my full attention to him, making sure he can read the intent in my eyes. If stereotypes had a face, he'd be the avatar for the Irish American…ginger hair and all. I have to give it to the guys, apart from a few scrapes and scratches, they didn't rough him up a whole lot. How considerate of them.

But sitting there in the middle of the empty warehouse, wrists turned palm side up and tied to the armrest along with his shins roped up tight to the legs of the chair, he just looks weak and scared. I mean, his instincts are on point because when you end up sitting above a drain, surrounded by the clean up crew for the Mancini mafia family, it means you're about to lose some bodily fluids...one way or another. And that should scare the fuck out of you.

Here's the thing, I want answers and I will stop at nothing to get them. Although I know he's chum in the food chain, I have no doubt he's got information I can use. This is the ultimate test for people like him. They're either loyal and ready to die on their hill of assholes or...they like pretending they are until shit gets real and nails start flying off. Either way, this man dies tonight. Even if by a long shot or by distant association, Shane Brennan was somehow part of the conspiracy that got Murphy killed and I won't let that go.

"Freak, huh? Sounds to me like you're a judgmental little prick." I speak, calm and unaffected, as I walk around, placing my helmet on the table that's been pushed up against the far wall. Then, I slide out my blade, shrug off my leather jacket, and pull off my riding gloves, only to replace them with latex ones. My hair is in a low braid that hangs down the middle of my back to avoid getting it stained with blood; it's too fucking hard washing it out.

Shane is watching me, not responding to my words or the clucking of my tongue as I approach him, slow and easy.

"The way I see it," I continue, bringing the knife to eye level and inspecting the line. I know it's perfect, that's not the point. I just like looking at the sharp, clean edges before I get it all dirty. "Of us all, you're the freak here, Shane." When I speak his name, I look him straight in the eye. "You're the asshole who likes to run bikers off the road then run like a little bitch in heat."

Shane rears back like I've slapped him then, when he realizes he's shown weakness by his shocked reaction, he spits a wad of phlegm in my direction. Fucking disgusting.

"I ain't got nothin' to say to you, Sha-dow." He splits my street name in two, saying it like a five-year-old who's trying to hurt his classmate's feelings. Except, we're not five and this ain't kindergarten. Also, I'm bored.

He tries to follow me with his gaze as I walk behind him but Binx has done a stellar job tying him up, so he doesn't see me coming when I slam my hand in his thick red hair and curl my gloved fingers around the dirty strands. I don't like touching men I don't know, but more than that, I don't need to leave my DNA on his body—even though I know damn well that this is one corpse no one will ever find.

Pushing his head to the side, far enough down to be painfully uncomfortable, I run my blade along the shell of his ear and whisper, "Where is Ronan?"

Again with the spitting, but in this position, he gets it all over himself. Fucking dumbass.

"I ain't telling you shit." Fuck, I really wished this one was a little smarter than the others.

My blade is so fucking sharp that it takes little effort to slice off his ear. "I don't think you heard me right, so let me ask again." Even though he's screaming his fucking head off, I still only whisper as I kick his unattached ear into the drain so he can see it there at his feet.

"You fucking cunt, you cut off my ear! What the actual fuck?" There's no helping my eye roll. Where the fuck did they get this guy? MadeMenWannabe dot com?

"Hmm, I wonder...do you know the origin of the word 'cunt'?" I blow on his open wound and grin when he belts out another screech of pain.

"Fuck you talking about? I don't fucking know!"

Looking to Shoo, I shrug like this guy's too stupid to live.

"One of many theories is that it comes from the Latin 'cunnus'." I pause for effect or else this just isn't any fun.

"Well good for fucking you." As he speaks and cries, the blood running down his face and across his mouth sprays all over his arm and hand. I'm still holding him down at a weird side angle so I can speak directly into his wounded ear. Or...missing ear? I mean, right now it's just a hole.

"I'm not done." I tap the side of his head and revel at the gush of blood and Shane's accompanying screams. "The word 'cunnus' means 'sword sheath'. Isn't that ironic?" Letting go of his head, I step up in front of him and show him the holster for my knife. "I mean, it's not a sword, but close enough."

When I crouch down to look him straight in the eye, I ask again. "Where the fuck is Ronan?" Shane's head is leaning back, bobbing, but I see the defiance in his flat, blue eyes, not missing the moment he decides to piss me off.

Jumping to the side, I watch the spit land on his thigh and shake my head. "You're pathetic."

My hand flies through the air, the knife slicing across his face and painting a slash of red across his cheek.

"Fuck you! You're not going to find him! He's not even in the fucking state, you stupid bitch!"

That gets my attention. But I can't show weakness, not now.

"Gag him." Without even looking at Shoo and Binx, I wait for them to follow my order. And because Shoo is who he is, he rips open Shane's T-shirt—bloodied and dirty from whatever hole he crawled out of—and pushes it in his mouth to shut him up. It doesn't take long for the cotton to soak up his blood, no doubt invading his sense of smell too.

"Out of state, huh? Are you hoping I'll play twenty questions with you?"

Shane thrashes as I speak, trying to get the gag out of his mouth, but it's no use, that thing is in for the long haul.

"It's funny that you would think loyalty to Ronan will give you some kind of power." Ignoring his cries of pain, I keep talking like he's not sitting there trying to get free. "It won't. You're going to die here today. The only choice you have is whether you go easy or hard." Shane shakes his head at my words, probably hurling insults at me, but I can't make any of it out, obviously.

Throwing the knife in the air, I keep my eyes on his as I catch the hilt and in one smooth move, plant the blade right through the middle of his palm. Shane's head snaps back, his eyes screwed tightly closed as every muscle in his body contracts all at once.

"Where. Is. Ronan?"

Shane is outright crying now, tears mixing with blood and snot as he shakes his head and convulses on the chair.

"This can all stop if you just give me something I can use."

With his eyes closed as he sobs, his chest heaves from the pain and the difficulty in breathing. He's only got himself to blame. Slowly, his lids open and it's clear the pain is about to make him pass out. I definitely do not want that shit. He's no good to me acting out a scene from *Sleeping Beauty*, I need him talking.

Raising the knife above my head, I make a big show of bringing it down on his kneecap, and that's when I see it. The moment when torture has taken its toll. The second they've given in.

With a nod, I silently tell Shoo to take out the gag so he can speak.

"I...I don't know..." Oh for fuck's sake, I'm about to lose my fucking patience with his idiot. "About Ronan." The way he speaks tells me he's got more to say so I give him the time he needs before judging whether or not he's worth my patience. "But I can...tell you who called me...that night." He squeezes his eyes tight and takes in a shaky breath and I fight the urge to give him the universal sign for hurry the fuck up. "The night...I ran you...over."

Shane's head lolls to the side and it's clear I don't have much time here.

"All right, Shane. I'll bite. Who was it?" Maybe it's useful, maybe it's a dead-end but I won't know until I know.

"Harvey...Cook." I frown at his admission because it rings zero bells.

"Who the fuck is that?" Shoo speaks first, sounding like he doesn't believe a word Shane's saying.

"I don't know." We're all looking at this guy and I realize, in this moment, that he really is useless.

"I don't have time for this shit. You boys can have fun." Wiping my blade on the only part of Shane's clothes that isn't already soaked in it, I lean into his good ear. "With a little luck, you'll pass out quickly because these two can play for hours and hours and hours." At my words, Shane's eyes spring open, his pupils constricting as realization dawns. He's going to pay for the sins of his crew and his affiliation to them. "No hard feelings, Shane, but that bike is my best friend and when you fuck with mine, you basically fuck yourself."

With that, I turn and walk out. I've got shit to do and calling Glitch is the first thing on my list.

Snapping my dirty gloves off as I step outside and slide the metal door closed—we don't want the sounds to filter out and catch the attention of a passerby—I then press the third contact on my list.

"What's up, Boss? Got something for me?" Glitch is chewing on something when he answers on the first ring and, by the sound of it, I'm guessing it's his Cheetos.

Gross.

A small smile curls at the corners of my mouth as the word crosses my mind alongside Hallie's grimaces. Before meeting her for the first time, that word wouldn't have been in my vocabulary. Now it's popping up in my head like a zit.

"Yeah, do a search for Harvey Cook and get back to me ASAP."

"Sure thing." The line goes dead as expected. Glitch knows I don't chit chat. He learned the hard way that once I've said what he needs to know, I'm out.

When I go back inside, Shane is two minutes away from losing the battle. The phone is back in my pocket and the knife in my sheath when I shrug on my leather jacket and push my helmet back on my head.

All the while, I watch Shoo as he nails the guy's bare feet to the wooden slabs planted on either side of the drain before Binx walks up with boiling hot water. I'd cringe at the sight, knowing the pain Shane is feeling is probably going to give him a heart attack, but any possible empathy I could have had was ripped away from me the day they killed Murphy Gallagher. The only decent man left in this world.

Now, my world is bleak so, yeah, I really don't give a fuck that he's hurting.

This is why we're told to choose our friends wisely. Because their fuck ups carry consequences.

Chapter Ten

J

"It's a good thing you're one of us, Fizz, or, I swear, I'd kidnap you and keep you locked in my apartment for all time." Tab runs his meaty palm over his chest and stomach as he stands to take his dirty dishes to the kitchen. "Fucking love crew taco night."

"You wouldn't have tried my tacos if that's the case, Tab." Fizz laughs and finishes off her bottle of beer as Crank clears her empty plate along with his. She's officially been banned from tidying up after one of our big meals together because the cook should not have to clean—and the rest of us pretty much suck at cooking anything more than ramen.

"Semantics." On his way back to our large dining area, Tab ruffles Fizz's hair lightly.

"Fuck off, Mountain Man." She slaps his hand away. "Go get the van ready for us. One of Tommy's men called in for a clean-up in Harlem. They should be almost finished with their job in the next hour."

"Who the fuck is To—oh, you mean Babyface? You got it." Tab salutes her, a wry grin on his face as he walks out.

I finish up the last of my taco, watching and enjoying the way my crew interacts. This made-family is something I never even dreamed of, yet, it's something I couldn't do without anymore. I can't help wondering how Hallie is going to fit in.

It's dangerous, sure, and my main focus was to keep her as far away from all my shit as possible, but that's not really working for me anymore. Or her. She needs me, I need her, so this has to work out. I'll make sure of it.

With the amount of death and destruction she's had to encounter so far, there's no longer a need to hide it from her.

"You still insist on calling the other capos by their real names, Fizz?" I can't help but ask and it makes me smile.

"Only some of them. I can't call George 'The Butcher' since Devon came on the scene, but I'm on board with calling Eddie 'Snake Eyes'. And Tommy's almost as old as I am now. Calling him Babyface doesn't feel right anymore." She stands at the same time as me and pushes her chair under the table.

"Fair enough. I do love that his crew call in advance when they're working though." And I really do.

"Me too. But they're always messy. Getting rid of evidence on his crew's jobs is something we have to be meticulous about." She shudders and grabs her jacket from the back of her chair.

I laugh and shake my head. "Yeah, they like to get slicey. Have fun though, I'm gonna go catch up with Glitch."

Who thanked Fizz profusely for dinner before taking it back to his cave.

Crank is washing up the dirty dishes as I enter the kitchen, having pulled the short straw this evening—literally. We don't take it in turns to wash up because, frankly, I'd rather take a shit in my hands and clap. It's pure luck every time, and I'm always the straw holder.

"What're your plans tonight?" I ask as I place my now empty plate next to the sink.

"I'm helping Binx tune up his new ride before going over the map of death sites, just to be sure we have it right before going in."

If I'd just asked Shoo the same question, I have no doubt he'd be explicit in explaining how he plans to jerk off this evening.

"Good. Thanks for doing that, Crank." I begin heading out of the room.

"No worries, Boss." He doesn't look around or stop what he's doing as he speaks, continuing to wash the dinner dishes.

The smell of tacos hits me as I open the door to Glitch's cave and there's still half of one sitting on his plate by one of his keyboards.

"Dude, crack a window open." I sit myself down on the swivel chair next to him.

"It's fucking cold outside at this time of night. I don't wanna freeze my systems." He continues tapping away.

"More like freeze your nutsack." I laugh. "So, what have we got?"

"You're gonna have to be a little more specific with the amount of balls we have in the air right now, Boss." He stops typing and turns to look at me, a smirk on his lips.

"Harvey Cook." The newest clue we have on anything that isn't a dead-end.

The Imperial March from *Star Wars* begins playing loudly from my pocket at the same time as my phone vibrates again.

"Why the fuck is it doing that?" I pull out my phone and stare at it until the music stops, showing me I have three unread messages from...

> **Daddy D:** How did it go with Shane?

> **Daddy D:** Did he give anyone else up?

> **Daddy D:** I'm coming over.

What the fuck? I check the number and have to resist rolling my eyes into the back of my head because this guy is asking to get his balls sliced off. I know for a fact that Marco's brother-in-law, Devon, calls himself that so no...just fucking no.

Glitch is chuckling to himself, sipping on his can of Redbull. "Is that your stalker? Because if it is, he's stepped up his game and I'm kinda impressed."

"Yeah. How is that even possible?" I quickly type out a response to the deluded man that is Dmitry.

> **Me:** You have no idea where I am, PIMFA.

"Let me have a look." Glitch holds out his hand and I pass him my cell. He taps for a few minutes before inhaling deeply and exhaling with a, "Wow," then handing it back to me. "He's bypassed the security I installed and has remote access somehow."

"Motherfucker." This is a killable offense in my eyes. My phone holds a lot of information that, in the wrong hands, could be fatal, and I don't know this guy for shit. Trouble is, I kinda don't want to kill him. He's intriguing, a challenge, someone I haven't been able to figure out completely. I immediately change his name in my cell to 'Fuckwit'. We'll see how he likes that.

"Are you growling?" Glitch is trying hard not to laugh and I glare at him, making him quickly turn back to one of his screens.

Shouting from somewhere outside catches my attention just as Binx throws open the door. "Boss, there's some dude here who says you can vouch for him. Crank has him up against the garage door right now. Says his name is Dmitry. What do you want us to do?"

"Fucking man has a death wish." I sigh heavily and stand before walking out of the room and toward the side door to the garage.

And there he is, wearing jeans that show off his peachy ass and a black *Star Wars* T-shirt, which hugs his heavily tattooed biceps. Oh, and Crank is holding a gun to the back of his head and has his face crushed against the door. I can't quite see his expression, but as I step further into the garage, Dmitry's huge grin becomes visible.

"What the fuck are you doing here?" My words are practically a snarl.

"Told you I was coming, and I always do what I say. Does your crew always welcome guests this warmly? He's kinda turning me on." Dmitry laughs, throwing a teasing wink at Crank.

"Crank, let him go. I know him." Resting my hands on my hips, I make sure at least one of my daggers is within reach.

Slowly, Crank lowers his weapon, narrowing his eyes on Dmitry's head as he turns to face me. "You try anything, I'll help her bury your body."

"Anything I do to your boss, she'll beg me for." Dmitry grins at me the whole time.

"Yeah, good luck with that." Crank scoffs as Dmitry walks toward me.

"Follow me. Touch nothing or I'll cut your fingers off." I turn and walk back through the house to where I left Glitch, knowing Dmitry's right behind me.

I shouldn't allow this man in, especially not into Glitch's room, but he knows everything anyway and there's no denying that fact. To be honest, as soon as I realized the crazy fuck had actually come here, I figured he and Glitch can put their technical heads together. Maybe then we'll be able to get the bullshit dealt with a lot quicker.

Trusting him isn't my issue, because I sure as fuck don't, and I know for a fact that Glitch won't hesitate in shooting him between the eyes if he screws up in there, but Dmitry's been somewhat helpful so far, so he can stay. For now.

"Nice setup, man." Dmitry appraises Glitch's batcave, nodding his head with respect in his eyes as he takes it all in, closing the door to the room behind him. "What's the processing power like on those?" He casually sits in the chair I occupied before stopping Crank from shooting him and Glitch doesn't even flinch, answering his questions.

He's in his element talking about computers and it's good to see. He wouldn't dream of being this open with someone I hadn't brought to him myself.

"Hang on a minute, why haven't you threatened him with the gun under your desk yet?" I at least expected a little intimidation to happen. Gotta say, I'm disappointed.

"Boss, you wouldn't have brought him inside alive if he was a problem. And I saw the messages when I was checking out your phone." Glitch turns back toward the screens and points something out to Dmitry.

The trust my crew has in my judgment is scary sometimes, but it's just one reason I'd die for any one of them.

The phone thing has got to be how he's tracked me here, fucker.

"If you two could stop orgasming over the computers, I still want to know what you've found out about Harvey Cook."

They both turn to look at me, now lounging back on the small sofa-bed after allowing them tech-talk time, and Dmitry's eyes immediately catch mine, holding me prisoner.

"We're setting up some facial recognition software, found some social media presence, some bills, but it's like he's been dead for the last ten years. Everything stops, but there's no record of death anywhere." Glitch is the one who answers me, but he's staring at his screen again as he does, all while Dmitry's gaze remains connected to mine.

We're in some kind of standoff and I refuse to lose by looking away first.

"So we still know a whole load of nothing?" I ask with a sigh.

Dmitry's eyes crinkle a little at the edges, like he's taunting me.

"Pretty much, Boss. But D's helping me set this up so it should work quicker and we'll have a hit in no time. I'm also working on some pictures, but I need time to cross-reference first to make sure it's the right guy. The number of Harvey Cooks in the US isn't fucking small."

"D? You only met him an hour ago."

Dmitry's cheeks twitch at my comment and he finally breaks the stare-off when Glitch taps him on the arm.

"What am I supposed to call him? He said his name is D, I call him D." Glitch shrugs, and if I could see his face I have no doubt I'd have to throat punch him for rolling his eyes at me.

I don't respond, pulling out my phone to send Hallie a goodnight message before she goes to sleep. It's something I've gotten into the habit of doing and I won't deny the warmth that spreads through my veins when she responds with her usual, "Goodnight, Mom. Love you."

"Okay, as soon as we know that's the Harvey Cook we're looking for, it'll start tracking him once we get a facial recognition hit. We'll have a location in no time." Glitch turns to look at me, patting Dmitry on the back as he does. "D's got skills, Boss. He sticking around?"

I glare at him, which should give all the answers that I'm willing to give to that question. Then my eyes slide over to Dmitry, who still seems to have that knowing smirk on his face. "Time to go." I stand and open the door, not needing to remind Glitch to keep me in the loop in real time.

"I'll send you a link to that website." Dmitry slaps Glitch on the back as though they've been friends for years and follows me out of the room.

Everyone else is either out working or back in their own apartments now, the rest of the house quiet from inactivity. Glitch is the only one who stays here regularly, he's taken residence in the master bedroom.

Once outside, I step up to my bike, completely ignoring the large man hovering behind me. I need to ride, clear my head a little.

"Take me to your place for dinner." His breath is warm against the back of my neck, and he's so close without actually touching me.

"No. You shouldn't even be here." The fact that he is, and I didn't try to stab him, is something I need to seriously think about on my ride.

As per my usual M.O., I ignore anything else he has to say, sliding my helmet over my head and lifting my leg over my blood-red baby. The engine is alive within seconds and

I don't even look back as I ride off, the vibration between my thighs like an elixir I will never tire of.

The mid-April night chill is thick in the air and I revel in the sight of the Hudson River on my route home. I don't head straight to my apartment, choosing instead to spend the next two hours riding through the streets of New York. My thoughts are consumed with things they shouldn't be. Dmitry. Why he keeps showing up, why he makes me feel the way he does, why I like it so much, why I haven't killed him yet for all the liberties he's taken with me. That one, I still don't have the answers to.

High on my to-do kill-list is killing Ronan and whoever remains in his crew, closely followed by finding the serial killer murdering Marco's soldiers. Somewhere among all that, we need to figure out what Harvey Cook has to do with anything and why Mr. Wright is such a sketchy tail-dodger that has my hackles rising every time he's near. Most importantly, above all else, I need to get my daughter back without getting the feds on our case.

Dmitry should absolutely not be occupying my brain space with all that I have going on.

Knowing he's been my texting stalker this whole time should be something I despise him for, but he delivered Riley Callaghan for me on a platter, has given me leads I'd never have without him, and is now even helping Glitch. He's an enigma, pushing his way into my life as if he's always been there, and somehow, he's not out of place in my world.

I can't figure out what his deal is, what he wants, what his end-game is. Whatever it is though, I won't hesitate in gutting him if he betrays me.

Pulling up outside my apartment, I go through the motions of locking up my bike before heading inside and jogging up the stairs to my door. A noise inside my apartment makes me pause, moving my hand to my back to grip the handle of my gun. I won't shoot the intruder because the noise would be deafening and the cops would be called and I don't wanna deal with all that tonight. It's past midnight and I just want to crawl into bed after I've stabbed whoever this fuck is. I'll call for my Reapers to help clean it up tomorrow.

I slowly turn the key in my lock and push open my door, the smell of cooking onions assaulting my senses.

What the...?

Now that my door's open, the sound of country music playing from my kitchen is clear. Then I hear his voice, singing along to something about whiskey. I take a deep breath because this fucker just won't stop.

It takes me mere seconds to walk into my kitchen, the barrel of my gun pressed against the back of Dmitry's head as he stands in front of the stove that has been used a grand total of never since I've lived here.

"Ooh, foreplay! Thought we'd do that after some food." He turns to face me, my gun now directed at his forehead, and steps forward, so close that my chest practically heaves against his. Then he wags his brows, his trademark smirk firmly in place.

"What the fuck are you doing in my apartment?" My words are low, quiet, barely a whisper, and the threat in them is clear.

"Thought I'd make us a snack before bed. Cooking is my love language."

"Presumptuous much? Just because I let you make me come *one* time doesn't obligate me to give you any more. Get. The fuck. Out." With each word, I take small steps toward him, pushing him backward into the countertop behind him. My gun is still against his skull and now I'm on my tiptoes, my nose pressed against his, my eyes narrowed on his pale green ones.

"Mmm, I love it when you threaten me. I'm starting to think it's *your* love language. I can work with that."

And he isn't lying, the feel of his hard cock against my stomach is doing things to my insides and my breathing has become heavy. But the fact he's used the word love three times in as many minutes is making me question his sanity.

He's invading every aspect of my life and I'm not used to this behavior. The standing firm against me, ignoring my simple requests, my privacy; he's stirring feelings inside me that I'm not sure I'll ever be ready for and it's fucking confusing. So I step back and hit him in the face with the butt of my gun, across the cheek, not hard enough to break anything, but his head moves to the side and I have to hide my smile.

Seconds pass before he lifts his hand to his face, slowly turning back to look at me again. The smile on his face is feral, sending heat straight to my core.

"Do it again."

He's fucking serious?

He begins stalking toward me, to where I've backed up and am trying to control my breaths. The look in his eyes is dangerous, addictive, and I do exactly as he requests, I go to punch him again.

This time, he blocks it, gripping my wrist and continuing to walk into me. We're now chest to chest again because I refuse to back up any more. Without another word, I swing my left fist into his stomach before gripping the arm he is holding me with and dragging him further into my living room to flip him onto his back.

"Get out of my house, Dmitry. There's no reason for you to be here." My gun is on the kitchen counter now, because I'm not going to shoot him. Something inside me wants him to fight back, but if he does then I know he won't be leaving this apartment.

"Oh, Little Demon, of course there is."

It happens so quickly I almost miss it, but the fucker throws a dagger at me, one that imbeds itself into the wall directly behind me.

"You fucker." I'm on him in seconds, throwing punches at him, straddling his waist until he grips my fists and flips me onto my back.

The sadistic asshole is laughing as he nips at my bottom lip, his solid cock perfectly aligned with my pussy before I manage to get an arm free and punch him in the ribs. This would be over in seconds if I reached for one of my knives, if I wanted to do some serious damage. He's winded from my last hit, and during the brief moment he is distracted from the pain, I slide my legs back under him and kick him off.

My breaths are heavy, fast, and adrenaline is pumping through my veins as he stands again, the dangerous grin on his face going nowhere.

"You're fucking incredible." His voice is full of lust, of promises I don't want, of need for something I can't give.

"And you're a fucking idiot."

He laughs again and moves toward me as I rush to the kitchen in the direction of the burning smell now filling my nostrils. The onions in the frying pan are a black mess as I turn off the knob at the same time as grabbing the knife sitting on the counter. I don't take my eyes off him as he leisurely walks over without a care in the world, a bruise forming on his cheek just below his scar.

When he's a few feet away, I throw myself at him, pushing him against the wall and holding the knife to his throat. "You need to get out while you still have your life, Dmitry. I'm not playing this game anymore."

"Who said I was playing a game, Little Demon?" He pushes his head forward, pressing his neck against the blade, and kisses me. No, this is not a kiss, he's devouring me.

His tongue demands entrance and I open up for him, allowing this crazy man to claim my mouth with a fiery passion until I regain some sense of control and pull back.

There's a thin line of blood along his neck where my knife broke the skin and a heat in his pale eyes that would make a weaker woman beg.

Deliberately and slowly, he raises a hand to his neck and slides his fingers across the small trickle of blood before bringing them to my mouth. My lips part for him, red flags popping up in my brain telling me a million reasons why this is a bad idea, but fuck do I want this man.

Just for tonight. I can allow myself that. I've earned the time out, haven't I?

I suck on his fingers and it's like melted butter on my tongue, then I bite him. Not hard enough to break the skin, but when I do, he groans. The sound goes straight between my thighs and when he grabs the back of my head with his free hand, yanking my head backward to give him access to my throat, I let him.

The throbbing between my legs is insistent, no longer allowing me to ignore one of my baser instincts. To fuck.

"Fine. You can stay." My voice is breathy, full of as much need as his responding growl.

He chuckles against my neck as he continues to nip and suck, the small bites of pain sending shocks to every nerve ending in my body. Knife still in hand, I grip his T-shirt and slice down the front of it, ripping it open and grazing his chest at the same time. He hisses at the contact and pulls my hair back harder so he can get to my lips with his again.

The kiss is desperate, feral, full of tongues and teeth and lips pressed against each other with need. Dmitry slides the zipper of my jacket down and pushes it from my shoulders, his other hand still gripping at my hair, controlling my movements. He releases my hair long enough for me to rip off my black tank top and push down my pants, only my panties left on my otherwise naked body. At the same time, he steps out of his jeans bending slightly to grip just under my ass. He lifts me and isn't gentle about slamming me onto the kitchen counter.

It's cold against my ass, but the chill is quickly forgotten as Dmitry takes my nipple between his teeth and bites down. He pays special attention to them before grabbing the knife from my hand for himself. With measured movements, he steps back a little and rakes his eyes all over me. Then he uses the tip of the knife to mark my chest by dragging it across my skin from my clavicle to my belly button. I now have the same faint red line as I marked him with.

"Fucking beautiful." His growl vibrates against my breast as he attacks my nipple with his mouth again.

"Shut up and fuck me."

"Soon, Little Demon." He chuckles again and works his lips down my stomach, squeezing one of my tits with his left hand and gripping my thigh tightly with his right.

The kisses are interspersed with tiny bites of pain that have me thrusting my hips to try and get some friction from somewhere. I'm not disappointed as his tongue finds my clit and I groan loudly. His teeth and fingers join the party down there and I'm a needy fucking mess already. He rips a hole in my panties instead of pulling them off or shoving them to one side, giving him the access I wouldn't have denied him anyway.

My body is a traitorous bitch, but I don't care, this feels fucking insanely good. His fingers work magic as he twists them in and out of my pussy, furiously lapping at my clit. It's like he's eating his favorite meal and can't get enough. The groans and growls coming from his throat are an aphrodisiac to my growing orgasm and I ride his face to bring myself closer.

He's still squeezing and kneading my tits in his palm, pinching my nipples each time he bites at my clit. The pain is followed each time with indisputable pleasure.

"Yes!" I scream out as an orgasm rips through my body and I buck against his relentless mouth.

It's not enough. I need more of this, of him.

"Stop screwing around and fuck me already." I look down at him and he meets my gaze with my clit in between his teeth.

He raises an eyebrow and slowly backs up a little. As if a thought has just come to him, he picks up the knife he dropped on the counter beside me and begins rubbing the hilt against my wet pussy, soaking it in my cum.

"Like this?" he asks, pressing the tip just inside me, his eyes still on mine as his palm grips the blade and he pushes it further.

I gasp at the sensation, my eyes growing heavy with lust as a small trickle of blood falls from his fist and he pulls the knife out. Hissing, he drops the bloody knife onto the floor, but that dangerous grin remains in place. He pushes his boxers down, giving me the perfect view of his now fully-naked body.

It's a fucking masterpiece. The Celtic design from his bicep travels across his shoulder and partially on his hard, smooth chest, and I can't help the tip of my lips when I notice the design blends into the Death Star over his pec and ribs on one side. Taking in his naked form is something I'd like to take my time with, because I don't anticipate seeing it again after this.

There's still a faint red line down the center of his chest where I scratched him with my knife earlier, and I want to lick it, to revel in the mark I gave him.

"Do you want my cock, Little Demon? My cock that is so hard for you it fucking hurts."

I nod, desperate to be filled by him.

"Words, Little Demon. This only works if you really want it." He doesn't step toward me, but I can see he really wants to. His restraint is impressive.

Raising a brow of my own, I grip my tit with my palm and pinch my own nipple, then slide my other hand over my clit and groan when I make contact. It's still tingling from my previous orgasm and won't take much to bring another one forward.

Dmitry's breathing gets heavier, more erratic as he glares at me with amusement.

"Fuck me now, Dmitry, or I'll do it myself." I moan lightly and push a finger inside myself, squeezing my nipple at the same time.

He doesn't need telling twice, it seems, because in the next moment he grabs my wrists and holds them above my head before lining himself up with my eager pussy. His mouth presses against mine in a searing kiss and my toes curl when he pushes inside me. We both groan loudly, as if we've been waiting our whole lives to feel this pleasure. I close my eyes for a second at the euphoria rushing through my system and dig my fingers into his back, holding on tightly with the hope that he never stops pounding into me.

Scratching into his skin seems to spur him on and his thrusts are vigorous as I feel the draw of blood beneath my fingernails. Our moans morph into screams, the sounds of pleasure filling the space around us, and I'm glad for the soundproofing I had installed when I bought the place. I have no doubt my neighbors would be calling the police with the noises we're making.

If at all possible, his movements as he pounds in and out of me are more frantic than before and I know he's as close as I am. He brings a hand up to my throat and collars me, putting pressure in just the right places, which nearly sends me over the edge of the cliff. Our mouths are practically sealed together as we taste each other, claim each other, own each other, and he continues to fuck me like his life depends on it.

"I can't hold it back anymore, Little Demon." He drops my wrists and squeezes his fingers into my hip while his other hand keeps a firm collar around my throat. "Come all over my cock."

I don't need to be told again as he thrusts hard and fast into my cunt, to the hilt every time, his pubic bone brushing against my clit, and I burst on a scream.

"Fuck! Yes!" My orgasm hits, making my toes curl, and my body spasms, becoming uncontrollable under his ministrations. I'm completely at his mercy in this moment and I don't give a shit. It's freeing.

"You feel..." He drags his cock almost all the way out. "So." Slams it back in. "Fucking." Slides it back out. "Good." He slams it in again, and the roar that escapes him is like music to my ears, I swear I could come all over again if I weren't spent.

My thighs fall to the sides, the muscles so weak I can barely control their movements, my arms trembling from any effort I try to force on them. All the while Dmitry continues to kiss me, slowly sliding in and out of my cunt as if he wants to draw out every last drop of pleasure. The kisses are slower too, more gentle, and I don't hate it. Then reality kicks in; this man I barely know, who has been stalking me, is in my apartment, in my pussy.

This isn't something I've ever done. No one except me has ever been inside this apartment, and I definitely haven't fucked anyone here before. But, truth be told, I'm too tired to fight it right now.

With a sigh, I break the kiss and pull away from him, his dick still hard as it slides out and I push off the kitchen counter.

"I need to shower. You should go home." Without waiting for a reply, I leave the kitchen and head into my bathroom, not even looking at his face.

That was a mistake. It felt fucking amazing, but it can't happen again.

When I'm finished showering, I wrap a towel around myself and pad into my bedroom. I'm a little disappointed that I sent him home, but it had to be done.

The disappointment quickly dissipates because he's in my bed, under the covers, his head resting against his palm and that dangerous fucking grin aimed directly at me.

Narrowing my eyes, I prepare to tell him to fuck off, but even after freshening up in the shower, I'm still too tired to argue. It feels like forever since I've needed my bed as much as I do now and I'm going to take advantage of that. I'll burn out if I keep going the way I have been.

I sigh and drop my towel before climbing into my bed beside him. He holds an arm out, encouraging me to nestle into him, but no. Instead, I rest my head against the pillow and turn my back to him, lying on my side before reaching across and turning off the lamp. The bed jiggles a little and his heat is suddenly right behind me, his tattooed arm falling over me and pulling me into him.

Again, I'm too tired to argue, so I release a deep exhale instead. "Fine. You can stay."

He chuckles into the back of my neck, my damp hair making the heat of his breath send a chill over my skin and I shiver as my eyes grow heavy.

"Goodnight, Little Demon. Fair warning, I'm a snuggler."

Chapter Eleven

J

The entire length of my body aches, a delicious kind of burn that starts at my toes and ends at the tips of my fingers, as I stretch across my bed. It only takes me a second to realize something's not quite right. There's no doubt I'm in my apartment but the chemistry is off. Although, judging by the cold sheets beside me, it's clear Dmitry has been up and gone for a while.

I'm choosing to ignore the slight, almost insignificant kernel of disappointment at that thought and embracing the relief that my apartment is once again all mine.

Blinking away my sleep, I pop open one eye, snarling at the curtains I forgot to close before going to bed last night. That being said, I was a little fucking preoccupied, wasn't I? Another thing I can blame on Dmitry and his stubborn ass.

Okay, so I can admit that it's also a fine, altogether biteable ass, but that doesn't mean I need him in my space.

Just as thoughts of last night flit through my mind like a high-end porno movie, the smell in the kitchen area assaults my nostrils and forces me to sit up. We burnt dinner in our haste to fuck last night, yet this smell is different. Less aggressive and a hell of a lot more appetizing.

Is that...sausage?

I know for a fact my fridge is empty and the only food I have in this place are coffee and pretzels.

Breakfast of champions.

Propping myself up on my elbows, I frown as the sight of Dmitry's bedhead and naked, tatted shoulders greets me in the kitchen. He's moving from side to side, his head bobbing up and down as he...what the fuck *is* he doing?

From my bed, I can't see over the bar area so I fold my knees and stand on my mattress to get the full effect of this man at my stove. It's when he turns to grab something by the sink that I notice the pods in his ears. And yup, this fool is cooking and dancing, wearing only his jeans, in my fucking kitchen like we're Mr. and Mrs. Homemakers having cute after-sex breakfast.

What world does he live in? He knows about Murphy, he knows about Hallie. If he thinks last night meant anything more than just me getting my orgasm on, he's living under a fucking rock on a deserted island in the middle of fucking nowhere.

But then he starts humping the counter, lifting one leg and throwing his hands up like he's in a music video right before he puts his leg back down and gifts me with a twerk.

That's when it happens. It's sudden and it's unexpected, stunning me into temporary shock as Dmitry freezes, turns to me, and grins like he's won the fucking lottery.

"Oh, Little Demon, did you just laugh?" His fingers pop out his buds before he places them carefully on the bar and picks up his black-rimmed glasses.

Shit, I've never seen him wearing those and for some ridiculous reason, I'm suddenly aware that I'm naked and turned on.

A small growl escapes me as I rip the sheets off my bed and bounce off the mattress, stand, then cover myself like I'm Caesar and this is Rome.

"Wipe that smirk off your face, Geek Squad. You caught me off guard with all that ass play going on."

He doesn't answer, just keeps grinning as he brings a piece of bacon to his mouth and snaps it in two with his teeth.

Flipping him off, I head straight for the bathroom, pee, then wash my hands before checking myself out in the mirror.

Damn. My hair looks like it went four rounds with Mike Tyson before giving up the fight, and while I love a good, rough fuck, I'm not usually a fan of the whole markings on the skin thing. Yet, the barely-visible cut from my knife is still there and taunting me.

Hmm, interesting. Of course, I don't bother to tame my hair or try to wipe away what little mascara has darkened beneath my eyes because what he sees is what he gets and if he's disappointed, then he clearly knows where the door is since he so blatantly used it last night without my permission.

Not gonna lie, walking back out only amplifies just how hungry I am. Plus, the closer I get to the stove, the more my stomach reminds me that I worked off every last calorie from Fizz's tacos last night fucking my stalker-slash-twerk meister.

My gaze lands first on the skillet, where scrambled eggs, bacon, and sausages are all sizzling to perfection, before spotting a box of weird Danish-looking things.

"What's that?" I point to said pastries, noticing some are filled with blueberry by the violet coloring and others are red, so either strawberry or raspberries, if I had to guess. The yellow filling one makes my mouth water and I decide I don't even fucking care what it is, I'm tasting it.

"Kolache; they're Czech pastries. Blueberry." He points to the violet one, then points to the red one. "Cherry…and that one is my favorite. Lemon curd." As he speaks, he picks up the pastry and brings it to my already open mouth.

The tangy smell of lemon is the first clue that this may become my favorite food ever. The second is the sweet and sour explosion on my tongue. I was expecting the dough to be flaky like a Danish but instead, it's dense and a little on the sweet side.

Holy mother of fuck, I'm in love.

"Good, right?"

My eyes are closed in ecstasy so I can't see his expression when he speaks, but I'm willing to guess that he's grinning like a fool because not only did he make me laugh, but he also made me moan and his cock wasn't even involved.

"Jesus, did you make those?"

He tries to take the pastry away but I growl at him. With a chuckle, he keeps it at my mouth and waits for me to take another huge chunk of my new obsession.

"Nah, I went out to Brooklyn this morning to pick them up. Ordered them yesterday so they'd be ready by nine o'clock."

I stop mid-chew at his admission.

"A little presumptuous, don't you think?" My words are barely comprehensible with the mouthful of pastry sticking to my palate and tongue and even my teeth, but I can't bring myself to care.

"I prefer the word preemptive." Gliding the tip of his nose along the column of my neck, he whispers as his mouth stops at the shell of my ear, "Told you, food is my love language."

Right. Leaning back, I narrow my gaze at him before taking another bite and shuffling along to the coffee pot. Dmitry takes out two plates—which is the exact total number of plates in this apartment—two forks and one glass, placing it all on the bar and serving our hot food like he's been doing this his entire life.

"I only found one glass and…can I say that Marco needs to start paying you better than this? Jesus, Jordyn, I had to buy basic condiments like ketchup and mustard. Who lives like that?"

I roll my eyes at his teasing tone but don't give him the information he's clearly fishing for. We fucked, we didn't get married.

"I have two of everything in case something breaks. Case in point, I broke a glass, still have another. I have everything I need here." I bring a forkful of eggs to my mouth and nearly orgasm at the spices he used on them.

"So what happens when you have company?" Watching me, he speaks around a sausage, biting half of it off and grinning like a kid. It's a little endearing and I don't want to like it. But goddammit, he made me breakfast.

I shrug at his question and decide that I'll give him this little tidbit, even though I know for a fact he's going to think he's special. "I don't bring anyone here so it's a moot point."

"Hmm, so I'm special." Predictable.

"No, you just showed up and refused to leave like one of those alley cats that decides your house is now theirs. Technically, you weren't invited." I narrow one eye at him, daring him to contradict me.

"I dunno. Your exact words were..." He looks up to the ceiling like he's searching his brain for the memory before snapping his fingers and grinning again. "Fine. You can stay."

Pointing my fork at him, I speak slowly so he can understand me. "Keep it up and you won't be finishing that meal."

Still looking like he's on cloud nine, Dmitry cleans off his plate and serves me more coffee, filling the lone glass with orange juice.

With only one glass, the ass makes a show of drinking out of mine, his eyes fixed on me and a smile so wide it causes his scar to crinkle.

"So what are the glasses for?" I use my fork again, making circles in the air at his whole hot-geek look going on.

"To see?" Christ, this man.

"Are you trying to piss me off?" Cocking my head to the side, I give him my best glare, the one that makes grown men kneel at my feet and beg for mercy.

"Fuck, yes. Is your pussy wet for me?" What? Is he insane?

When I rub my naked thighs together, I frown.

"I wish I could say this was a ploy to get you all hot and bothered for me but they really are prescription." He pops a stray piece of bacon in his mouth, his eyes never veering away from me.

"So why's this the first time I'm seeing them?" I sip at my coffee and take in just how fucking hot he really is. It's not necessarily the light-green eyes or the strong, Roman nose, or those fucking talented lips. As my eyes roam his features, I decide it's all of it. The combination of it all, including his scar and quirky personality, makes him all kinds of irresistible.

"Contacts." His answer halts my inspection of him, my gaze narrowing on his mirth-filled eyes.

"I'm guessing you planned to stay the night and brought all you needed with you?"

Dmitry reaches out and taps me on the tip of my nose and I swear to fuck, if I weren't chewing on a cherry kolache, I would have bitten his finger right the fuck off. "Bingo."

"Take your shit back with you. This is a one off so don't get used to it." Fuck, tart cherries on the sweet dough are just as delicious as the lemon, which reminds me. "How'd you find this place?"

Dmitry shrugs. "I make it a point to know the location of all the good Czech bakeries."

"Because...?" Do I have to spell it all out for him?

Leaning in, he crosses his arms on the counter and grins. "Because, silly, my parents are Czech. It's my heritage. Never lived there but I still have dual citizenship." Interesting. I'll have to get back to that.

"Now, if we're playing twenty questions, I believe you still haven't answered mine. Is your pussy wet for me?" Dmitry goes from playful to lusty in two point four seconds, his eyes boring into my chest. When I look down, I roll my eyes.

"Fine. My pussy is wet for you and yes, my nipples are hard. What can I say? I'm a woman with needs and last night you gave me what I wanted." I speak in a bored tone, like we're talking about the Dow Jones and how stable it's been as of late.

Dmitry stands, one hand on his belt buckle as he pops it open and slides the leather, slowly, from the throngs of his jeans.

"What you wanted." He repeats my words like he's testing them on his tongue, measuring their worth. "Let's see if I can give you exactly what you need." At his tone, my thighs clench and my pussy is immediately ready for him. Fuck, how does he do this?

Fingers fisting my hair, he pulls me back into his chest and plants a kiss on my lips, no tongue, as he reaches out for something. I can't see a damn thing in this position—no doubt a calculated move—but as soon as he lets me go, I notice the ketchup and mustard sitting right next to my plate where my uneaten sausage lies.

"You know, in certain cultures, it's rude to not finish your plate." I don't respond to his little role playing, curious where he wants to take this. "In fact, working for the Italian mob, you should know that." My gaze follows his every move as he flicks at my sheet, letting it fall like he was personally offended by it, then picks up the ketchup bottle, opens it, and lines it up with my nipples.

He wouldn't...

Oh, but he would.

A streak of red hits the right tit, immediately creating goosebumps from the cold. He repeats his action with the mustard, leaving twin lines on each nipple.

"Not to mention, I cooked you breakfast, and in my country, it's frowned upon to not finish your meal." His voice is soothing, like he's reading a bedtime story, when he picks up the sausage and dips it into the ketchup, then the mustard, before bringing it to my mouth. "Open."

Obeying doesn't come naturally to me but I do it anyway because I'm fucking turned on for some crazy reason. I bite, chew, then swallow.

"Hmm, I like feeding you, it makes me hard." He's not kidding, it's right there, just above my ass.

Pulling back the rest of the sausage from my mouth, he lifts it to his own lips then hums.

"It's missing something…" he says absently as he leans in and licks a path from my collar bone, up the column of my neck, and stops at my jaw. "Let's see if I've figured it out."

His hand between my legs, he slides the sausage up my slit before circling my clit. I stiffen, my mind going to a million different scenarios of good hygiene and possible yeast infections. If he tries to fuck me with it, I will shove the entire country of Germany up his sausage-loving asshole.

"Relax." Easy for him to say. But when his hand comes up to his mouth, I realize he was using my cum as a condiment. I do relax then. No one is getting fucked with food today and thank fuck for that. Except, when Dmitry moans in my ear, murmuring how delicious I am, I have to control my desire to fuck his face with my cunt.

Actually, no I don't.

"Screw it." Jumping off the stool, I push him back, then back some more, until he lets himself land backwards on the bed, grin and all. Straddling him, I press my palms against his chest and kneel my way up to his face, my pussy hovering just above his delectable mouth. Green eyes sparking from below, he licks his lips and winks right before I lower my cunt and get what I need from him.

"Be a good boy and finish your meal."

With one of his hands on each of my ass cheeks, he tongue-fucks my pussy like a starved man, his tongue licking everywhere, his teeth nipping at my clit and my lips just as his finger pushes inside and curls.

Leaning over him, my hands pressed against the wall, I move my hips as if I were fucking his cock and, to be honest, this is just as enjoyable. Hell, more than that...it's fucking fantastic—even though I'd never tell *him* that. The man's ego is inflated enough as it is, no need to do more damage.

My thighs widen when his finger travels from my pussy to my ass, circling the tight rim before pushing inside, slowly. In and out, little by little, until my ring of muscle lets him in completely. Goddamn, that feels good. So. Fucking. Good.

Below me, Dmitry moans his own pleasure into my pussy, the vibrations making my head spin and my body sing. Fuck, yes.

"Don't fucking stop!" I'm not sure who I'm talking to, him or me because, to be honest, I'm the one in control here, the one fucking him, even though he'd like to think he's topping from the bottom.

Hell, maybe he is. Do I really care? Not even a little. The only thing that matters is this, right here. This feeling growing inside me, taking over my muscles and nerve endings. This power that's making my eyes blur and my ears pound with my very heart beat.

This.

This...

"Oh, fuck!" I convulse, my pussy practically suffocating him as I take my pleasure from his mouth. Dmitry's torso rises from the bed like he can't get his mouth deep enough, needing to bury his entire face inside me.

The idea of him so desperate takes me to the point of no return.

I fall. No...I fucking crash. My mouth drops open but no sound comes out as I let the orgasm take over my body, my mind...my fucking sanity.

By the time I regain my senses, I'm lying on my back, my eyes closed and my lungs begging to take in more air.

"Fuck, Little Demon. I think I know why breakfast is the most important meal of the day."

After that insane orgasm, Dmitry hauled me to the shower, carrying me like a fucking sack of potatoes, where he fucked me from behind against the tiles as the shower pummeled our slapping skin and muffled the cries of our sudden religious tendencies.

For the first time in years, I forgot about everything. I forgot about the Italians, the Irish, and the fucking Greeks. I forgot that outside these walls a world was there to remind me of the injustices I've been dealt.

A world where Murphy no longer exists.

So, when the phone blares the theme song to *World War Z*, I roll my eyes and accept Zavier's call. Mr. Wright is back at the casino, so I don't hesitate to throw Dmitry's clothes at him—apparently he's a walk-around-naked kind of guy—and tell him to get his shit and let's go. By the time I get to the casino, I'm in work mode and ready to get some fucking answers. I'm tired of using kids' gloves on this guy and from the vibes I'm getting from Z, he's done with him, too.

Heading straight for the roulette table, I sit my ass down and stare straight at Mr. Wright, who is sweating like a fucking pig at a barbecue.

"Funny meeting you here," I say, accepting a bottle of mineral water from the eager waitress and checking the cap is sealed before thanking her.

"I was thinking more along the lines of annoying, but whatever." He's been drinking, his eyes are a little unfocused as he pushes his chips forward onto red before slamming back what I'm guessing is whisky in his glass.

Roulette is all about probabilities. There are thirty-eight slots, eighteen of which are red. The payout isn't as fulfilling as betting it all on a single number but it might even him out. Unless, of course, he's been losing all fucking night and this is just one more push into debt.

An employee brings me two thousand worth of chips, courtesy of Zavier, I'm sure. I'm okay with that. I don't mind betting other people's money. As I place three hundred on number eight, black, I sit back and watch the man we can't seem to figure out. The table is almost full, only two seats are empty. Luckily, one is between Wright and myself so I don't beat around the bush anymore.

"Tell me, Wright. What is your deal? Why can't we find anything on you?" Sometimes, you just need to go straight for the carotid.

The idiot scoffs, wiping his forehead with a handkerchief before slicing a glare my way. "Because I'm smart and you people are a bunch of amateurs."

His answer intrigues me. He's not even hiding the fact that something's not squeaky clean about him. In fact, he sounds almost disappointed that we're still trying to figure him out, like he's playing the kiddie leagues when he believes he belongs in the majors.

"That's a little condescending coming from someone who can't seem to catch a break at the casinos yet comes around three times a week to…continue losing." I take a sip from the fancy bottle of water, pausing for effect. "You know, Einstein was onto something with his theory on insanity. You doing the same thing over and over again expecting a different outcome says a lot about you too." My phone pings with a text message, and even though we're not supposed to be on our phones, I still take it out and read it. Clearly, I don't give a fuck. Is Z going to kick me out? Yeah, I don't think so.

Glitch: Incoming

Glitch: Harvey Cook

I'm guessing it's a picture, and just as the grainy image pops up on my screen, Dmitry slides in next to me and kisses my neck, whispering. "Did you miss me?"

I almost smile at his antics, elbowing him in the ribs while keeping my eyes on the screen.

It's not very clear but there are three people in the picture. A man, a woman, and judging by the height and braces, a teenage girl with cornrows down to her neck standing between the two.

Dmitry's hand palms my chin, lifting it so my eyes meet his stare and licking a path across my bottom lip.

My eyes narrowed, I catch his tongue between my teeth and bite hard enough to get his attention but not hard enough to cause real pain. The fucker winks at me.

"I'm working," I tell him, my eyes back on the phone.

"Are you betting, ma'am?" My head snaps up and I snarl at the croupier for calling me that.

"No."

"Yes." Dmitry and I both answer at the same time as he pushes all my tokens onto number twenty-four.

I frown but return my attention to the picture. There's something about the guy...I feel like I've seen him before.

"No more bets," the employee announces, waving a hand over the table before spinning the wheel in one direction and the ball in the other.

"Why did you bet all of it on that number?" I mean, it's their money, it's not like I care. They are the house.

"The twenty-fourth is the first time I ever laid eyes on you." My eyes snap to his, my brows furrowed. *What the fuck?*

"What are we, in middle school?" In my peripheral, Wright slams back another whisky as the ball drops into black and he loses...again. He's agitated and I can tell this loss is making him crazy.

"Look." Taking my eyes off Wright, I see that the ball has landed on twenty-four but my mind is still on the old man as pieces begin to click into place and my brain finally puts two and two together.

My gaze drops back to the picture as Dmitry drags his chips toward us.

Then it hits me.

Motherfucker.

When I look up, ready to pounce, he's gone.

Turning back to Dmitry, I push him in the chest and grit out a long, frustrated string of curses, all of them aimed at him.

Wright and Harvey Cook are one and the same.

Chapter Twelve

J

"How in the ever loving fuck is Mr. Wright, Harvey Cook—whatever the fuck his name is—connected to the Irish mob?" Flower picks the lock of the town house we discovered belongs to Cook, asking me the exact question that has been on my mind since Glitch sent me his photo last night.

The curtains are all drawn so we haven't been able to get a glimpse inside. We're hoping to catch him sleeping, but with the way this front lawn is overgrown I've got my suspicions that he's not here anymore.

"If we're lucky, there'll be something inside to give us answers." A musky smell invades my senses as I step through the now open front door. "Although, it's not looking good."

It seems the place has been empty for a while if the coating of dust on the windows and in the corners of the room is anything to go by. We both remain quiet and walk in different directions, making sure the house is clear of people before we begin our search in earnest.

Upstairs is deserted so I meet Flower back in the main living space, if you can call it that. The house is barren of things; the bare essentials and nothing more. Well, not even all of those. There is a crusty mattress in a tiny box room, a rotten toothbrush in the bathroom, and a lawn chair downstairs next to a kitchen table. That must be where he sits and eats his tasteless cereals, of which there are several boxes in the pantry. It's a squatter's ideal location and I'm surprised it isn't already full of them.

"Anything?"

I shake my head at Flower's question as I pull out my cell to text Glitch and let him know what we've found, or in this case, haven't found. Then I stop ignoring the messages from D and open them up.

> **Fuckwit:** WUU2? I don't have eyes on you.

And there's the reason this man is an absolute stalker. And also the reason I still haven't killed him.

> **Fuckwit:** I know where you are. Want some help?

> **Me:** When I feel like a damsel who needs a man to help her, I'll let you know.

I absolutely will not let him know, because being a damsel in distress has, and never will be, my thing.

> **Fuckwit:** Whoops, too late.

> **Me:** WTF is that supposed to mean?

"Who's got you grinning like the Cheshire Cat? Because that is not your Hallie smile."

"My Hallie smile?" Instead of outright snarling in my friend's face to shut her the fuck up, I'm deflecting.

"Yeah, we've all noticed that one. We know when you're texting her. This smile's different though. Has our Shadow taken a lover?" Flower extends and rolls the last word and laughs before quickly moving toward the back door, away from my easy reach.

So much for deflecting.

"No." I narrow my eyes at her, being very clear about the fact that this subject is off the table, and she holds her palms up in surrender, tipping her head slightly in acknowledgement. She's still fucking grinning though.

"Daddy's home!" The front door swings open and Flower and I both point our guns at the intruder. At the same time, two daggers fly toward the opening, one grazing his forearm as he tries to block them and move out of the way. "Well, fuck. I thought we'd save the foreplay until later, and I definitely didn't think you were into sharing." Dmitry stands up from his crouch and his gaze flicks to Flower before returning to me with that smile on his face that does things to my insides.

"What the actual fuck, Dmitry? We could've killed you." I'm trying not to shout because it's almost midnight and there are other houses nearby, but fuck me, this man is a pain in my ass.

"You didn't though. Aim must be a little off." He winks, stepping further inside the house and closing the door behind him. I want to punch the smirk from his face.

There's an equally punchable smirk twitching at Flower's lips too. "I'm gonna go, Boss. There's nothing here, place is deserted. I'll check in with Glitch on my way home." She heads for the door, and as she passes Dmitry, she looks up at him and pauses. "Good luck, new guy. She's gonna rip you a new asshole." Then she chuckles—more like cackles—and walks out through the front door.

The two of us remain, in another stand-off stare-off situation, our eyes locked together.

"Wanna help me bring my equipment in?" He tilts his head to gesture outside and the stupid dick better not have parked in front of the house and blown this whole thing. Harvey Cook may not be here right now, but this is a residential area and nosy neighbors talk.

"No, not really." It's on the tip of my tongue to ask for more information, like why he's here and what kind of equipment he brought, but I'm choosing not to engage.

"Didn't think so." Turning his back to me—which is pretty fucking stupid in most situations—he opens the front door and steps out, leaning down to the side and picking up two large silver cases. He holds them up like a prize before bringing them in and closing the door again.

Rolling my eyes, I give in and ask, "Okay, what are the cases for and why are you here?"

"Glitch said this was Cook's place so I figured we'd wanna keep an eye on it. Digitally." He lays the cases on the floor and flicks the locks before lifting the lids.

There are wires and tiny cameras and a few dozen other items that I'm sure Glitch would have a field day with.

The same Glitch who needs to keep his fucking mouth shut, though I can't be mad. The only reason we have more information now is because of Dmitry.

"Okay. And you'll be sharing all of this intel with us." It's not a question, I'm stating a fact.

"Of course, Little Demon. I have no use for it myself. This is all for you." There's that wink again, and the way it makes his scar move makes me want to lick it. I'm still curious where it came from.

Shaking my head in disbelief at his boldness, I sigh. I won't deny that even though this could be a fruitless task, it could also not be.

Dmitry pulls some items out and moves to the front door as he installs one of the cameras just above it, his back to me once more. Stepping up beside him, I grab the handle of my dagger, still stuck in the door frame, and yank it out.

"What's your deal, Dmitry?" I walk toward the kitchen counter in this open-plan space and perch against it, placing the tip of my knife on the surface and spinning it to see how long it stays upright.

"I love how you say my name. It's sexy." He finishes with the camera above the door and takes another out of his case, heading for the corner of the room.

"Deflection. How original."

He laughs as he connects the camera to I don't know what. I thought these kinds of setups would be a lot easier than he's making it look.

"Wanna play a game?" His eyes connect with mine for a second and he grins before he continues to do his tech-geek thing.

"No." I put my dagger away and pull out my butterfly knife to play with. I could go home, leave Dmitry to it, but I won't.

"Come on, twenty questions. I'll go first. What do you look for in a man?"

It's my turn to laugh, quietly of course. "If we're playing twenty questions, I'll be asking them, okay?"

"Sure thing, Little Demon. That's one, nineteen left to go." He moves toward the stairs with another device and I follow, leaning back against the railing at the bottom and flipping my butterfly knife around.

"How did you get that scar on your face?" Might as well make use of my time in this shitty little house.

"Ooh, you don't hold back, do ya?" He chuckles and looks right at me, his face turning serious, his pale eyes narrowing on mine. "Okay. I'll tell you, but you have to promise not to laugh."

Now I'm really curious.

"Nope, can't promise not to laugh at something. If my natural reaction is to laugh and I do it by mistake, then I'll have broken my promise and I don't do that." I shrug. It's bullshit, of course. Keeping my emotions in check comes almost as easy to me as breathing, but I'm still not making a promise I may not keep.

"Fair point." He still looks completely serious, straight-faced as he begins to speak. "When I was at college, I did a little hacking into a small bank, nothing major, but I was caught by the police and knew I was going straight to jail. Thing is, I got let out on bail very briefly and I didn't wanna go back and become someone's bitch for having a pretty face. Because you've gotta admit, my face is pretty." He winks, yet again, and I swear I'm going to poke a matchstick in his eye so he can't do it again. "Anyway, Z was my roommate at the time, we got completely wasted and he offered to help me. Turns out, what was supposed to be a cut through the eyebrow to give me an edge ended up with a slip of the knife and ta-da!" He shrugs and heads back downstairs to grab some more things from the now near-empty cases.

"That's kinda badass. Stupid as fuck, but did it work?" I follow him all the way upstairs and watch him install a camera at the end of the hall.

"Actually, yeah. That and the fact that I'm ripped and gave some very lucrative investing advice meant I was mostly left alone. Made some friends, got into some fights, established the hierarchy. I survived, so there's that." We go toward the one bedroom up here, the one with a rotted single mattress in the center of the room.

"How long were you there?" I continue to play with my butterfly knife, the movements calming.

"Couple of years. That's four questions, sixteen to go." He reaches up to the top of the wall with his latest camera and I can't help peeking at the skin showing between his black T-shirt and jeans.

"Are you really counting down the number? What happens when it gets to zero?"

"Yup. When it gets to zero, you win a prize." He wags his brows at me suggestively and I roll my eyes again. At this point, there's no denying where my daughter gets her attitude from. "That was two more questions by the way, only fourteen left."

I growl at him under my breath and he fans himself. "I love it when you get growly, Little Demon."

"How would you get rid of a dead body?" It's something each of my Reapers has given me the answer to, by doing rather than telling, but still, I'm curious.

"What happened to questions like, what's your favorite color?"

"Dmitry, if you want a girl to ask those kinda questions, you're in the wrong place."

Slowly, he turns his head to look at me. "Oh, Little Demon, I'm never in the wrong place with you."

"Really? That's cheesy as fuck, Dmitry. Just no." It's going against everything I know about myself, but the way he is with me doesn't make me want to run away. He's growing on me. Like a weed, but still.

"Yes, really. And I'd probably buy a pig farm like Brick Top. A pig can chomp through bone like butter." Finishing up with the final camera, he pulls out his cell and I'm assuming this is where all the video feeds are being streamed to.

"Who the fuck is Brick Top and why isn't he my friend?" I smile, because he sounds like the kinda person I'd like to know.

"You know those count as separate questions, right? You've got ten left once I've answered these." He looks up from his cell before heading back downstairs and delving into one of his silver cases. "Brick Top is a character in a movie called *Snatch*. Fucking great movie, by the way. So he's not your friend because he's not real." He flashes his white teeth at me with that dangerously addictive grin of his and I shake my head. "Ten left."

"Why did you deface my motorcycle?" He's lucky I'm letting him keep his fingers for that stunt, but the fact he gave it back to me, fixed-up, does make it semi-forgivable.

After closing the silver cases, Dmitry stands and meets my eyes. There's a moment of hesitation there before he speaks. "You mean the D on the tank? Marking my territory." He wags his brows again. Every time he does it, there's a suggestion in his gaze that I keep denying myself.

"Is there something other than the D that you did to my bike?" His reaction to my initial question makes me think there is, which is the *only* reason I'm ignoring his marking the territory comment. I step toward him, the only sound coming from my boots hitting the floor until we're toe-to-toe. "Because you'd tell me if you did something else, wouldn't you, Dmitry?"

His lips tighten in a sheepish smile. "Well…" He shrugs.

"Well, what?" He backs up against the wall, and I follow. "What did you do, Dmitry?" I had Crank check it over, but it's possible he missed something.

"That would be telling." His dangerous grin is etched onto his face.

"Yes, it would." Raising my hand, I grip him by the throat and hold him against the wall. "Do you have a death wish? What are you hiding? Because you're shit at the whole not showing what you're feeling thing."

The movement beneath my hand when he swallows makes me push harder, and my pushing isn't the only thing that's hard...the other thing is pressed against me and I don't want to move away from it.

"You know I love it when you're rough with me, Little Demon, but I'd prefer to stay alive." The vibration of his chest as he chuckles lightly makes my nipples ache. "I may or may not have put a tracker on it." He holds his palms out in surrender as my grip on his throat gets tighter.

Crank specifically looked for a tracker.

"Where?" The word is spoken through my gritted teeth. I'm very clearly not happy about this development, and again, if this were anyone else I'd have ripped his head off by now.

I hate that he's making me behave like this, but shit, the way he's capable of making me lose myself at the same time is so foreign to me.

"Brake light casing." He shrugs before leaning forward against my hand and gripping my bottom lip between his teeth. Sucking it into his mouth, my grip loosens a little as he kisses me fiercely, then he drops to the floor, fucking commando rolls, and runs to the back door. "You've still got two questions left, but you can save those if you like." He wags his brows then blows me a kiss before saying, "Catch me if you can, Little Demon." The back door is open in the next moment and he's gone, into the forest of a backyard.

Unless he's climbing fences, he's not getting very far, so I don't rush. He absolutely deserves a kick to the groin for putting a tracker in my bike, and I plan on delivering said kick when I find him.

It's dark outside, no street lighting, and the mass of trees and bushes in this yard makes it difficult to move, let alone see. Rustling of dead leaves makes me continue forward. The yard is longer than it is wide, and I'm guessing Dmitry is as far from the door as he can get.

"Come on, Dmitry. Stop running from me. I'll only make you bleed a little." There aren't any surrounding yards to this property, it's set off a little from the rest on the street, but I'm still conscious not to be too loud. It's ironic that I'm stalking him right now and I can't help the thrill of excitement that begins in my pussy.

"I expect better than a little, my Stabby Queen." His whispered voice comes from the left, so I turn toward it, the rustling beneath both our feet making this feel more dangerous than it is.

The wind picks up, but considering we're in April, it's not causing me to freeze my tits off. There's movement behind one of the few trees by the fence, so I slowly stalk toward it, careful with my footing. A stick snaps beneath my boot and I inwardly curse myself, but it makes Dmitry move.

Thing is, I move quicker. I grab the collar of his T-shirt and sharply pull him backward, making him fall down so I can easily straddle his hips and hold my palm over his mouth. The adrenaline from the quick chase is thrumming through my veins and I let go of his shirt to pull out one of my daggers. Removing my other hand from his mouth, I hit him with a glare and cut open his top, baring his tattooed chest.

When he tries to speak, I hold the knife over his lips and whisper, "Shh."

It would be a shame to fuck up his tattoos, so I find a clear space on his sternum and begin the first cut. His whole body tenses at the pain, but he doesn't complain, taking his punishment like a good boy.

When I'm finished, I cock my head to the side and grin.

"Don't fuck with my bike again." I practically spit the veiled threat into his face, and before he can pull his kissing-me-to-distract-me trick, I let go of him and stand with one leg on either side of him.

"Okay. But I'm gonna fuck *you* again." Quick as a flash, he slides out from under me onto his knees and rips my black combat pants down to my ankles.

I'm a little stunned and completely turned on as he shoves his nose into my cunt and sniffs, groaning, then flicks his tongue over my clit. Gripping my leg, he pulls one of my boots off, followed by my pant leg and panties. They're still on the other leg, my boot stopping them from coming all the way off, but that doesn't bother either of us, it would seem.

He catches me off guard yet again when he stands and grips my thighs, shoving me against the tree trunk and lifting my legs over his strong shoulders. My head falls back into the tree as he buries his face in my pussy and goes to fucking town on me. I'm grinding against his face, my jacket riding up a little behind me with the friction against the tree, but the pain from the bark mixed with the pleasure of his tongue only makes me come quicker.

The growls of satisfaction coming from Dmitry's throat add to the euphoria spreading through my body and my nipples are so hard and in need of attention I can barely catch my breath.

"Fuck me, Dmitry."

"I plan to, Little Demon." His words vibrate against me, sending a small aftershock through my body and making me twitch against him before he removes my legs from his shoulders.

The strength he has is fucking immense, and I'm in awe of how he seems to move me around so easily. He wraps my legs around his waist next, his palms clutching at my ass, squeezing tightly as he lines himself up.

One short, sharp movement is all it takes before he's inside me. His cock fills me so completely that I hate the thought of him ever leaving. Then he starts moving, in and out so quickly I can't hold back my gasps. It's difficult to stay quiet when being pounded into oblivion against a rough tree trunk, but I'm nothing if not dedicated to trying. If we get caught, we're not just spending a night in the holding cells.

My jacket rides up some more as Dmitry moves one of his hands from my ass to squeeze my breast, pinching at my nipple before claiming my mouth with his. It's like he knew a louder scream was pending and he's stolen the sound for himself, our tongues tangling in a dance like nothing I've ever experienced.

Just as another orgasm begins to build, he pulls out of me then detaches my legs from around his waist while still managing to kiss the shit out of me. I slap his arm because I was enjoying that, but he surprises me by taking charge yet again, groaning into my mouth before twisting my body around. He chuckles against my neck as he begins kissing from my shoulder to my jaw, leaving a trail of painful nips in his wake.

"Hands against the trunk."

I purposefully mistake what he's saying and reach behind me to grip his cock in my palm, squeezing him, pumping him torturously slow. But I'm just as needy as he is so I quickly aim his tip for my entrance, bending over to give him easy access before resting my hands against the bastard trunk.

"I won't call you a good girl," he whispers into my ear as he slides into me. "Because you'll never be good, but you are fucking unreal. My bad Little Demon." He pulls out almost all the way before slamming back inside me, bringing his hand around to my mouth just in time for me to bite on his fingers instead of screaming out loud.

My palms get just as scratched up as the bottom of my back as he pounds into me again and again, his balls banging against my clit and causing my whole body to shake in anticipation of the next orgasm.

It builds from the tips of my toes and they curl, then it flows up my legs at the same time as electric shocks travel down from my neck, and they meet up in the middle, right inside my pussy, before it all explodes. My body involuntarily spasms against him and I continue to ride the high, the aftershocks making me groan as he gives one final thrust, slapping my ass before squeezing it hard.

"Still so fucking addictive," he rumbles into my ear and I shiver against him.

"You'll get bored soon."

"Never."

After our session in the overgrown backyard of Cook's abandoned house, we both went our separate ways. I felt like I needed to set a boundary with Dmitry, so as we covered ourselves up I went straight back to business, telling him to inform me if there's movement and all that.

Now I'm home, in my giant bed, and my only focus is on my need to change the sheets. They still smell of him. The last time he slept here may have been the best night's sleep since I can remember, but that doesn't mean I want to be reminded of the fact.

My phone vibrates on my bedside table and I almost ignore it, but it could be him. Or Hallie. And I don't want to miss either of them.

Fuck. That's something for future me to dissect, because right now I just don't want to.

It's not a text from either of them. It's an app I don't recognize telling me there's movement by my front door.

What the...?

The sound of a key turning in the lock makes me grab the knife under my pillow, ready to launch it at whoever's about to come through that door. However, I'm not a stupid woman, I have a hunch I know exactly who it is so I don't aim for his head when the door does finally open.

I still throw it, but more as a warning. "Dmitry, you can't keep turning up wherever I am and think it's okay. It's kinda fucking creepy." The knife slams into the wall beside the door and he turns to look at it before glancing back at me with a raised brow and that damn smile.

"You like creepy. Take that tank top off and roll onto your stomach." He pulls a small tube of something out of his pocket before getting very, *very* naked and climbing into my bed beside me.

"Dmitry—"

"Top, roll." He gestures with his finger for me to turn over and I sigh.

He straddles my legs just as something cold touches my skin. I don't flinch though, because it's actually quite calming. Especially when he begins to massage it into my back and the cool of the cream soothes the heat from the tree-trunk grazes.

"Thank you, Dmitry." It's out of character for me to be grateful like this, but everything about this man pushes my boundaries.

"Just doing what any man would do for his woman, Little Demon, so thank *you*."

I'm going to let the *his woman* comment slide for now because he has magic hands and I can feel myself slipping into sleep. A sleep I so desperately need. When his hands finally stop their movements and he climbs off me, I don't fight him when he drags me into him and kisses the back of my neck before darkness claims me until morning.

Chapter Thirteen

D

"Quit watching me sleep, you creeper." I just grin at her words because she's so fucking adorable when she hisses, especially when she's half asleep. That said, I would never tell her that while lying this close to her. I like my balls right where they are and in mint condition.

"What can I say? I'm a sucker for a beautiful woman who snores like a little kitten." One of her eyes pops open and I'm not sure if she's trying to snarl at the snoring part of my comment or the cute comparison. Probably both.

"You're annoying." There isn't even a bite to her words and it feels like a win as a victorious chuckle begins to form.

But then her body shifts just enough for her tit to pop out from behind the crisp white sheet and my mouth waters on command. I'm like one of Pavlov's dogs when it comes to her. Always have been.

N.O. ONE

That first day she walked into the casino looking like a fucking queen in her red dress, assessing every corner of our space, she glanced up at the camera right above the door and winked. It was a statement to whoever was behind the screens watching her, a sexy middle finger that I felt travelling up and down my entire fucking body.

I recorded that moment and jacked off to it enough times that I noticed every exposed inch of her skin, tattooed every goosebump to memory and replayed her flirtatious *fuck you* over and over again. I recognized the moment for what it was and, as I lie here, in her bed, trying to work yet being completely and inexplicably distracted by her as she sleeps, I know I was right.

Jordyn O'Neill is the only woman for me. She's isn't the north star to my heart, she's the entire fucking compass. No matter what direction she points to, I'll be there with her.

Does that make me sound like a pussy? I hope so. Pussies are strong and powerful and owning my feelings for her only makes me more worthy of her.

With my back pressed against the wall—this woman doesn't even have a bedframe—and my legs crossed along the mattress, I follow her every movement as she springs out of bed, checks her phone, and heads straight to the bathroom to piss. It's still early on a Wednesday morning and Hallie should be calling her, like clockwork, in about twenty minutes.

I wonder if I can get an orgasm out of my little demon before that...

The thought makes me instantly hard, which isn't anything new. I've been here for the last three nights and just being around her gets my blood shooting south until she either sucks me off or fucks my brains out.

Sometimes both.

And yes, I always return the gesture in kind because eating her pussy is my favorite meal of the day.

The shower turns on and I know I've got about ten minutes of productivity in me. Breakfast was delivered twenty minutes ago, I met the driver downstairs to avoid waking up my girl. I fucked her good and hard last night and just like I'd hoped, my sleep deprived demon needed to conk out for a good eight hours.

I take this time to finish up a little research on Harvey fucking Cook. Glitch and I have been digging around every corner of his digital footprints trying to figure out why and at what point this man magically became Charles Wright. No one changes names for no reason and the fact that he's been fucking with us about some land we've yet to see is the reason I refuse to give up.

If there's something out there, I'll find it, and when I do, I'll hand it over to J as a late birthday gift. I'm a few months late but I've got a good excuse...I didn't know her yet.

When the shower turns off, I grin, slapping closed my computer and carefully placing it on the bedside table along with my glasses. This apartment is so fucking small I can feel the heat from her shower just as the door opens and she walks out wrapped in a barely-there towel.

With every step she takes, I watch her. I can't and won't pretend she doesn't fascinate me.

I know Murphy was a great guy, an excellent father. Watching them, I saw the way he looked at her, the way he worshiped her. In fact, I was more than jealous and had resigned myself to loving her from afar, knowing that she loved him too. Yet, there was always that little voice in the back of my head reminding me of how different their worlds were. How her needs were probably too violent, too broken and morbid for someone as pure as he was. Sure, he worked for the mob, but really...he worked in an auto body shop as an accountant and when he went home, his hands didn't feel dirty.

J needs someone who can walk through fire and revel in the burn. A partner who won't bat an eye when she comes home covered in some guy's blood and asks if he can get rid of her ruined clothes while she takes a shower. Opposites attract but that doesn't mean it's for the best.

"You got breakfast?" Her question is rhetorical, she can see the fucking food on the counter, but I answer anyway.

"Can't let my girl starve on hump day." The fact I can see the kitchen from her bed is turning out to be a great advantage.

"Whatever. It looks good." Even though she's complimenting my efforts, her tone sounds like an insult, all mumbled and dismissive as if her social skills are nonexistent.

"So, you think Hallie will like me as a step-dad?" I'm fucking with her, getting a rise out of her is my favorite sport. That's what I'm letting her believe for now because I have every intention of making her mine until the day they put me six feet under. And because Jordyn no longer exists without Hallie in her life, I'm looking forward to being whatever her daughter needs from me. I'll never replace Murphy, I'm too fucked up for that, but I can make a mean smoothie.

My body freezes as a sudden breeze at the side of my face is quickly followed by a thump in the wall. Slowly, I turn, my gaze falling on the hilt of a knife. Fuck, this woman will be the literal death of me and I'm okay with that.

"You're lucky I don't want my Reapers up here cleaning up the mess that is your dead body but the next time you bring up my daughter in that context, I won't miss."

Yup, I'm fucking hard and J notices right away.

"All I'm hearing is that you missed on purpose and I'm choosing to believe it's because you love me." She scoffs at my words, her glare a living, breathing thing only making my dick harder.

"Don't confuse a good fuck with a forever, Dmitry. The only reason I allow you in my space is because a good orgasm is hard to find." I have so many fucking jokes I could throw out but it's my turn to be pissed off.

I'm up and off the bed faster than she can say, *fuck me harder*. With the size of this place, I'm in her face within the next two seconds, one hand at her throat, pushing her into the fridge while my body is at a slight angle to avoid getting kneed in my nuts.

"I'm gonna need you to listen carefully, Jordyn O'Neill." My face is so close I can feel the heat of her mouth on my lips and the *thump thump thump* of her racing heart as I speak slowly and clearly. "You may allow me to stay here, but make no mistake, I'm allowing you the time you need to come to terms with the inevitable." I lick a path from her delicious collar bone to that intoxicating space where her neck ends and her jaw begins. I want to lick it then bite it, and because patience has never been a virtue of mine, I don't deny myself the pleasure.

"Oh yeah? And what's that, pray tell?"

This is turning her on, I can smell her pussy and it's only making me harder by the second. My little demon craves the push and pull, the levity and the darkness. Not only does she want it but she needs it to keep her balance in this fucked up world.

"You and me, we're happening." My mouth latches on to the soft, pliable flesh of her neck and I suck on it, flicking my tongue then sucking even harder, knowing damn well I'll be leaving a little present to remind her I was here. "You may not see it right now, Jordyn, because you're hurting and you've got shit going on, but..." I bite her neck this time and revel at the sight of my teeth marks marring the perfection that is her skin. "Do not ever disregard this thing between us. I will have you because I've been in love with you since day one."

We are locked in a stare down, her ocean-blue eyes searching mine, and I can see the sadness, the loss, the confusion that she hides on a daily basis. Somewhere deep inside her is that scared teenage girl who lost her parents in the most tragic of ways. She hasn't told me the story herself but from the pieces I've gathered and the rumors I've heard, I have no doubt it was traumatizing.

For a brief second, her armor falls, her muscles relax and a tear falls from one eye. Pressing her against the refrigerator where the humming of the motor is the only sound besides our heavy breaths, I whisper, "Can you feel it?" In another moment, she would have cracked a joke about my hard dick pressing against her, but this isn't about that.

This moment is about her knowing I'm not going anywhere. No matter the time it takes for us to jump in feet first, we are inevitable.

"Murph is dead because of me. Hallie lost the only parent she grew up with. It doesn't matter how you feel, Dmitry. It doesn't matter how good you make *me* feel. This guilt festering inside me is like a flesh-eating amoeba devouring my humanity one cell at a time. I don't have the will to fight it because I deserve this agony." It's the first time I've seen J vulnerable, the first time she's let down her walls and spoken her truth. And my fucking God, she's magnificent when she's honest and completely naked of all pretenses.

Pushing her chin up with the crook of my hand between the thumb and forefinger, I force her head up so all she sees is me.

"Then I'll fight for us both. I'll hand you the sword when it's time for you to slay your dragons then wash the blood from your body." The silence that follows my words is deafening, reminding me that no matter what I'm sure about, ultimately, this is all her decision to make.

When I feel her finger tracing the now-healing letter J that she carved into my sternum just three days ago, I smile to myself. In these quiet moments, she opens up without even realizing it.

"It's healing." Soft words caress my skin.

"It is." And that's all we need to say.

A half a second after J blinks, we are on each other. The poor excuse for a towel drops to the floor when her legs wrap around my waist and my hands cup both of her ass cheeks. Our mouths come crashing together like two armies in a battle led by Napoleon. It's ruthless and long, saying so much without uttering a single word.

Reaching down with one hand, J pushes my sweats down just enough to get my dick out, the pad of her thumb running softly against the head of my cock. I swallow my own gasp as I deepen our kiss and chase her touch by thrusting my hips forward.

It doesn't take me long to get my cock inside her, and when I do, I go deep. I pull her down on me by the handfuls of her ass, never missing a beat in our kiss. This is the first time we're not fucking out of anger or frustration. We're fucking because this thing between us is an entity of its own and it will never go away.

It can't. It's too strong.

"Fuck! Yes!" I hear a phone ring in the distance but it's no match for my heart beating in time with J's.

Every time I thrust into her, the fridge moves, bumping into the wall and making whatever it is she's got on top move and wobble. We're too far gone to actually care, our lips and teeth moving in a choreographed dance, nipping and sucking and licking at every turn.

The phone rings again and this time I feel J pause for a brief second, but the haze of lust is too great for us to stop. My groin is rubbing against her clit every time I slam home and my entire body shakes with the need to come inside her.

Hips pistoning, bodies slapping, we are frantic with every move we make. I'm afraid my legs won't hold so I pivot just right and sit her on top of the kitchen counter. At this angle, I lose all semblance of control as I fuck the vulnerability and the doubt right out of her. Her cries echo in the small space while my grunts sound more and more animalistic.

When J hooks her arm around my neck and brings her mouth to my collar bone, biting down hard, she frees us both of this pressure we've been building.

We both come in sync, her slick walls soaking my cock as I fill her up with my cum. Streak after blissful streak I pour into her and imagine her pussy wide open, leaking out from how well I filled her up.

Panting and sweating, we look deep inside each other, knowing damn well this was something more. Something meaningful.

The phone rings again and the moment is shattered.

"I have to get that."

The Shadow is back and my soul sighs. It's okay though, this was progress.

I serve us breakfast on the plates and pour orange juice as I listen to J talk with her daughter. Her voice is unique when she speaks with Hallie. It takes on an airy feel, like she knows Hallie needs to be reassured that everything here is going okay.

Their conversations are always short since she calls behind her grandparents' backs between the time she arrives at school and the bell for first period.

"What do you mean?" That airy tone is now ice, which makes the hairs on my arms stand to attention. "No, Hals, they never liked me. Yeah, okay. Okay. Bye, Kid. Love you too." As soon as she ends the call, she's back in the kitchen, picking up her towel and wrapping it around her torso.

"Problem?" I bring a piece of toast to her mouth and smile when she opens wide and bites down with gusto.

"Dunno yet. Hallie has a gut feeling that something is happening. Then again..." She chews a couple of times then washes down the toast with her coffee. "She's convinced the world is going to implode because she got an A minus on her algebra quiz."

I grin. I made my math my bitch.

"She's slackin'." I get a death glare and I know things are back to our normal.

Her phone dings with a text message, a frown creasing between her brows.

"What now?" I finish off my orange juice as we both stand at the counter, eating like we were raised by heathens.

"That was Marco, we've got another body." Our eyes meet and my disappointment is like a punch to the gut. "We can't clean this one up 'cause the cops got there before us."

"Fuck. Want me to hack into their system?" J narrows her eyes and shakes her head as she bites into another piece of toast.

"No, we've got eyes on the inside but we prefer dealing with this the quiet way." I nod at her words as I finish off my glass of orange juice.

Then I remember. "Are you staking out the other capo's club tonight?" I can't remember the guy's name.

"Eddie, yeah. He's still out, losing his son is breaking him." J's lip curls at the mention of Eddie having to deal with a dead son, the color in her cheeks drained as though it all makes her physically ill.

"All right then, let's get to work." We just need to get dressed, we should be out in a jiffy.

"Yeah, let's. I go to my job and you go to yours." She's walking back to her closet, presumably to get dressed. Shame...truly. She couldn't be more perfect like this if I'd created her myself.

"Silly wabbit, casino opens at one. I think I'll stay here while you go earn the big bucks. I'm not opposed to being a kept man, as long as you keep me...coming."

"You're an ass." There's barely any venom in her insult, it's cute. And now I'm hard.

"Why, I think that's the nicest thing you've ever said to me."

Chapter Fourteen

J

"Rack 'em up, Boss, it's my turn to break." Shoo chalks up his cue before taking a swig of his beer, almost slamming the bottle back onto the table once it's empty.

He's not like me. Shoo will happily drink on the job. While I'm against it for myself, as long as my Reapers get the job done, I don't give two shits how they go about it.

More than a few of Eddie's soldiers have turned up dead around their regular hangout, which means we've had to watch this bar in hopes of catching the fucker picking off our men. Tonight's our fifth stakeout and it's starting to get old. We're a fresh set of eyes since his own soldiers have found nothing yet.

Marco wants all of his capos and their crews working together on finding the serial killer fuck, and I'm all for it. Our soldiers turning up dead all over the city is really pissing me off.

"Ah, fuck. Missed."

It takes me a second to assess the table and which ball I'm aiming for first. Seeing as Shoo has pocketed four balls, all stripes, I know I'm solids. Because I'm bored as fuck—we've been at this for the last hour—I'm going to annoy the shit outta Shoo. The number one goes down first, then I calculate my next few moves and begin sinking the solids in number order, two through seven.

"Right side, far corner." I point to the pocket I'm planning on shooting the eight into, lining up my cue and smoothly sliding it between my fingers. The ball bounces off the left rail before falling easily into the pocket with the cue ball stopping in the middle of the table. I blow at the end of my cue stick as though any chalk is left there and raise a brow to a now faux-grumpy Shoo.

"Yeah, alright. I set 'em up easy for ya." He laughs and begins rolling the leftover balls into random pockets before handing his cue over to Ricky, who declared he wanted to play the winner next.

Ricky is one of Eddie's newest recruits and he thinks he's hot shit. Trouble is, he hasn't been around long enough to really know who I am. He knows that I'm mafia, that I'm welcome here, but that's as far as it goes and I haven't seen him here the last few times I've been in with my crew. This means Billy-Big-Balls thinks I'm an easy target, because of course he's a chauvinistic pig. Which is a shame. He's a looker.

After watching me clear the table, Ricky seems somewhat humbled and I fucking know this cunt's about to try and one up me. Causing a scene is the opposite of my intentions while I'm technically on a stakeout, so I refrain from slicing his ball sack off and patiently wait for him to offer me a deal.

Clearing his throat, Ricky places his cue on the table and tilts his head toward the dart board. "Let's see if you're as good at darts as you are pool. If I win, you let me buy you a drink." Okay, his offer wasn't quite as bad or crude as I was expecting. I get it though, he wants to save face by choosing a game he thinks he can win against me.

Bless him.

"And what if I win?" I didn't miss the fact that he didn't give that as an option, and in this case, his confidence isn't sexy.

He pretends to think about it. "If you win, you can buy me a drink." He grins and moves over to the dart board a few feet away from the pool table, pulling the darts out and handing me three.

Taking them, I smile, but it doesn't reach my eyes. "How about, when I win..." I pause and lean closer to whisper in his ear. "I don't break your fingers for touching me." So it was only his fingers on mine as he passed the darts, but whatever.

"Dude, you do know who that is, don't ya?" one of the older guys that I've seen in here every night pipes up, laughing and slapping Ricky on the back.

"What? Who?" Seems Ricky does have something about him because he doesn't try and posture his way through his lack of knowledge.

"I know you've heard of the Shadow, man." The guy laughs again and shakes his head before turning to me. "You hustling our newbs, Shadow?"

"Hey, he approached me. No hustling here." My smile is real this time.

Ricky's eyes widen and he turns to me, to really look at me. "Ah shit. Sorry, Shadow. Can I get ya that drink now or...?"

"Fuck the deal, Ricky. Just play. We'll start at 501." I tilt my head toward the board and throw my darts, two of them landing in the triple twenty and the third in the bullseye. Shoo notes down the scores on the small whiteboard on the wall beside us as Ricky sighs and begins to play.

Spending time in bars is not something I particularly enjoy, especially not when I am on constant alert for something that doesn't fit, but playing pool and darts has been killing time. Plus, it makes us look like we belong, which is exactly what we need our serial killer to think. Maybe whoever it is will believe me or my crew are the same as the newbs they've been focusing on so far.

It isn't long before the game is over and Ricky's shaking my hand—not quite the douche he first came across as. He's actually good at darts. His aim is a little off but he's got great potential.

I check my phone to see if Binx and Tab have texted with any updates from out front where they're staking out from the van. Our target may not ever actually come into the bar, which is why outside is being watched too.

There's nothing from them, but there are two unread messages waiting. One from Hallie and one from Dmitry.

Hallie: I miss you.

I immediately reply.

Me: Miss you too, Kid.

It breaks my heart every goddamn time she says that. The only thing that helps is knowing I'll have her back as soon as I've found a way around her grandparents. And I will find a way.

> **Big Magic D:** Your ass looks great bent over that pool table.

> **Me:** Perv.

The fucker's changed his name in my phone again, so I quickly change it to Big Delusional D. The timestamp on his message says it was sent about an hour ago and I'm kinda surprised he hasn't just shown up again. I guess the corner of the tech-cave Glitch cleared up for him gave him enough of a hard-on to stay for a while. They were working on trying to figure out information on the other people in the picture they found of Mr. Wright—Cook—and what we think is his family. If we can find them, maybe we'll have a clearer picture on his background and links to the mob.

Speak of the devil and he shall appear; Cook is sitting at the bar talking to Craig, nursing a bottle of beer between his palms. What is this guy's deal?

So, I know he has land that Z wants—wanted—to buy, which is why Z didn't want me to teach Cook a lesson the first night I beat him at poker. I know he's a slimy fuck who seems to be a fucking ninja at evading a tail, and I know he told Shane Brennan where I would be the night I was taken off my bike. What I *don't* know is why he's got my hackles up so much. I mean, grassing up my location to the mob is enough for me to want him dead, but maybe he just needs some rehabilitation.

I get the impression he's got a bit of a gambling addiction, and considering how long he's been talking to Craig over the bar, my impression is basically confirmed. Eddie's crew deals with a lot of gamblers across the city, often needing to borrow money and generally, these days, the majority of people are good about paying their debts off. The mafia may be into a bit of extortion, but we don't want to see our city go to shit. The deals Eddie offers are always fair unless the borrower fucks him off, then all bets are off.

"Is that Cook?" Shoo hovers behind me as we pretend to watch two people playing pool.

"Yup. See if you can get close enough to figure out why he's here."

Shoo doesn't verbally respond to my request as he begins making his way to the bar, sitting himself down a seat away from Cook and ordering himself a drink from Margie—Craig's still busy.

When he comes back, drink in hand, he stands directly in front of me so I can still keep eyes on Cook over his shoulder without it being obvious that I'm staring.

"He was asking to borrow more money, but he's late on his last payment so he was trying to barter with some land. Craig said he'd have to check with Ed before he made a decision, so Cook's just waiting now. Or Wright or whatever. This shit's making my brain hurt."

I nod in response, my mind whirring with possibilities and explanations as to why Cook keeps popping up every-fucking-where.

Fuck it.

"Let's bring him in. I'm sick of him taking up valuable brain space. Let's figure out his deal. Tonight."

Shoo downs the rest of his beer before slamming it down on the table beside us, in complete agreement with my decision. Unlocking my phone, I send the group chat a message.

> **Me:** Bringing takeaway in about ten.

Tab: Can't wait.

Binx: So ready for it.

Flower, Crank, and Fizz are staking out another location where we've noticed the serial killer seems to be active and Glitch is at the crew house with Dmitry doing whatever it is they do with computers.

A few minutes later, Craig returns—presumably after speaking with Ed on the phone about lending Cook more money—and he's shaking his head, telling Cook no, which doesn't seem to go down too well. Cook jumps off his stool, shouting, "What?" His arms are raised and his stupid thin face is turning red.

"Time to work, Shoo."

We both move quickly, each of us standing on either side of Cook. I tilt my head at Craig as I link arms with Cook, and Craig knows exactly what's about to happen. Extraction.

"Hey, what the hell?" Cook struggles as Shoo and I lead him toward the back exit. He's stronger than I'd have given him credit for, but he's no match for us. This is actually more fun than I thought it would be. Something feels right about finally bringing him in and I know he hasn't realized

I'm one of his captors yet. "*You.*" There it is! His voice is so full of venom aimed in my direction, and I smile, completely ignoring the dick. "Get off me. You have no right. You're just a stupid gi—"

Shoo slams his fist into Cook's face, effectively shutting him up, but also making Cook turn limp as he passes out.

"Fuck sake, Shoo. You could've waited until we got him in the van."

"Yeah, but he was being disrespectful, Boss."

I shake my head, but a smile is firmly in place. I fucking love my crew.

The van is idling alongside the bar, so there's no street traffic or people seeing us hauling an unconscious man, which is perfect. Not that anyone hanging around here would call us in for this anyway. Binx is waiting with the back doors open, ready for us to throw Cook's limp body inside, and there's surprise on his face when he sees who it is.

"Is he the man we've been after all this time?"

"Nah, but he's pissed the boss off enough for us to bring him in for questioning. We'll come back again tomorrow for another stakeout for the killer." It's Shoo who answers, leaving me to grab my helmet and shove it onto my head.

"Can I come inside with you tomorrow? Tab had chili for dinner and I swear his ass is rotten."

Tab chuckles behind the steering wheel of the van as Binx helps Shoo secure Cook with our custom-built chains.

"Take him to the warehouse by the docks, I'll follow behind on my bike," I instruct as I pull out my phone to check for messages. I do this way more often than I ever used to and I'm blaming a certain D.

Glitch has sent me a long text message that makes me pause, not quite believing what I'm reading as I wait for the picture he sent with it to download properly.

Holy fucking shit.

Cook has a step-sister, and we know who she is.

What the fuck?

Chapter Fifteen

Three hours earlier

"Fuck that, man, it's just not right. You can't love *Star Wars* and *Star Trek* equally." Shaking my head at the ridiculous notion that Glitch hurdled at me fifteen minutes ago, I chomp on my Twizzler out of pure frustration. Usually, I like to keep it in my mouth for a while, it helps keep the cigarette cravings at bay.

"I got enough love in my heart for both, dude. Deal with it." If the guy hadn't carved me out a little space for my toys in his nerd cave, I would have thrown a mouse at his head.

"Nope, not buying it. It's like saying you love your wife and mistress equally. Lies, all lies." I shrug as I scroll through hours and fucking hours of video surveillance around Cook's house. The equipment I set up in there is top of the line, the camera eye having a motion detector and following movements as it senses them.

"That doesn't even make sense. If you have a mistress, you're a fucking douchebag who's incapable of love." He's right. I need a new metaphor.

"Okay, I'll give you that. How about this…" My voice trails off as I narrow my eyes at movement in the bottom corner of the screen. "Wait…what is that?"

Glitch slides his chair along his burnished concrete floor and looks over my shoulder for a minute.

"Ah," we both say at the same time. "Mouse." We watch it for a while, placing bets on where it'll go and if it'll get into Cook's food stash.

It's not like he's there often anyway, but he does go back. We've seen him twice. Never stays the night, just sits at his table like he's waiting on something, then goes into his pantry, comes out with cereal. Eats. Waits some more then leaves.

My guess? He's a fucking sociopath. But I don't have anything to back up my diagnosis, so I wait and watch.

"We need eyes in that pantry, he fucking stares at the thing like he's got a ghost in there." My words are mumbled as I try to think of viable reasons for his behavior.

"Who? Cook Wright?" That's what Glitch calls him.

"Yeah, something's off. And I mean besides eating plain Wheaties. Who does that?" I mock shiver although the thought makes my mouth dry.

"Sociopaths, that's who." We fist bump without even looking at each other. Called it.

"So, you and Shadow, huh?"

I raise a brow at Glitch, throwing him a quick glance before returning to my screen.

"Pretty sure she'd make your use of condoms redundant if she knew you were asking about her private life." As much as I appreciate Glitch, the subject of J and me is off the table.

"Technically, I'm asking about yours." He grabs a handful of plain popcorn and chews like he's five.

"No can do. That subject is off limits, even to you."

Glitch chuckles, probably knowing I just saved both of our lives.

"All right, so let's get back to this shit show, then." Glitch turns his attention back to the wall of screens, three of which are displaying the dive bar somewhere in bumfuck Brooklyn. Nothing says "dirty deals going down" like four concrete walls and a leaky roof on a plot of dead grass and full of puking alcoholics. Lovely.

Shaking my head, I scope out the camera angles and grin when I see my little demon pointing her stick over the green velvet of the pool table. From my vintage point, it looks like she's aiming for the two, a solid blue, into the corner pocket. The shot isn't impossible but with the orange stripe ball encroaching on her line of sight, she'll have to aim carefully. Which, of course, she does.

Watching her every move, I take my time appreciating how her leather pants hug every curve of her body, reminding me of what's underneath.

Before I can stop myself—and let's be honest, the thought never crossed my mind—I pull out my phone and send her a good luck text.

> **Me**: Your ass looks great bent over that pool table.

"If you get a boner in my nerd cave, I will ban you." Glitch murmurs without ever taking his eyes off the screens.

My smile is wide and earnest. "I wouldn't dream of it."

"Right." With a snort, he throws a piece of popcorn in the air and catches it like he's been practicing that move for years. For all I know, he has.

In one corner, Glitch has an ongoing *League of Legends* game happening on Twitch, where he's just a spectator tonight. We've got too much shit happening to be responsible for a champion but it's always fun to watch others get their asses handed to them when it's not your team taking the hit. The stream volume is on low but it's easy to make out the players screaming about protecting their Nexus and hurrying their asses to the fountain.

Fuck, I love that game. Nothing like MOBA—multiplayer online battle arena—to get your blood pumping. Well, that and a certain hot blonde in leather pants.

"Any bites on the facial rec from that picture?" When we found the picture of a much younger and less-bald Harvey Cook, we decided to dig around and find out where the others ended up. From the clothing and his aging, I'd place the photo in the mid eighties. There's just no ignoring the neon clothing and the *Like A Virgin*-era Madonna T-shirt.

"Not yet. It's taking a while to clean the grain and smooth out the creases. We should get something soon though, it's at seventy percent now." Glitch's fingers are flying across his keyboard, his eyes scanning the screens and one leg bouncing up and down like he's had ten too many coffees.

For the next hour, I continue going through the most boring fucking videos of pure nothingness, my blood pressure rising every time a fucking mouse strolls out and goes grocery shopping in Cook's pantry.

"Look at that little prick!" At Glitch's words, I turn in my seat, following his line of sight, and frown. As if I could change anything from where I am, I lean in closer and memorize every inch of this douchebag who's looking at my girl like she's his next dessert.

"Who is he?" Young, good looking in that his-balls-just-dropped-about-five-minutes-ago kind of way. Mostly, he looks naïve and if the smirk on my little demon is any indication, he's about to get devoured and spit out faster than you can say spawn point.

"Newbie from Eddie's team. He's about to learn a valuable lesson in humility." We both chuckle at his words and, on cue, we watch as some old dude pats the kid on the shoulder and mere seconds later, his face drains of all color.

"Bingo. The Shadow strikes again." There's no denying the awe and respect in Glitch's voice when speaking about J. In a world created by men for men, Jordyn O'Neill has whipped every single motherfucker there into place.

"Fuck. You're hard right now, aren't you?"

I don't bother looking at him as I answer. "Yup."

Fifteen minutes later, I'm still going through tapes and growing more and more convinced that the pantry has an important role in this crazy ass situation when my phone beeps. Before I even glance at the screen, I know it's my girl.

Little Demon: Perv.

I'm about to type something back when Glitch jumps out of his chair and puts his headphones back on.

"Binx, did you see that?" My attention is immediately on the screens as I try to figure out what the fuck.

"Is that...?" I let the question trail off because I already know the answer. I can't hear what Binx is saying in Glitch's ear but there's no mistaking it. Harvey Cook, or fucking Wright, just walked into Eddie's bar and went straight to the counter without passing Go, but I'm guessing there's some collecting going on and it's nowhere near two hundred dollars.

"Binx is waiting on J to give orders." We both watch, wishing we had some fucking sound, but when I suggested it, J said there was no need. Next time, I'm taking charge whether she likes it or not.

I'm guessing not. Too bad.

From the angle of the camera, J is assessing while Shoo walks to the bar all casual and looking to buy a drink. It's clear he's listening in on the conversation but Cook is too twitchy and worried to pay any attention.

What the fuck is he doing there and seriously, what are the odds?

"I thought he had ties to the Irish. If he's looking for money why isn't he just going to them?" Glitch shrugs at my question and I assume it'll go unanswered but, seconds later, he gives me his take on it.

"The Irish are too close to their cash, they don't shit where they eat. If you're working for them, they won't lend you a damn penny."

I nod. It makes sense. He comes to the Italians to get some gambling money, I presume. It's fucking stupid but it makes sense for someone battling his addiction.

I'm about to go back to my yawn-inducing surveillance when Glitch curses and calls out Binx's name.

"Shoo just clocked Wright...erm...I mean, Cook."

Again, I can't hear Binx on the other side but Glitch lets me know that J has given the order to take him in for a little chat. That's code for someone's gonna bleed, and fuck if that doesn't turn me on.

After a couple of hits from Shoo and a permanent snarl on J's face, Cook is dragged out of the bar and there's a long beep from the tower where the facial recognition software is running. Glitch and I both look at each other and grin. Game time.

Our toys are working.

Leaning into the screen like two teens watching porn for the first time, I freeze.

"Holy shit," comes from Glitch.

"Is that...?" I ask because I've only seen her once, and briefly, but J's talked about her a few times.

"Sure as fuck looks like it," he confirms, and I try to understand how any of this is fucking related.

"But...how?"

"I don't fucking know." We both jump onto our own computers, fingers tapping away furiously.

"I'll check Harvey Cook's family history," I tell him, and his grunt is my cue that he's searching out the girl's information. If our software works, then our search history will match.

"His father got remarried when he was in his late teens." I'm thinking out loud but also feeding my findings to Glitch.

"Yeah, her dad died when she was a kid, her mom remarried when she was in her early teens," Glitch confirms, and shit just got fucking real.

"I have to send this to J before she goes to the warehouse." Glitch's fingers are flying across his phone, the image being downloaded and dropped into an app he created that keeps their files and conversations private and incognito.

Then Glitch makes a call.

"Fizz? You need to go to the warehouse and help out the crew." I frown. Why isn't he saying something about what we just found? "Shadow's orders."

We look at each other, a little dumbfounded.

"Hey, Glitch? How did you not already know this?" They work so closely together, trusting each other, it's beyond me that she wouldn't have already seen his picture or that they wouldn't have some kind of clue about her past.

"We don't talk about our shit here. It's never a thing unless we make it a thing."

While we stare, unblinking, at the picture that was created from the artificial intelligence and turned out to be spot on, the sound of a team winning on the far side of the room erupts from the speakers.

Meanwhile, Fizz and her step-brother, Harvey, are about to have a family reunion.

Chapter Sixteen

J

"What's up, Boss?" Fizz has just arrived at the warehouse, her dark curls loose and wild, and I hate that I'm about to dampen her spirit.

Having her step-brother in our custody doesn't mean good things for him and I'm not sure how she's going to take it. Still, he hasn't technically done anything worthy of dying for, and now that we know he's Fizz's step-brother, that means he's family in a way.

How all this goes down from here depends on Fizz.

"I know you have been busy working on other things while we've been dealing with the Mr. Wright job, so you won't be up to date with what we've found out so far. Most importantly, that Mr. Wright isn't his real name."

"Well, damn. Is it someone we know? Someone *I* know?" She's a clever woman, quietly observant, and her being here having this conversation isn't the norm for these jobs. She usually stays clear of the physical stuff.

"We found an old family photo and Glitch did his tech thing. You're in the photo, Fizz. His name is Harvey Cook." I don't hold back on the information, there's no reason to do so. We need to move quickly, hope Cook can give us some information on Ronan or any of the other members of the mob, then hurry the fuck up with finding our serial killer.

Fizz's eyes go wide and her hand flies to her mouth at hearing his name and she immediately reaches for the seat beside her. Luckily, it's on wheels, because I'm not sure she'd have moved it to her in time to sit on it otherwise. I'm glad for the comfortable office space to have this conversation. It seems the news is harder for Fizz to hear than I could have guessed.

It quickly becomes clear that this isn't going to be a happy reunion between step-siblings because I can read my crew like a book. She's silently crying into her palms, shaking her head, her whole body trembling, and I feel awkward as fuck. Everyone knows hugs aren't my thing, but Fizz is my family and seeing her like this melts a little bit of the ice from my heart.

I move to crouch in front of her, grasping her hands on the side of her face and bringing our heads together.

"Talk to me when you're ready, Fizz. Take as long as you need, okay?" My words are whispered but firm and she nods gently.

The door bursts open and Crank waltzes in. "When do we get to try and make the fucker talk?" He pauses when he sees me crouching in front of an obviously distressed Fizz and is beside her in a flash. He grips her arm, pulls her up, then sits in her seat and brings her onto his lap, wrapping her in his arms.

I've always known these two have a special kind of relationship, but this confirms just how close they are as she nestles into him and begins to sob. He's ten years younger than her, but it's not obvious by the way he always takes care of her. He knows more than the rest of us about her past, why she's not good with jobs that involve kids, so it stands to reason that she's comfortable in his arms.

"What the fuck happened, Boss?" Cradling her head into his chest, he looks to me, fear and worry in the crinkle of his eyes.

"Mr. Wright is Harvey Cook. Fizz's step-brother." I stand and lean against the edge of the desk. This is a handy office space to have at the warehouse. Sure, for conversations like this, but mainly for our don, Marco, to use when he needs to do business unrelated to his hotels.

"I'm gonna kill him." Crank growls and the hand he was rubbing up and down Fizz's back turns into a fist.

"No." Fizz's voice is quiet and she sniffs before lifting her head to look at him. She sighs heavily then says, "I want to do it."

The new determination in her soft voice surprises me as much as the words.

"Okay, this got dark real fast. I'm not saying I'm against it, but I kinda need to know why he's a dead man." I cross one ankle over the other, getting comfortable for the new information about to hit me, because there's no way this isn't a big deal. Fizz may be mafia, but she's one of the kindest souls I've ever known. The fact that she wants her step-brother dead isn't a simple age-old sibling rivalry.

Sitting up on Crank's lap, Fizz wipes at her damp, puffy eyes with the sleeve of her olive-green sweater. She doesn't attempt to move any farther away from him, content to let him keep his arms wrapped around her waist.

I wait patiently for a few minutes while she gathers the energy and courage she needs to tell me what's going on.

"His dad married my mom when I was a teenager. He's six years older than I am so I think he was…nineteen? Maybe twenty. He hated me." She pauses, as if the memory is causing her physical pain, before inhaling deeply and closing her eyes for a second. "To start with, he just found ways to get me in trouble with our parents. But that wasn't enough for him. After a while, he started hurting me, told me he'd kill my mom in her sleep if I told anyone the bruises were from him. Then it turned into...he..." She sighs heavily and closes her eyes again. "He made me do things to him and raped me consistently for years before I ran away. I found Marco's dad and he kept me safe, gave me a job, made me into more than nothing." Her tear-filled gaze meets mine and there's so much guilt swimming in their depths that I break my no-hugging rule, leaning down and wrapping my arms around her neck.

"Don't you dare let what he did to you make you feel ashamed. You have never been nothing. Do you hear me?" The hug is quick and I grip her head between my palms once more, staring her in the eye. "What are you, Fizz?"

The tears are streaming down her face, but she narrows her gaze with determination as she sniffs.

"What. Are. You, Fizz?"

"I'm a bad-ass bitch." She huffs a gentle laugh and shakes her head.

I won't lie, when River told me her mantra for herself years ago, I took it upon myself to make sure the women on my crew knew it too.

"Yes, you fucking are." I speak directly to Fizz, knowing Crank is listening intently to what I'm about to say. "I'm totally on board with him dying, I would never deny you that, but I need to see if we can get any info on the Irish from him before you land the final blow. You gonna be good with that?"

She nods and I mirror it in acknowledgement. "You wanna come in once we've got what we need or you coming in for the whole thing? Completely your choice."

"I think I'll sit out here for a bit. I'll come in soon though. Is that okay?"

I wink. "Whatever you need, Fizz." Letting go of her face, I stand and head for the door. Might as well get this whole thing moving along because this fucker deserves Hell for what he's done.

"J?"

I stop with my palm on the door handle and look over my shoulder. "Yeah?"

"Make it hurt." Fizz's small, wobbly grin gives me hope that she's not entirely broken by this man and I'm reminded of the fire I love so much about her.

"Of course."

Shoo winces and grasps his junk as I use the blow torch to cauterize the end of Cook's dick, the tip of it lying on the ground beneath his head. He's currently hanging upside down from the ceiling. We've been at this for a couple of hours now and he still hasn't given anything up about Ronan and he keeps passing out from the pain. It's fucking annoying.

Cook's screams have died out again and I sigh, releasing his swinging body from the chains holding him up so he falls to the floor. I drag his limp, naked form by the leg to the wall and tie him to the metal chair. Tab helps, because of course the weak-ass ballbag has passed out again.

"Why d'you always have to go for the family jewels, Boss?" Shoo shudders and begins clearing up the chains that were hanging from the ceiling. They will be thoroughly cleaned before being put away for future use, but not until we've finished with this creep.

"Not always, but he practically asked for it." I shrug as I finish tightening the chain on his left ankle and step back, conscious of the words I just used. If men can say a rape victim asked for it, then I can say the same about cutting off the tip of a rapist's dick. Tit for mother fucking tat.

Cook's head slowly lifts from his chest; he's waking up as I move over to one of the cabinets and begin pulling out some tools. Toothpicks, a rusty saw, a large can of gasoline, and a dirty-as-fuck sack.

"Why do you still want him?" Cook's voice is croaky and low, not really aimed in any direction.

"Okay, I'll give you something. He stole something from me and I don't play well when others take what is mine." I raise my brows because he's getting fuck all else out of me, but at this point, a small exchange of that information is a new tactic. Everything's worth a shot.

"Ha." Cook shifts his gaze to mine, where I'm standing in front of him, toothpicks in hand. "Your kind are so selfish. Always thinking of yourselves."

Before he can continue his tirade, I grab the dirty sack and shove it over his head. Then I grab the gasoline can, walk back over, and yank his head backward, pouring the liquid over his face. His choking sounds are music to my ears, but I know I have to stop.

Leaning down, I speak into his ear. "Tell me where Ronan is and I promise this stops." I don't tell him he's going to die anyway, but I won't break my promise. I'll stop pouring gasoline on his face.

"Fuck you."

His spluttering begins again as I pour more liquid over his covered head, then I stop and rip the sack off, controlling where his face is looking by gripping his ear.

"Tell me. Where Ronan is. And I promise I'll stop." This is also one I won't break. Just because I'll be stopping, doesn't mean the rest of my Reapers will.

He's still coughing, struggling to catch his breath, and I move to put the sack back over his head before he stops me. "Wait. He's in Georgia. Somewhere around Savannah in a fucking bunker. That's all I know. Now you have to stop if I know anything about a promise made by the mafia." He spits at me and I manage to move back quickly enough to avoid the dirty bastard's bodily fluid.

The smirk on his face tells me he's severely underestimated this situation. He actually thinks that's it. I suppose I could have promised to stop sooner, but if I'm honest with myself, I was enjoying it.

I sigh, annoyed that I have to give up my torturing to Fizz now, but it's her turn to do whatever she needs to get rid of her demon. The whole thing is still blowing my mind and I'm surprised that I kept my cool as well as I did.

He's been beaten, burned, cut, had literal salt rubbed into the wounds, and the old fucker's still going. But he's Fizz's kill and I'd never take that away from her. If anything, the revelation with Fizz just made it easier to question him. Knowing he is going to die anyway meant I could be a little sloppier with my methods.

"I suppose I should thank you for the information on Ronan, but it's about as useful as tits on a fish." I believe that he doesn't know anything else. It's pitiful, but it's *something* for Glitch and Dmitry to work with.

Since when did Dmitry working on shit become normal? I shake the thought away, something to deal with at a later date. Although I would never admit it to him, I'm beginning to kinda like this new normal.

"It's all I've got and all you're getting." His confidence is astounding and I almost laugh.

The door creaks open behind me and there's suddenly a new look in Cook's eyes. The cockiness has gone, replaced by fear.

He knows he's fucked. This time, I let myself smile.

"I'm going to keep my promise, but that doesn't mean that you get to live. Your life is now in her hands." I step back as he begins to struggle against his restraints, like he actually thought he'd get out of here alive before he laid eyes on Fizz.

"What...you're...*you*." His voice is trembling, full of anger and fear, and the sense of karma that fills me is warming. He's now experiencing what he made her feel all those years ago.

Fizz tentatively moves into the room with Crank behind her and I see the moment she steels her spine now that she's face to face with her abuser. She doesn't say a word, just stands there in silence and lets Cook stew in it. Her nose twitches up and her face contorts into one of disgust and I'm guessing the smell of his urine, sweat, and tears has hit her.

Slowly, I walk toward my oldest Reaper, vowing to learn more about what troubles each of them, because if running from my past has taught me anything, it's that revenge is fucking tasty.

Fizz, the woman who was never meant for this life but was forced into it anyway; the woman who is loyal to her core, but has been running from her demons her whole life, just like me; Fizz, who is now standing in front of me, about to do something she will never come back from.

I couldn't be prouder.

N.O. ONE

Life begins on the other side of fear, and facing it head on is something I wish I'd done years ago. I'll get my chance when I kill Ronan and get my girl back. For now, this is Fizz's moment.

"Just nod if you want out. Okay?" I know she won't take the option, the determination in her face is solid, zero cracks, but the offer's there. I know Crank will too happily kill this motherfucker if given the chance.

She nods, letting me know she understands, gently touching my shoulder before she begins to walk toward him.

His features scrunch in disgust, but the fear is still oh-so-clear and I fold my arms across my chest, leaning back against the wall next to Crank as we watch.

"So, this is who you've been running with, little sis. I did wonder. Shame I—"

It's over so fast I barely had time to blink. Fizz has pulled out a gun from her waistband and shot him between the eyes. The loud shot is quickly followed by four more, one to each of his kneecaps, one to his dick, and one through his heart.

He's dead in seconds, parts of his insides now on the ground with the growing puddle of his blood.

It's a little anticlimactic for my taste. I was hoping she was going to draw it out a little, but considering this isn't usually her thing, I get it. Over and done.

Fizz places the gun back into her waistband and sighs before turning to face us. There's a small smile tipping the corners of her lips as she walks in our direction, stopping in front of Crank and looking to me.

"Better?" I ask.

"Thank you." She tilts her head in respect and wraps her arms around Crank. The tears in her eyes linger at her waterline and he takes a deep breath. "I know you wanted to make him hurt, but he didn't deserve to breathe the same air as me any longer. And he definitely didn't deserve my words. I'll make hoagies for us all on Saturday." Her smile is still a little wobbly, but I don't call her on it as she lets Crank lead her from the room.

Relief floods my veins that she's okay. I care about my Reapers far more than I'll ever let on. That doesn't mean they don't know it, though.

"I guess Fizz isn't driving the van tonight?" Shoo chuckles, dumping the tools we've used today into the box we store them inside before they get cleaned.

"Dick. Binx is on his way in with the chemicals and Tab is about five minutes away with pizza. Get started on the clean up. I need to call our nerds with the Georgia info."

I lift up my phone and open the door to step out.

"*Our* nerd*s*, Boss? He sticking around then?" Shoo emphasizes the our and the plural part of nerds, wagging his brows and overstepping his boundaries, as usual, but instead of telling him to fuck off, I surprise myself with my answer before disappearing from the room.

"Maybe."

Chapter Seventeen

D

"May the Fourth be with you, too, Mom. Have fun at the LARP convention!" With a sigh, I end the conversation with my parents only to look up and see Glitch's gaze fixed on me like I've grown two more limbs and a second head. "What?"

We're back at Harvey Cook's place, packing up my camera and audio equipment all nice and neat in the original boxes. I'm a little anal like that.

"Are your parents at the San Francisco LARP Anonymous Convention?" Of course he'd know. For people like us who grew up gaming, this gathering is epic.

"Yeah, they've been attending since year one. I was like, I don't know, two years old?" I shrug, pointing to the different cameras J and I set up at Cook's house. "That one is brand fucking new, man." I'd wanted to test the limits of that equipment and decided doing recon on this house was a good start.

"You're an asshole! I've been calling in favors right and left trying to get that set-up before it goes retail." I laugh, knowing exactly how he feels. The XD two-fifty is the latest Japanese technology and it blows everything else out of the fucking water.

"A friend of a friend is, uh, one of the concept technicians." I feel more than see Glitch freeze and I'm pretty sure if I turn around his mouth will be hanging open like a damn fish out of water.

Definitely testing that theory, placing a bet against myself.

When I turn to face him, he's doing exactly that and I mentally high-five myself.

"How am I just learning about this now? You've been on surveillance for the last week, man. That's fucked up." Shaking his head, he tests the sturdiness of the lone table in the middle of the kitchen. Once satisfied that it won't break under his weight, he jumps on like a frog and stands facing the tiny camera encrusted in the wiring of the seventies-galore lamp shade hanging from the ceiling.

"Not my fault your attention to detail is shit." Placing the original box for the camera on the table beside him, I give in to my curiosity.

That fucking pantry.

Cook never came here at regular intervals. It wasn't a specific day of the week nor a special date in the month. It was random, or at least that's how it seemed on the tapes.

The only rituals he had were the cereal he ate and that fucking pantry he kept his eyes on, barely ever blinking.

"There's gotta be something in there, Glitch. Why would he come to this fucking dump just to eat cereal?" My question is aimed at Glitch but, really, I'm just talking to myself as I walk over to the small, damp room and open the door.

When J and I came here the first time, we'd checked it all out. All three bedrooms, every bathroom—there are two and half—living room, basement, and yes, this empty pantry. There wasn't a damn thing that seemed out of the ordinary. An abandoned house with dust everywhere except for the kitchen table and the one chair. The refrigerator isn't even turned on, which made me want to gag every time I saw him eating Wheaties without a single drop of milk.

"Sounds like a sociopath to me." By the soft tone of his voice, I can tell he's just saying whatever he thinks I want to hear because his entire attention is solely on the tiny camera that's probably giving him a boner right now. "Fuck, look at this baby." Called it.

"If you jack off to images of it later tonight, I may have to disown you as a friend." Beyond his chuckle, I don't hear anything he says because my only focus is the empty shelves, save for the row of cereal boxes, and wood paneling that decorate the walls. A thick layer of dust coats everything except the shelves in front of the boxes, which makes sense. Every time he came here, he pulled one out then slid it back in.

Putting myself in Cook's shoes, I reach for the white box, ignoring whatever joke Glitch is throwing my way, and pull it away from the wall behind it. I don't know what I was expecting, a magic lever that opened up to a magical world of wizards and creatures, maybe?

Nothing happened.

I try the next box, then the next. Pulling out, pushing back in. No magic, not even a sound that would tell me I'm on to something.

Maybe I'm wrong. Maybe Cook was a complete psycho and had a thing for Wheaties and empty pantries. I mean,

I saw some weird shit in prison that makes this look like picture-perfect sanity.

I remember this tall, bald guy in the cell across the hall from me had befriended a cockroach. Named him Cap, like Captain, and cut out a tiny cape for him to wear with the letter *A* drawn with his blood. He wasn't allowed to have a pen so he improvised. His words.

So, maybe Cook wasn't out of his mind, maybe it was just a quirk.

I'm about to turn around and walk out when something catches my eye. I stop, ignoring the sounds of Glitch behind me as he jumps off the table then pushes it to a different corner of the kitchen before he's back up and working on another hidden camera.

Just behind the first box is an oval…what is that? With my phone in hand, I tap the flashlight icon and point it at the wall. It's a half-eaten piece of Wheaties, reminding me that a mouse has been squatting in this place for at least as long as we've been watching it.

Shaking my head, I decide to take all the boxes out and throw them out. With no living next of kin, Cook's house had been placed up for auction, and by the power vested in my hacking skills, it is now part of Zavier's holdings, along with the land he'd been trying to buy for months.

Leaving these boxes here would only encourage the entire population of mice to take up residence.

Grabbing all four, I press them together and back away. This time when I glance at the wood paneling, I realize something's not right. The line isn't straight, the cut isn't sealed. There's a big gap between the wood and the shelf and I don't have to be an expert in DIY to know that's not normal.

"Glitch," I call out as I put the boxes back on the shelf and forget their existence all together. My gut is screaming at me that I'm onto something here.

With the flashlight pointed at the open space, I get closer, seeing mouse pellets all around and half of one between the slats of the wood on the back wall.

It's definitely an opening.

"Glitch." This time I call out a little louder as I pick up a knife conveniently placed along the wall. Too conveniently, in fact, and I'm certain Cook used it to open this wall space.

As soon as the little door pops open, I freeze. It takes my brain a few minutes to register what exactly I'm seeing because holy fucking shit, this is anything but normal.

"Glitch, I swear to fuck, you need to stop flirting with the equipment and get your ass over here." My eyes are glued to the sight in front of me. Fascination, disgust, intrigue, confusion. Every one of those emotions are swirling inside my brain like a perfectly timed drain, circling, circling, circling.

"What's up, did you find—" I know the exact moment Glitch sees what I've been trying to understand.

"Yeah." I whisper my answer as if this is too much for loud words.

"Jesus, man. Who does that?" I know his question is rhetorical but I feel the overwhelming need to answer.

"You were right. Harvey Cook is a psycho." We stand in silence, letting my words linger like the rancid smell of a fart after a hefty chili dinner.

The wall has been cut out, with shelves all around and clear jars lining the space. "I'm going to take a wild guess and say that's formaldehyde in there." I lean in and shiver as a blue iris, wide and staring, turns on itself, the nerves still attached and swimming like tiny snakes.

"I'd have to agree." In my peripheral, I see Glitch take out his phone, snap a few pictures, then send them to their group chat.

"What'd you tell them?"

"I think we got a twofer," he answers, the tone of voice giving nothing away. No inflection, no shock, no disgust. Just another day at the office.

"Yep. Gambler by day, serial killer by night." With Marco's soldiers all being found with their eyes carved out, it was easy to put the two pieces together to get the whole picture.

Like I said, I don't believe in coincidence.

By the time we got all the equipment out of the house, we debated on whether to bring the jars of floating eyeballs but agreed it was bad juju to carry them around in our car. Getting pulled over with over a dozen sets of eyeballs would surely call for a trip with the Five-O.

Before going to prison for hacking into a bank where blood money from at least five different wars spanning the last three decades were being kept, I was just a guy fascinated by anything with a hard drive. Passionate about three-dimensional world building and comfortable hanging out with likeminded people.

They say prison changes you but your core remains the same. Sure, I had to learn to defend myself, but mostly, I used my brain and my skills. The greatest violence I'd ever inflicted on anyone was through a screen with well-designed weapons made of pixels and imagination.

When Zavier hired the best lawyers he could buy and still wasn't able to get the charges dropped, he did the next best thing. Made me his partner in all things casinos on the very day I walked out. Although I was arrested in San Francisco, the bank was in New York City so…Ryker's became my home for the next two years.

I'd always known he'd grown up with the inheritance of the Greek mafia, but until I stepped foot into this world, I had no idea what that meant. Was I afraid? I probably should have been, but working behind my screens meant the world was in a different realm from where I sat.

At the time, I didn't need to interact or smile and be funny. That was Z's job. Me? I just had to be good at my job. And I am.

Except, one night, J happened and all my plans disintegrated from just that wink. That one shameless act of defiance ruined me for all others.

Now, I'm in her world and every day I discover just how dark her existence can be. I'm not afraid of it, although I probably should be. To be honest, I don't really give a fuck. All I see is her. Every one of my senses is fixed only on her.

That's not to say that floating eyes and swimming optical nerves don't make my stomach revolt. They really fucking do and if I don't ever see them again, I will be okay with that.

"So what do you think, Dima?" I spin around at the sound of Z's voice, seeing a red Aston Martin pull up behind him and none other than Marco Mancini stepping out. To my surprise, he walks over to the passenger side door and opens it, holding out a hand for who I'm guessing is River, his wife.

I shrug at Z's question. I'm no expert on viable land, but an apartment building facing the East River with the Manhattan skyline? I don't need to be a financial mogul to know we're standing on prime real estate.

"I wouldn't say no to breakfast with this view every morning."

Marco and River slowly make their way to us, hand in hand, and I don't miss the way he stands proud with her by his side.

Sliding my hands into my jean pockets, I straighten my spine in response to his presence. There's no indication Marco's going to pull out a gun and shoot us but there's something in his eyes, a determination, or maybe the protective instinct of a lion, that demands respect.

"Marco. Mrs. Mancini." Zavier shakes Marco's hand but only bows to his wife since her right hand is being held hostage. I can't help my smirk when she breaks free of her husband's hold and presents her hand to Zavier. They shake as Marco and I do the same. When it's my turn to greet Mrs. Mancini, I grin at the firm grip.

I know J considers River to be a force of nature, and I can see why. She has the grace of a swan and the presence of a hurricane and I immediately like her.

"You'll have to excuse my husband, he tends to trust no one, especially when it comes to me." Marco's jaw clenches as his gray eyes bounce from me to Zavier then back to me.

"I have a meeting in forty minutes." Well, I guess we're moving this along, then.

"Right. So, my partner Dmitry and I were able to acquire this land from its previous owner." Zavier's not lying but he's also not being completely transparent. By "acquire" he really means his partner—me—hacked into The Office of the City Register and changed ownership from Harvey Cook to Zavier Galanos.

River snorts as she takes in the view around us, making the corners of my mouth tick up. She's not stupid and neither is Marco, but sometimes Zavier is too confident. Most times, he underestimates his opponents.

"And did you...*acquire*..." Marco pauses on the word giving it a weight of its own. "This land before or after our Mr. Wright—"

"Harvey Cook," River interrupts without even looking at Marco.

"Yes, apologies. Before or after Harvey Cook descended into the deepest, darkest depths of Hell?" Marco's tone is all business, no fluctuations and not a hint of anger. But I'm not fooled by his calm. A cobra doesn't get agitated before a deadly strike.

"Hell is too good for him." On that River and I agree wholeheartedly. I'm guessing the Reapers got them up to date quickly since Eyeballgate was only a few hours ago.

"I won't lie, I've been after this lot for months now and well, I won't deny myself a good opportunity. Especially since you and I had a deal." Zavier doesn't back down from Marco. In different circumstances, Zavier would be Marco's equal, a mafia prince in his own right.

Except, he gave all of that up for a life of freedom.

"Hmmm, you know, Zavier," Marco begins, his index finger tapping against his lips as he pauses, making sure our attention is solely on him. "Funny thing about opportunity. It comes and goes. And what I allow to come to you in this city, I can take it away."

River walks back to Marco's side and together they are two towers of immovable strength.

"What my husband is trying to say is that we don't appreciate liars, Zavier. And more than that? We don't take too kindly to manipulators. If you want something, you come to us. We assess, we decide." At River's words, Marco's head bows in her direction like he's showing reverence and I see it. It's right there.

The awe and the love. It's so fucking clear and I feel it in my gut.

It's the exact same feeling I get every time Jordyn O'Neill walks into a room. Goddamn, it's blinding.

"You're right. You're absolutely right. You have my word, Mr. and Mrs. Mancini, it won't happen again." Smooth, Zavier, very smooth.

"No, it won't." Marco ends the conversation with those three words.

"Enjoy your property and make sure you show us the floorplans. Who knows? We may need an apartment one day." River grins then looks to her husband. "I'm hungry."

Our goodbyes are swift and not five minutes later, Z and I stand here staring at the slowly descending sun over the skyline.

"This place is going to make us a fortune, Dima." My chuckle is low but genuine when Z predicts the future.

"Good, you can pay for the plastic surgeon to fix your fuck up." We both laugh, knowing damn well, I'd rather cut off my limbs than go under the knife to fix my scar. In fact, I've got a little soft spot for my scars and I can't wait to get my new tattoo in the morning.

"Like you ever would."

"Nah, Jordyn loves me just the way I am." I grin and he rolls his eyes. I know he had a thing for her but he just wanted to fuck her, I want to build a throne for her and kneel at her feet. Not the fucking same.

"Think you can handle her?" Z turns to fully face me, the banter gone, the big brother vibe fully in place. "She's...a lot."

I grin because he doesn't get it.

"No, Z. She's everything."

And just so we're clear, I may not be used to violence, but for her? I'd fucking slice open my best friend's neck if he ever laid a hand on her.

Thankfully, I fell in love with a woman who'd do it herself then come to me for a hard fuck.

"Duly noted." And that's that. With these few words, Zavier now understands where I stand and I know he's got my back just like I've got his.

For the next hour, Zavier tells me all about his plans for this land, the high-end apartments he wants to erect, the name he wants to build for us. We throw around ideas for a company brand that would be separate from the casinos and people in the business we want to work with.

Through it all, half my brain is on other matters. While Z imagines his empire, I go through a mental list of all the things I need to do to make sure Ronan Callaghan isn't anywhere near Hallie. I put a plan into place that allows me to hack into the city cameras in Savannah, Georgia as well as Cocoa Beach, Florida where Hallie's staying with her grandparents.

Speaking of those two rats, I'm keeping a close eye on them too because no matter their ages, I don't fucking trust them.

After all, instead of discussing their wish to take Hallie away from the toxic environment that was the Irish mob, they literally ripped her out of her mother's arms.

People with worthy souls don't do that. I know it. J knows it.

It's time to help my little demon get her daughter back.

Chapter Eighteen

J

"School here sucks and Grandpa is being weird."

Hallie sighs down the phone, and while I'm fully aware she's a teenager and everything will "suck" for her, I still want to fix it all.

"Why is your grandpa being weird? What's going on, Kid?" With everything else happening around us, Glitch hasn't had a lot of time to dig into the grandparents properly yet so I can get my girl back without having the police or feds on my back. We know they're connected to the Irish mob, but it has never been directly. When I was younger, they always seemed to look down on me and my parents and I just assumed it was because we were lower down the food chain than them. From what I remember, they were suppliers of something, and if Glitch can just find out what, we may finally have the thing on them we need to get Hallie back.

"Ugh, there was a stupid party at the house on Friday and Saturday, with like a million old men in stuffy suits and Grandpa made me talk to their sons, who were also like, totally ancient. When I told Grandpa I was tired and didn't wanna do it anymore, he got mad and told me I had to stay or he'd take my phone away. So, like I said, weird."

Okay, now this is worrying. I have an idea why he's doing this and I don't like it, but I'm not going to panic my baby girl over it.

It has, however, become a priority to get her out of there. It's no longer the safest option to let her stay until I've sorted my shit out.

To be honest, there's always going to be shit to fix in my world, there's never going to be a perfect time to bring her home to me, and while I'm totally unprepared to be a full-time mom, that no longer matters.

She does.

"Oh, gross. I'm so sorry. Did you have to wear dresses?" I faux-shudder, loving the little giggle she responds with.

"Yeah, ugh." She repeats my faux-shudder and we both laugh. "Anyway, bell's about to ring, so I should get to class. Talk to you soon, Mom." That word still sends a tingle straight to my heart every time.

"Talk to you soon, Kid." Placing my phone down on the kitchen counter, I pour myself a fresh cup of coffee from the pot and inhale deeply.

The scent is like a balm to my soul and I enjoy every burning sip in complete silence as it glides down my throat. Dmitry has been here every night since the first time, and sometimes he's still here in the morning, while others he isn't. I still haven't decided how I feel about it, but I really miss the smell of sausage on the mornings he's not here.

When he let himself in unannounced last night, he explained what he and Glitch found in Cook's pantry. Glitch had already given me a run-down, but Dmitry felt the need to go into detail. It pissed me the fuck off to know we had the serial killer in our palms and didn't make him suffer more. Still does.

Marco's relieved that he's dead, as are the other capos, but that doesn't make the knowledge of who he really was any better. What we still don't really know is the why.

Why did Cook murder our soldiers the way the Greeks did years ago? How did he do it, considering most of our soldiers are ruthless? Did he work alone? How did he keep losing our tails? All his death has done is pose more questions. The least I could've done was make his suffering last a few more hours, get some answers from the gambling psychotic fucknut.

"Honey, I'm home!"

I look over to the door, watching Dmitry work his way inside with brown paper bags and what looks like fresh coffee. Downing the rest of the black liquid from my mug, I move to stand from my stool. I've given up on throwing daggers at him. All that does is encourage him.

"Don't get up, Little Demon, you need to rest that ass up for the pounding you're getting later." He's by the counter and in front of me in seconds, placing the bags and coffees down before grabbing my face in both hands and kissing me like a starved man. His tongue plays with mine like they're old friends and when I grip his biceps, he sucks my bottom lip into his mouth and pulls away. "Mmm, delicious. Vanilla or caramel?"

I narrow my eyes at him. "Vanilla or caramel? As in, coffee? Tell me you didn't destroy the coffee with syrup?"

"Destroy? Nah. I'm telling ya, you'll love it. Did you know, vanilla is actually a really complex flavor? It gets a rep for being plain and boring, but really—"

"Okay, shh. I'll try one." I grab a cup at random and take a sip, surprised that I don't hate the sweetness.

"See, I knew you'd like it." He picks up the second cup and taps it against mine. "Bottoms up. Or at least, they will be later."

"That's what you think." I raise my brows at him accusingly just before my phone begins ringing. It's not a number I recognize and I know Dmitry notices my confusion before I answer the call.

"I know you're there. How rude to answer the phone and not even say hello, Jordyn. It's Jonathan Gallagher."

I sigh and prepare myself for whatever shit show is about to ensue, pushing aside the twinge of pain from hearing Murphy's surname on someone else. "What do you want?"

"And this is why you don't deserve that girl in your care. No manners, whatsoever. Just like your parents." His deep voice is grating on me and I want to kill him.

"What. Do. You. Want?" I won't apologize. These people had me beaten, shot, then stole my little girl from me at her father's funeral. They deserve nothing but my complete and total ire.

"I'm just calling to let you know that we know Hallie has been speaking to you." My heart drops to my stomach. I don't want her to get into trouble. "We're allowing it because she's being pliant, for now. But mark my words, if she becomes difficult, all contact will stop. Do you understand me, Jordyn?"

Fuck you would be my usual response to this kind of threat. Fucking try me is my usual stance on these matters. But this is my thirteen-year-old kid's happiness on the line.

"I understand." And I do. All too well. I understand that I need to get her out of that situation as soon as physically possible.

"Good." The line goes dead and I pull my phone away from my ear, staring at it as though I could reach through it and rip Mr. Gallagher's fucking head off.

"Little Demon, we'll fix it. I already have access to the surveillance around her school and their home. And I'm working on finding something on them. There's no way they haven't messed up somewhere and I'm telling you I'll find it. Now..." He pauses and leans in to kiss my forehead. "Eat that kolache while it's still warm, then you can teach me how to ride a damn motorcycle. I'm thinking of getting one so we can go on road trips with Hallie." He wags his brows and my mind is whirring at a thousand miles per hour from pretty much everything he just said.

That dangerous grin I've grown to love stretches across his stubbled face, the scar over his eye crinkling in a way I can picture with my eyes closed, and I open my mouth to question, well, everything. There's a kolache between my lips before I can speak and Dmitry laughs as I growl at him and narrow my eyes again, biting into the doughy softness.

"Don't talk with your mouth full."

I chew on the soft lemon curd pastry, which has become my new obsession, before swallowing it down. "What do you mean you already have access to surveillance? And why?" I'll address the motorcycle lesson once I know his reasoning for this. I'm surprisingly not mad that he's taken it upon himself to get involved, because of course my own personal stalker knows everything going on in my life.

"Because it's important to you." That's it. That's all he says as he begins munching on his own blueberry kolache. As if it's that easy.

But why can't it be that easy?

Life has been nothing but an everlasting rollercoaster, rolling in all the directions, and I've just been along for the ride. Dmitry seems to hold the key to getting off, to making things seem much simpler than they've ever been. There's no guilt, no secrets between us, and I have to admit to having more than a few feelings for this man who slid into my life as easily as his dick slides into my cunt.

"Okay. Update me when you have something." I catch his eye and he grins again, giving a small head tilt of acknowledgment as I pick up the rest of my own breakfast.

"I did a thing."

Fuck, I hate it when people start off with this type of warning, especially Dmitry since he's the king of over-the-top.

"You do a lot of things." My gaze follows his every move, weary and expecting some crazy shit to happen in the next few seconds.

"I do. I'm happy you've noticed." His arm reaches up and behind his head as he fists the cotton of his shirt then pulls his entire T-shirt right off, giving me the best morning view possible: his naked, tattooed chest. The clear cut of muscles and the swirl of colorful tattoos make my mouth water and just when I'm about to help myself to a little dessert, I register a brand new tat, right there in the middle of his sternum, assaulting every one of my brain cells.

"Is that...?" No words.

"Yup. Didn't want to waste the perfect opportunity to show, not tell." With those words, I'm able to rip my stare from his chest and look him straight in the eyes.

"Show what, exactly?" I think I know, but holy shit.

"Every fool on this planet who's ever been in love has had some kind of verbal declaration." He shrugs, then continues. "I'm showing you the only way I know how that you're it for me, J." It's like those words just come so easily to him.

"So, tattooing the letter J on your chest is your way of showing me you love me?" Fucking hell, this man.

"To be fair, you carved it with your knife, I just made it permanent."

So what does that say about me?

Having Dmitry on the back of my motorcycle with his arms wrapped around my waist and his dick sticking into my lower back feels kinda symbolic, especially after that weird-yet-meaningful little conversation from earlier. I know the Sons of Khaos motorcycle gang that we sometimes have dealings with would say this means Dmitry's officially my old man—not that they generally have female members—but I'd probably rip their tongues out if they tried to say anything of the sort.

Teaching him to ride this afternoon didn't happen, mainly because I don't trust a newbie on my baby. I don't give a fuck that he had it fixed for me, he can learn on something else. He pouted, but we found a dealer with something we can use and we've just dropped it off in the van to Crank for a check over.

Dmitry insisted we stop and have a celebratory drink on the way back to my apartment, so that's why I pull up in the parking lot of a random dive bar twenty minutes from home.

Until I have more information on Ronan or Hallie's grandparents, right now I'm kind of at a loss with what to do. There are no bodies to clean up, and I'm itching to do something. Anything.

Squeezing my ass, followed by a slap, Dmitry climbs off from behind me and holds his hand out for me. I don't take it, which only makes him smirk as he slides off his helmet at the same time as me.

"I don't know why I let you talk me into coming here." I shake my head and begin following Dmitry inside.

Before walking through the door, he pauses and turns to me. "We're gonna play a game tonight, Little Demon. I don't know you, you don't know me. I probably should've asked this before now, but do you have any hard limits?"

Is he being serious? He is...

I raise a questioning brow. "Dmitry, you've fucked me with the hilt of a knife, run a blade across my skin, and you're asking me about hard limits? Is this a sex club?"

"No," he laughs. "But consent is sexy." He winks and flashes that damn grin, making me shake my head, trying desperately to hide my own growing smile.

"Okay." I've never thought about hard limits before, I feel like I'm pretty much down for anything, actually... "Gun play. I'm not fucking stupid and I don't want a loaded gun pointing at me or you while we're fucking. That's about it." I shrug, truly unable to think of anything I wouldn't want this man to do to me.

And fuck, that's scary...the trust I have so quickly given to Dmitry is the total opposite of how I have lived for so long.

"That's a good one. Same. I may be handy with a knife, but guns aren't my thing. After you." He opens the door and gestures for me to pass through first, slapping my ass again as I walk past him and head straight for the bar. It stings a little, but it's a delicious sting, and he's lucky not to lose a hand.

"What can I get ya?" The busty bartender with flowing dark hair rests her palms on the bar and smiles, but it doesn't reach her eyes and she's obviously bored.

I don't know this place or the people in it, so I'm careful with my drink choice.

"Bottled water, please. Leave the cap on."

"Really? Why come to a bar and order water?" She scoffs and grabs my drink from the small refrigerator behind her, clearly not reading the room and the trained assassin standing right in front of her.

I turn to see what Dmitry is going to order, but he's not there. He was right behind me when I walked in and now he's gone. I don't know whether to go back out and search for him or wait. Did he say he was going to the bathroom?

Fuck it, he can look after himself.

The bartender places my bottle of water in front of me, knocking it over when her eyes practically bulge out of her head as she looks over my shoulder. She's lucky the lid is still on.

"Hey, sexy. Do you have a name or can I call you mine?" Dmitry's voice is low, sultry, and I'm trying not to laugh at his cheesy pick-up line when I notice the bartender is still standing there, and she might as well be drooling.

"I'll be yours. And I promise I'd never laugh at you like she just did." Her smile reaches her eyes this time, and she must have adjusted her breasts to look bigger because she's just a head on tits at this point.

Something inside me switches, and I have to hold myself back from reaching over the bar and smashing a glass to shove in this woman's eye. I lower my head, glaring at her through my lashes, and I can't control the snarl that escapes before I turn around. Dmitry is right there, so close but not touching, and I realize what he's doing. The whole strangers meeting in a bar thing. It's cute, and if it shuts this big tittied cunt up, I'm all in. That's the only reason.

I run my hands up his chest and unzip his jacket, sliding my hands inside and feeling the warmth beneath his black T-shirt. Pushing off his jacket, I silently caress his biceps, all while our eyes are locked together. It's like pure reverence emitting from his pale-green irises, and his gaze alone seems to hold a power over my entire body.

"Er, excuse me. I asked if the gentleman would like a drink." Her now nasally voice makes me sneer and Dmitry's lips tip up at the corners as he grips my waist, hoisting me onto the bar and stepping between my legs.

"I'll drink from your pussy. *Mine*, nothing else will quench my thirst." I'm all for a bit of exhibitionism, but

I'm going to draw the line if he actually tries to go down on me on this unsanitary slab of wood. It's no secret that people, in general, do not wash their hands after pissing. My naked ass isn't getting anywhere near that. Maybe that should be one of my hard limits.

His lips are on mine in seconds and he devours me, doing to my mouth what I now want him to do to my pussy—and I'm beginning to come around to the idea of doing it right here as he tightens his grip on my waist then pulls my head back by my braid to bite my neck.

"Hey! You can't do this here. I *will* call the police."

That's it.

I rip my mouth away from Dmitry and push him away a little to jump off the bar.

"Can't a girl get dicked around here? You call the police and I'll cut your huge fucking nipples off with the bottle opener. Okay?" The green-eyed monster makes an appearance, and I know I'm being irrationally jealous, but it's uncontrollable. Dmitry is under my skin, through and through.

Fuck.

I won't deny that I like it. I can't.

The bartender's eyes go wide before she puts her head down and scurries away to serve another customer. It's a

Monday night so it's not busy, but there's a steady flow of customers.

"You getting jealous, Little Demon? Kinda ruined my game, but I *am* hard as a fucking rock, though." The glint in his eyes tells me he knows the answer to his question.

"Wanna get out of here?" My panties are soaked and I'm more than ready to get pounded.

"Yeah, service here is shit anyway." Dmitry smirks and winks at me, again, and I swear I'm addicted to the way it scrunches up his face when he does. Putting his palm against the bottom of my back, he leads me outside. "Ever been fucked in an alley?"

I furrow my brow a little then look up at him beside me. "Random, but no, actually."

"Think you can ride wearing a butt plug?" The smirk never leaves his lips as we stand beside my motorcycle.

I actually take a second to think about it, because that's not something I've ever tried. "Dunno." I decide to be honest, shrugging.

"Oh, Little Demon, we're gonna have some fun tonight. Go down that alley beside the bar, put your palms against the wall, and close your eyes." He slaps my ass yet again, encouraging me to move, and I take a deep breath.

This is a trust moment. And because I can't control myself around him, I choose to go with it.

"Fine."

He chuckles behind me as I walk away, flipping him off at the same time.

Gotta say, the smell of an alley isn't something that's ever turned me on, but on the grand scale of alley-smells, this one isn't too bad. There's a dead-end, blocked off by a couple of dumpsters, and the bar's back entrance is a large black steel door sunk into the brick wall. The opposite wall is bare and there's a space lit up like a spotlight that is perfect for whatever Dmitry's planning.

Placing my palms on the cold brick, I face the wall and spread my legs a little, sticking my ass out for good measure. I wait for two, then five minutes, quickly becoming impatient. If this fucker's left me here, I'll slice his dick off.

While I'm silently grumbling to myself and thinking of ways to damage Dmitry, I have lost concentration on my surroundings. The scuffle of feet makes me lift my head, suddenly alert once more until his scent hits me.

"Don't turn around. Face the wall."

I do as he asks, a smile tilting my lips when he steps behind me and shoves his nose into my neck. He sniffs, taking me in.

"Fucking divine." He moves his head away and the sound of a blade being unsheathed makes me raise a brow. Bending down, he begins gently running the tip from my ankle to my ass, where he pauses to cut out what feels like a large hole from my pants.

"What the—"

"Shh. Just take it, Little Demon. Stop thinking for once and let me work." His dark chuckle sends vibrations straight to my clit as he continues his trail over my back with the dagger. If he slices this jacket though, I'll kill him. He must sense that because he doesn't, but he does wrap his arms around my front, pressing his hard cock into my ass, and takes his time cutting through the front of my top so I'm bare to the elements.

"You're still thinking too much. Trust me to make you feel good."

I think I'm being plenty trusting by coming into an alley and standing with my back to him, but he's right, I'm on edge, so I sigh. Closing my eyes briefly, I try to relax in his hold, which is surprisingly easy.

It always is.

It's not something I care to try and understand just yet, but this man has become a new solid fixture in my life and I don't think I can let him go.

He dips a finger into my pussy. "So wet for me," he murmurs into my ear, adding another finger and hooking them just right. His palm presses against my clit and I'm close to combusting already. Dmitry seems to know exactly what my body wants and when, pushing his fingers in and out, grazing my clit again and again before he pulls his fingers out. Then I hear him sucking his fingers into his mouth and I smile.

"Oh, fuck!" I gasp as his dick quickly thrusts inside me from behind, right as one of his hands palms my breast. The other hand has dropped the knife and he's now gripping my hip with a bruising hold.

The anticipation has already made me wet and the way this man handles a knife would make any woman like me light up like a bonfire. The way he fucks me is pure, needy, and I think I need him just as much.

It's quick, it's brutal, and it's fucking perfect as Dmitry pounds into me, pinching my nipple and marking my skin with his fingertips. Then he bites down on the back of my neck and I scream out an orgasm, pushing back against him with as much force as I can handle. But it's not enough, I need to see his face as he roars out his own orgasm because it's become one of my new favorite things.

Trying to move, to turn around, I'm stopped as he grips harder, saying, "Nah-ah," before the palm gripping my hip disappears and slaps across my ass cheek. "I bet that looks so fucking pretty and red." He soothes his hand over the now warm spot on my ass, squeezing hard again as his movements become erratic.

Our joined screams and curses echo through the alley and I dig my fingertips into the wall, pushing back on Dmitry with abandon. The world falls away and it's just us, joined in a way so carnal, so natural, it's impossible to deny our connection.

He roars out his release, holding himself deep inside me for a few seconds and resting his head against my shoulder. We're both breathing heavily as he gently slides out, squeezing my nipple again for good measure.

"Let's go finish this at home. I wanna try spanking you when I can see that ass turn red."

Chapter Nineteen

D

With a Twizzler sticking out of my mouth, I hum to the tune of some old-school Black Sabbath. The speakers are on surround sound, positioned at the sonically ideal spots for my listening pleasure. My office was my playground when we remodeled the casino with Zavier, and as soon as the walls were painted, no one else was allowed to touch it.

I've got a total of eight computer monitors on my U-shaped desk with television screens on the wall for the different cameras I tend to keep an eye on.

Usually, I watch Jordyn. With the GPS hidden in her bike, I always know where she is, and when I get worried, I provide aerial surveillance in case she needs back up.

Or sometimes, it's just because I want to see her tight little ass doing very bad things in the city that never sleeps.

Right now, however, I'm keeping an eye on the house in Cocoa Beach. In other words, I'm making sure Hallie is safe down there in Florida.

For the last three weeks, since Jonathan Gallagher—Hallie's grandfather—called Jordyn and basically threatened her, I've been keeping tabs on who's coming and going. I've got the street cam on my phone so even when we're back at J's place, we check on Hallie on a regular basis.

Every time I get a glimpse of the teen coming home from school, I record the stream and show it to J in the evenings. She doesn't cry but I can tell the image of her strong, beautiful daughter chokes her up.

So I just hold her, pinch her nipples, and fuck the sad right out of her for as long as possible.

Just as Ozzy starts to sing about warlords taking over the world, I suddenly stand—my chair flying backward and hitting the door—an air guitar poised between my hands as I sing, proud and loud, pretending I've got musical talent, playing in front of twenty thousand fans.

On the rare occasion I look up at the screen, what with the head banging and scrunched up eyes—it takes talent to pretend you're a rock star—I don't see anything out of place.

Until, that is, with my body arched back during the solo, my fingers flying across the invisible guitar and the speakers making me feel like I'm a fucking god, I see it.

I stop dead in my tracks, dropping my fantasy and screeching back into reality where something is definitely not right.

With three clicks of my mouse, the sudden silence is deafening as I watch a man dressed in a three-piece suit and flanked by three huge guys heading down the walkway straight to the Gallagher front door.

Oh, fuck no.

Using the second keyboard, I zoom in on the image, activating my facial recognition software to make sure I'm not fucking hallucinating.

I'm not.

Fuck.

There is no mistaking that is Ronan Callaghan ringing the Gallagher bell like a fucking door-to-door salesman.

Without taking my eyes off the screen, I swipe my phone from the desk and send out a quick text message to J. I'd call, but she's likely to ignore it while she's in her capos meeting with Mancini.

Me: Call me

Thirty seconds later.

> **Me**: Fucking call me, now.

Jesus fuck. Do I know anyone in Florida who can run interference? Of course not because I'm not a fucking mobster and don't have anyone in my life except my best friend out on the casino floor scoping out a good mouth to suck his cock, and my LARPing parents who speak dubious English, at best.

> **Me**: J, THIS IS NOT A FUCKING DRILL
>
> **Me**: fuck fuck fuck

Shit. I'm calling her. The messages should tell her to fucking answer. It rings four or five times before going to voicemail.

Fuck me, I didn't realize her capos meeting was a no-phones-on shindig. I call again for good measure because this is a motherfucking emergency.

As I do this, I search the internet for flights down to Florida in case we need to fly down because no one in our immediate circle actually lives there.

Ah, fuck it. This is not good. He's there, he's fucking there with Hallie, less than a month after some big to-do party hosted by her grandparents where skeezy old men were talking to her and she was being forced to play the meet-and-greet game.

Hallie is thirteen years old. What the fuck is wrong with people?

Fuck this. I'm not wasting time because of a fucking meeting of the heads.

This is stupid.

No, it's not.

Well, it is though, isn't it?

Probably. Definitely. But do I give a fuck? Not even a little bit.

The whole way to La Guardia Airport, I second guess myself about a half dozen times.

When I tried to book a flight like a normal human being, I scoffed at the flight times and the one, sometimes two stops along the way. By the time I'd land in Melbourne, Florida, Ronan would be long fucking gone. Orlando was an option but it's twice the driving distance to Cocoa Beach and the airport is fucking huge, which, again, would suck up all my time.

Hell, despite all of my efforts, Ronan may be long gone no matter what itinerary I choose, but I can't stand by and do nothing. Sitting on my ass is not an option.

When it became clear I wasn't going to go commercial, I called Zavier and told him I needed a chartered flight. It only took him fifteen minutes to find a friend of a friend who had a plane on standby for a flight to Houston and didn't mind doing a little detour to the Sunshine State.

Generous motherfucker. I'll have to buy him a case of very expensive and very illegal Cuban cigars.

> **Me**: J, I swear to fuck, pick up your phone.

I call again, but no answer, so I try Glitch, but he can't get a hold of her either. He assured me that one of the Reapers would drive up to the Upper East Side but traffic in Manhattan is a constant. His advice is to wait for J to get his message. She'll know what to do.

But time isn't on our side and even leaving right now we're taking the risk of losing Ronan.

All the way to the airport, through security, down the tarmac and up the small steps to the eight-seater plane, I have the phone to my ear or my fingers flying across the screen telling her I'm about to board and fly down to get Hallie.

I add on that I brought my knife so she doesn't worry. Too much.

Yes, this is fucking stupid. No, I don't give a shit.

Z's acquaintance is at the top of the stairs, greeting me with his year-round tan and million-dollar smile that looks less than two years old. I suppose when you've got enough money for a private jet, you have enough to reconstruct your teeth and get big shiny white ones.

More power to you, man.

We shake hands and I don't miss his slight recoil when his eyes land on my scar before he quickly looks away.

It's all good, I'm used to it and I don't care. It keeps irrelevant people away and I'm okay with that.

"Thank you for this, it's an emergency and commercial wasn't looking good for me." I bend at the knees to avoid slamming my head against the entrance and whistle low at the interior of the plane. It's all beige and white, glossy built-in furniture with eight large, comfortable looking leather seats, four on either side of the cylinder-shaped cabin with a work table separating them.

By the time the plane takes off, I've sent no less than fifty messages to Jordyn and called half that many times. My service dies mere minutes after take off and I spend the entire flight wondering if I've lost my fucking mind.

That being said, if I can get a private flight down there, J can figure it out as well. If not, I'll go in like a Navy Seal and grab Hallie before high tailing it out of there. What could possibly go wrong?

I don't even entertain that thought because the sheer number of things that could go wrong is a list as long as my cell mate's rap sheet.

Dude was in for life.

An hour and forty minutes later, we're touching down on the hot tar of the runway and I'm practically blinded by the sunlight streaming through the portholes, turning me into *that* guy…the one who slides down the shade because the sun is too bright.

Stepping out of the plane and thanking Jeff, Zavier's friend of a friend, profusely, I pull up my app and order a driver to take me to Hallie's. I've downloaded everything I need to know on my phone and just when I turn it back on, the incessant dinging plays like a concert for a solid five minutes.

Fuck me. Just a glimpse at Jordyn's messages tells me I'm about to get my fucking ass kicked.

> **Little Demon:** What the fuck? Is she okay? What is going on?

> **Little Demon:** Are you out of your fucking mind?

> **Little Demon:** A knife to a gunfight? Fucking cliche, JFC.

> **Little Demon (forty minutes ago):** We're on Tyler Walker's private plane. DO NOT FUCKING MOVE from the airport.

> **Little Demon:** I'm serious. Stay put.

That last message makes me pause, she's worried, but she's still an hour out and I can't waste that kind of precious time.

Knowing damn well she has no service up there, I run to the front exit, trying my best to not suffocate from the wall of humidity that attacks my lungs. Fucking hell, how do people breathe in this state? California is hot but at least you can breathe while your skin burns off.

It's a forty minute drive to Cocoa Beach. I put on a random location for drop off, some Welsh pub catering to the surfers and tourists, as I fix my gaze in the direction of the Gallagher home.

I have no luggage, no bags. Just my knife in a sheath hanging from my belt like I'm about ready to wrestle a fucking alligator. Fitting, I suppose.

When I get to the house, I walk by the drive once and check for cars through the gate. Every doubt I had about flying down here on a whim flies out the window when I spot Ronan's car still sitting in the driveway. Fucker is still there. Hopefully he's staying long enough that when J gets here, she and the Reapers will take him out and we'll take Hallie home where she belongs.

The end.

Crossing the touristy two-lane street, I'm happy to see that the house shares one side of a wall with a public access to the beach. The greenery has overgrown and curious eyes can't really see me if I try to scale said wall. Hell, there's even a tree branch low enough for me to use as a ladder.

This is the universe telling me I have to go inside and make sure Hallie is okay, I'm sure of it.

As I climb the tree, I take one last look around to make sure no one is coming around before I step onto the top of the cement wall then jump down to the grass below. Fuck, I hope there aren't any snakes or else my Navy Seal days will be over before they even begin.

The entire perimeter of the property is lined with palm trees and the south-facing wall has only one window that looks like a bathroom, judging from the size. I crouch just in case, practically crawling to the back where a screened-in pool is all set up and ready for the summer.

There are definite voices inside but nothing alarming. In my pocket, my phone vibrates and, without making too much noise, I take it out and read J's message.

> **Little Demon**: Where the fuck are you?

> **Me**: Don't freak out.

> **Me**: I'm at Hallie's.

> **Little Demon**: Fuck, D. Just…fuck.

> **Little Demon:** Don't do anything stupid. We'll be there in thirty minutes.

It's a forty minute drive but I'm guessing one of the Reapers will deal with the end-of-May traffic by driving like a psycho on hot wheels—understatement, I'm sure. Fingers crossed they don't get pulled over because I can't imagine the number of weapons they'll have stashed in the trunk.

I'm about to type out a message asking her to be careful when I hear the high-pitched, distinct sound of a scream. Female. Young.

Hallie.

My entire body goes still and my instincts kick in.

Chapter Twenty

J

Two hours earlier

"Turns out Cook was a runner for the Irish for the last twenty years. Never amounted to anything more because of his gambling habit." Ray "The Stinger" Martini, Marco's underboss, has been looking into the whole Cook thing since Dmitry and Glitch found the eyeballs in the pantry. "He was a great getaway driver, which is probably why he managed to lose the Reapers' tails. I found some files on his phone that suggested Ronan wanted a turf war between the Greeks and the Italians, but they were from about eight years ago, before the whole Greek boss being shot by his brother situation."

There are a few snickers around the dark walnut table because Aleko Kastellanos actually did us a huge favor. Until Zavier came on the scene, the Greeks had been all but invisible since that day.

"It seems Cook took it upon himself to carry out the order once Zavier came into the city. He knew he was a relation of the original Greeks and, I'm speculating here, he thought he could finally rise up in the ranks of the Irish if he completed this order. Fucker was too dumb to realize the eyeball taking was only a Yiannis thing and we'd catch on real fast that it wasn't the Greeks making a comeback."

When Marco chose Ray to be his underboss, his second in command, I knew it was a great choice. Ray is sharp as a blade and resourceful as fuck. His reports are always so articulate, which is completely unexpected just to look at him. His sharp nose that's clearly been broken one too many times, his unkempt hair peppered with dark gray, and the casual hoodies he practically lives in don't scream "mafia", but he is one of us to his very core.

Tommy, Eddie, and George are all nodding, listening intently to what Ray has to say, while Marco appears unperturbed, taking everything in and quietly assessing.

"He wasn't working alone, either. Petey Callaghan, Ronan's grandson, was helping. Between them, they injected their victims somewhere in or around Eddie's bar by bumping into them. Then they waited. And we know the rest." Ray shrugs with a heavy sigh.

Eddie's deep rumble of anger can be felt throughout the room, but we all know why and I'm actually surprised he's even here. Most of the soldiers that were taken were his, one being his son, and he and his wife have been holed up in their house since it happened. There were a few of Tommy's soldiers killed too, but only the ones that frequented Eddie's bar.

"We're pretty sure Cook was the instigator because there haven't been any more murders since he was introduced to Hell almost a month ago, thanks to Shadow's Reapers." He nods respectfully in my direction and I return it with a smirk.

Marco sits forward in his seat at the head of the table, quietly letting Ray know he's about to say his piece.

"Petey got on a flight to Florida within a few days of Cook's death, so we've put the feelers out to some of my contacts to keep an eye out, but there's not a lot else we can do. However, J..." Marco pauses, setting his icey-blue gaze on me at the same time my stomach drops. Hallie is in Florida. I know it's a big state, but coincidences are fairytales that I don't believe in. "You should move forward any plans you have to get your girl back because I don't trust it. We know Ronan is out that w—"

The large oak door to this cozy conference room is pushed open, slamming against the pale wall behind it, and my eyes widen when I see Shoo, closely followed by Tab, barging in. They're both out of breath and Shoo manages to speak before he gets shot in the face by one of the six deadly mafia leaders sitting around the table cocking their guns.

"Ronan's in Florida. He took some men to the Gallaghers'. Dmitry is on a flight."

"Say that again, big man. With breaths between sentences this time." Marco remains the epitome of calm, but I know he's sizzling underneath just as much as I am. After Hallie and I spent some time staying with him when Murphy died, he built a fun little relationship with my daughter. Mainly sneaking her chocolates and cookies when I wasn't looking, but it was their thing.

It seems that, in the time it takes everyone to put the safety back on their weapon, tucking them back away on their person somewhere, Shoo realizes the severity of what almost happened when he stormed in.

"Damn, what a great entrance." He has the sense to look a little guilty before he continues. "Check your phone, Boss. Dmitry saw Ronan and some goons arriving at the Gallaghers' about an hour ago. He's been trying to get a hold of you, and because he couldn't, he jumped on a flight to Florida and told Glitch to get us all to meet him there. We don't know anything else, we got here as quickly as we could."

I'm actually dumbfounded, rendered speechless, my world crumbling before I've even had a chance to make it beautiful. This is what waiting for the perfect moment does…fucks you up the ass with a shovel. My fists are trembling and it's taking everything within me to breathe evenly, going through every scenario in my mind to fix this.

"Tyler? I need your plane as soon as possible…Florida…it's for J…yeah…if Enzo and Devon are available, we could use them too…thanks." Marco's voice cuts through my thoughts, and listening to his call with his brother-in-law, Tyler, may or may not have put a lump in my throat—I'll deny it until the day I die.

They're ready to go to war with me. Without knowing anything about the situation, they're fucking ready.

"Eddie, do you want in on this one seeing as you've been hit by the Irish too?" Marco's attention is on Eddie, who has been silent throughout the meeting, scoffing here and there, but he lost his son to these crazies, he has a right to deal with it just as much as I do.

"My wife would probably crumble if I left now, but I have a few soldiers that would love to get their claws in some Irish mob scum." His face scrunches up in anger and I can understand what he and his wife are going through. Losing a child is one of the most excruciating pains a person can go through, and to even keep breathing is a major feat.

"Ray, you will need to hold down the fort, keep things running here for the next couple of days. Make sure there are at least five sets of eyes on River at all times. J, get the rest of your Reapers to meet us at the airport. I'll text the address, it's private. Devon and Enzo are on their way and Tyler has secured us a plane." Marco is standing now, sliding his arms into his charcoal-gray suit jacket and typing madly on his phone. There's a reason he's a great don, and his ability to multitask like this is just a bonus.

"The rest of you, get back to your crews, your families, and we'll finally get this shit behind us."

Ray, Tommy, George, and Eddie stand, taking turns shaking Marco's hand before leaving through the still-open door. Tab has to move aside because he fills the doorway with his bulk, and they each tilt their heads to him in acknowledgement.

"I texted the valet, they're bringing your Harley around to the front with my car, we'll head out right away." The valet parking at this hotel is the only place I'll ever trust with my baby. They know to walk her to and from the parking lot rather than try and ride her. Perks of my boss owning the place.

"Marco, River's pregnant. You should stay here." What he's doing for me means everything and it just reminds me of the family I've found here. I'm fully aware he can take care of himself, and he's my boss, but I don't feel right about him risking himself like this for me. We don't know what kind of situation we're walking into in Florida.

"J, you and I both know River would have my balls if I didn't help you get your girl back. Let's go." Without another word, he's through the door, leaving Shoo and Tab waiting for me to make a move.

This kind of situation is usually something I thrive in, but when it's this personal, it just hits different. With a deep breath, I stand, pull out my phone from my pocket, grab my helmet, and walk out of the conference room toward the hotel entrance.

There are at least thirty missed calls, twice as many texts, and a lot of voicemails. I read what I can before my bike is wheeled toward me, each text like a knife being pushed into my heavy-beating chest. Shoo and Tab jump on their motorcycles and wait for me to mount mine, ready to have my back the whole way.

Dmitry's texts are erratic, panicked, so I listen to the voicemails because I need the information now.

The voicemails don't help calm my soul at all. Lifting a leg to straddle my motorcycle, I call him back, again and again, but there's no answer. It doesn't even ring and I almost kick myself because I know he's on a plane. I send a few erratic texts of my own because the crazy fuck just said he was getting on a fucking plane.

> **Me:** What the fuck? Is she okay? What is going on?
>
> **Me:** Are you out of your fucking mind?
>
> **Me:** A knife to a gunfight? Fucking cliche, JFC.

Fuck this shit. We need to get to the airport.

We land just under two hours after taking off and I'm restless. Sitting and doing fuck all on the flight over felt like torture. It's good to see Enzo and Devon. Enzo used to be Marco's underboss until he knocked Marco's sister up—well, one of her three men knocked her up. Devon is a fucking master with knives and I can tell he's itching for a bloodbath almost as much as I am; whereas Enzo is a quiet and lethal kinda guy who made sure we have a stack of weapons ready and waiting on the plane, silencers and all.

Fizz and Binx are heading here in the van with a shit-load of cleaning supplies. It'll take them almost a day, but it's necessary for us to do our jobs efficiently.

Without knowing what we're walking into, we need to be prepared for any number of possible scenarios, and a clean up is going to be needed, no matter what. Because someone is going to fucking die today.

I've fucked around long enough, thinking it's all the best for Hallie's safety when the only option has ever been to have her with me. It's where she wants to be, it's where I want her to be, and I think I've just been making excuses up to this point, afraid that I'll fuck up her life somehow because I don't know how to be a mother.

Well, now all bets are off. Guilt and sadness have ruled me for far too long. She's coming home with me. Dmitry's coming home with me. And I'm gonna allow myself some happiness.

There are two black Camaros waiting for us, thanks to Glitch, who is our eyes and ears for this. He stayed back at the clubhouse where Dmitry gave him details on the cameras around the Gallagher property. His text update tells me that Ronan and three other guys are still there. There's been no movement, no one has left since they arrived.

I look around for Dmitry, but there's no sign of him so I drop him a text as I climb into one of the cars. Shoo is driving with Tab, Flower, and Crank in the back seat. Marco, Enzo, and Devon are in the other car.

> **Me**: Where the fuck are you?

> **Future Husband**: Don't freak out.

> **Future Husband**: I'm at Hallie's.

My heart drops. I can't do this again. I'm not equipped to lose anyone else.

> **Me:** Fuck, D. Just...fuck.

> **Me:** Don't do anything stupid. We'll be there in thirty minutes.

It's a forty minute journey, but with Shoo driving, it takes the thirty I predicted and we pull up to park behind Marco and the others. We're a street away from the house and Glitch texts over a map with the best route for us to get there without being seen.

We all load up, silencers for our guns, knives for our sheaths, rope...because we want to be prepared. With a plan of action—to basically fuck shit up, save Hallie and Dmitry, and keep Ronan alive—we all move as one toward the house.

My Reapers and I enter via the back yard, using a tree beside the side wall to climb over. The security here is shit and I can't believe I ever thought Hallie would be safe with her grandparents. The people who took her from me in the worst way.

Yeah, I was fucking stupid. Lessons learned and all that.

Marco, Enzo, and Devon use the front door because Devon likes to make an entrance. I'm more of a sneak in the back kinda gal.

Pushing the handle down on the back door, I open it slowly before stepping inside. The small corridor is empty, but I can hear muffled voices coming from the kitchen on the other side of this wall.

I can't make out what they're saying, but there's laughter, and that makes my blood boil.

Marco, Devon, and Enzo enter through the front door, which I can see from my position, and I watch them silently round the corner, headed for the stairs.

Moving closer to the entrance of the kitchen, my Reapers close behind, I take a deep, fortifying breath before showing myself, gun raised.

"Where is Hallie?" I'm faced with Mr. and Mrs. Gallagher, Ronan, and one of his goons. The other two must be somewhere else in the house.

They all turn to look at me, the goon reaching for his gun before I shoot him between the eyes.

"What are you doing, girl? Do you have any ide—" Mr. Gallagher's rant stops suddenly as a bullet flies through his throat, and he grips at it, trying to hold his blood inside his body, but it's no use. I know I hit an artery with the amount of blood spurting from between his fingers.

Mrs. Gallagher screams so loudly I'm close to putting a bullet inside her too, but within seconds, Tab is behind her, a hand over her mouth to shut her up. We could do without the neighbors calling the cops before we're done here. Being in Florida means the New York mafia doesn't have quite the same pull.

"Where is Hallie?" My voice is low, steady, calm; everything I'm not feeling inside.

"Ha, what do you think you're going to do, Jordyn? You're scum." Ronan, who is stupidly unarmed, folds his arms across his chest, remaining seated on the stool at the kitchen counter.

"Says the man who's been hiding from me for months. I told you I'd find you, Ronan." I take slow steps toward him, lowering my gun and allowing a manic expression to take over my face.

"Go on then, you found me. So kill me already." The fucker's shitting himself and it makes me laugh. Not a real laugh, but the kind that says you're so pissed off you can't do anything else.

"Oh, Ronan, no." I elongate the no, toying with him now. "I'm not going to kill you...today. Not even tomorrow. No, I'm going to keep you alive for as long as I can be bothered to know you're breathing the same air as my daughter, and you're going to be in excruciating pain for every second of it."

During what I'm calling my evil villain speech, Flower has moved behind him and he almost jumps out of his seat when she grabs his arms and ties his wrists behind his back. Shoo helps, pushing Ronan's neck down so his face is on the countertop.

"You thi—" Flower shoves a rag from beside the sink inside Ronan's mouth. We don't need to hear him speak right now. That can wait until we're ready.

I turn my attention back to Mrs. Gallagher. "What is *he* doing here?" My words are clear, precise, full of venom for this woman who was supposed to be protecting my daughter. Instead, she let in the man who killed her father so they could share a cup of fucking tea. I nod to Tab, silently telling him to remove his hand from her mouth so she can answer me.

Tears are rolling down her wrinkled face and I'm debating letting her live.

"He-he came to speak to my husband. That's all. I-I don't know any-anything. I swear."

She's lying. My ability to read people like a book notes the subtle twitch to her right eye and the shift in her body like she's trying to come up with an answer that won't get her killed—there isn't one. As soon as I find my daughter, I'll find a way to punish Mary Gallagher.

"Where is Ha—" A commotion upstairs stops me mid-sentence. Upstairs is where Marco and his team went upon entering the house.

Then I hear her scream.

I don't need to tell my Reapers what to do next. Flower keeps her grip on Ronan and Tab shoves his meaty hand back over Mrs. Gallagher's mouth, while Shoo is quick to follow me out of the room and up the stairs, taking two at a time.

Following the noise brings me to a very elegant-looking room, it must be a spare or belong to the Gallaghers. Attached to one post of the four-poster bed is Dmitry, and his smile is a little sheepish as his eyes connect with mine, but the danger is still there. This man tried to save my girl.

He failed, but he tried.

His back is to the post and his arms are tied behind him, attached to the bed by a set of handcuffs. He's also covered in bruises and his dark-blue long-sleeve T-shirt is ripped open in several places. My eyes land at the center of his chest. The exact replica of my little carving project, now a permanent tattoo, reminds me of all the things this man does to show me his feelings.

"Hey, Little Demon. You got my messages then?" He chuckles, his grin making his pale-green eyes crinkle.

"Fuck off."

My response only makes him laugh harder, and if there wasn't still a goon on the loose, I'd be able to relax.

On another of the posts, with her chest facing it, Hallie's tied with her hands in front of her, and while it still boils my blood to see her like this, at least she's not as uncomfortable as I know Dmitry is.

My view of Hallie is obscured by Marco, who seems to be blocking her from the man on the floor, unrecognizable with the amount of slashes to his face, and I'm assuming he's one of the two goons left for us to get. So two down now, only one to go.

Easy.

Devon has a wicked grin on his face, which is dripping with blood, completely unnecessary considering he's only killed one man, but I've done his clean ups a few times now. I know he likes to get messy with it.

Enzo is shaking his head at him as he works on freeing Dmitry from the handcuffs.

"Devon, there's one left. I don't know where he is." I move toward my girl, where Marco has now untied her, the last of her restraints coming loose.

"Mom!"

N.O. ONE

My arms are filled as quickly as they open, and for the first time in forever, I relax with my baby girl. She squeezes me so hard I almost break, and I squeeze her back just as hard, promising myself that I'll never let her go again.

"Can I get me a piece of that hugging action?" Dmitry is beside us and he doesn't wait for an answer, pulling us both into his arms and holding on to us as though we are his everything. He sniffs into my hair and I feel his muscles relax.

For a moment, it all feels like too much.

"Got him!" Devon's voice is followed by a loud thump on the floor and I'm more thankful than I can put into words for these people. Devon pops his head around the doorframe and wags his brows. "Haven't killed the cunt 'cause he was shaking like a dog. They're no fun like that. Tied 'em up though so he can be carried like a bag. Tada!" He moves further into the room and uses both hands to lift his new man-shaped bag to show us.

Pulling away from my baby girl, I grip her shoulders and scan her beautiful face, holding back a snarl when I notice the light bruise forming on her cheek.

"Who hurt you, sweetheart?" I'm barely controlling my anger at the sight, but I'm holding myself together for her sake.

Hallie lowers her eyes to the floor before bringing that back up to meet mine. "Grandma hit me when I said I'd rather marry a lump of shit than her friend's grandson. I'm sorry, I shouldn't have cursed but I was so angry, and that Petey is just so ol—"

"Don't ever apologize for protecting yourself. Okay? You stay with these guys. I'll be right back." I grip her head between my palms and lean forward to place a tender kiss against her forehead before leaving the room.

With a calm reserved only for death, I walk down the stairs breathing in through my nose and out through my mouth. Palming my gun, I check the silencer is in place and step into the kitchen. Blood covers the floor from Mr. Gallagher's death, and it's mixed with piss that looks to have come from Mrs. Gallagher—Mary.

My eyes do a slow, dangerous sweep across the room to meet Mary's, a snarl curling my top lip. "I thought about letting you live, but you laid a hand on my daughter and tried to marry her off to the fucking mob. You sealed your own fate, Mary Gallagher." I don't move my eyes from hers as I address my crew next. "Tab, step back." I lift my arm and, without hesitation, I give her the same wound as her dead husband, shooting the cunt in the throat before she has a chance to defend herself or even stand from her stool.

A lightness fills my body and I can finally breathe again as I run back up the stairs to get my girl. My head has been whirring at a thousand miles a minute since Shoo and Tab burst into the capo meeting. I haven't thought straight, my usual cool, calm, and collected planning went to shit, but the people in this room and downstairs in the kitchen—not including the now-tied-up ones, of course—have really come through for me. In a way I never expected.

The parallels of storming into this house and storming into Murphy's house begin to fill my mind. Scared isn't an emotion I'd usually associate with myself, but I've been tested almost to my limits again and again. Losing Murphy broke something inside me, having my daughter ripped from my arms broke a little more, and I'm barely hanging on by a thread. Somehow, Dmitry has wormed his way in, and no matter how much I try to keep him at arm's length, he keeps pushing forward. I don't know if I can let another person get so close, because I simply can't handle it when they're gone.

With the life I've lived, I'm not sure I'm deserving of this kind of peace, of the happiness that being around him brings.

He squeezes Hallie and me closer to him, and even though it scares the shit out of me, for now, I allow myself to relax.

We're safe.

Chapter Twenty-One

D

First off, this plane is dope. Much better than Z's friend of a friend. My opinion may or may not be based on the fact that there's an actual bedroom in the back with a change of clothes that, thankfully, fits me. The whole ripped shirt and bruises all over my body isn't a good look. The black eye is definitely too much; like the scar wasn't enough?

Despite the battered body and swollen eye, I'm feeling like a proud monkey as I'm getting roasted by Jordyn's daughter. Like, full-on story time and I'm Tom, the cat who can't get shit right, and J is obviously Jerry, the mouse who smirks fifty times per episode because she knows what the fuck she's doing.

"So, I scream because Grandpa has thrown me in the bedroom and told me to stay there and be quiet." She turns to her mom, eyes wild with that unmistakable gleam of exhausted excitement. "He took my phone!" Because that's the epitome of wrongness in a teen's mind. "The only thing I could do was read the required chapters for English class on Monday." She looks at me and raises a brow in challenge. "Do you like *The Red Badge of Courage*?"

Now, this question feels like a trap. No doubt about it, she's testing me, and if I fail, my dream of being an amazing step-dad will go to shit. J leans back in her seat, a smirk firmly planted on her lips, while Marco chuckles as he sips from his glass—whiskey I'm betting. Still, I decide the best course of action is honesty because this kid is too smart to manipulate.

"Well, let's see...I like the character arc, the way Henry's view of war changes from this romantic notion to the reality of what wearing the red badge really means."

"Yeah, I guess, but I still think he's like this naïve puppy dog looking for pats on the head...just because." She shrugs, her eyes rolling just enough to remind me that she's thirteen. There's so much of her mother in her it's scary. Then, like that little aside didn't happen, she goes right back to her story...about me.

"Anyway, I'm sitting there reading the part about Jim getting hurt when there's a tap on my bedroom window and this guy's looking at me like a creeper." Her thumb is pointed at me but her big hazel eyes are fixed on her mother, incredulous.

"Yeah, it's his thing. He's got stalker tendencies. You get used to it." J winks at me and I lick my lips, reveling in the fact that my girl is a badass in and out of the bedroom but also, she's going to be an amazing mother. I can't wait to learn it all with her.

"I'm about to scream again. I mean, who does that?" Hallie's looking at me again like I should be answering what is clearly a rhetorical question. So I shrug, because yeah...I'd do anything for these two.

"Apparently, *he* does." Marco quips, laughter breaking out all around me, and that's when I realize everyone on the plane is listening to her story. Well, everyone except Ronan and trussed-up guy sitting next to him. They're both passed out from one-too-many blows to the face.

"And his scar was scary. I thought he was there to kill me but..." Her eyes go soft, a little sheen gathering at the corners when she whispers, "He looked at me like he wanted to protect me. He looked like Dad when he crawled..." Her voice cracks and she's immediately engulfed in J's arms as she murmurs something only her daughter can hear.

Minutes later, J's question reignites the story's plot line.

"So you let him in, Kid? Do I need to teach you about self-preservation?" Chuckles ring out but I'm too caught up in her version of what happened to care.

"Yeah, I walked over to the window—"

"With a letter opener," I interrupt, proud that she armed herself, and raise a brow at J for emphasis. J grins, her chin lifting with pride because that's her girl. Damn right.

"Well, duh, I wasn't about to let a strange man into my room empty handed. That's amateur even for me. So, anyway, when I open the window, this guy starts whispering about my mom and the Reapers and that he's here to save me. And I'm all... 'You're here alone?' and he's all 'Yeah, your mom's on her way' and just when I think it's all going to work out, he falls—FALLS—through the window, landing with a big old *thump* on the floor." She turns to me with a grin because I know where this is going, obviously. "That's when two of the big dudes burst into my room and find us there crouching on the floor. They have guns and D here, has a knife pointed at them while he's pushing me behind him." I won't ever admit it to anyone but I was scared shitless. Not for myself, but the mere idea of putting Hallie in more danger than necessary and causing J any pain was physically intolerable.

"Ah, excuse me...can we skip to the part where I sliced him a new ear?" The guy took one look at my knife and scoffed. When he approached, I didn't think, I jumped up and stabbed him, taking half his ear with me. My only saving grace as the guy howled with pain and probably dreamt of the hundred different ways he could kill me, was the strict order from Ronan to keep Hallie safe. That didn't keep him from beating the shit out of me while his buddy tied up Hallie then came back and held me down. Ball sacks. Both of them.

"Oh shite! That's why the little cunt was already bleedin'!" Devon calls out, whistling. "There might be hope for ya yet, Geek Boy." Nah, I don't think so.

"Yeah, I'm gonna need a more imaginative nickname. Geek is so...passé."

Everyone in the plane howls with laughter. Marco's grin makes him look mortal for once but when I turn to see J's beautiful face, there isn't a trace of humor on her features. I let my gaze drink her in as she stares at me, from the vast ocean in her eyes to the natural dark-pink hue of her lips. They're slightly parted and I know that, although she's grateful, right now she's mostly horny. I know that look. Jordyn O'Neill wants to thank me and right now she thinks her mouth on my cock is the best way to do that.

Little does she know that I don't need her thanks. All I want is her until I'm six feet under or buried in a cement casing and dropped in the middle of the Hudson, doesn't matter.

I want this, I want her, and I want Hallie. That's it.

"And the rest is history, as they say." I speak to everyone but my eyes are only on J.

Hallie yawns and I want to hug Marco when he tells her to go back to the bedroom and take a nap. After kissing her mother, she comes over to me and wraps her arms around my neck, squeezing to the point of blissful pain. "Thank you for thinking I'm important enough to get in trouble with my mom." And fuck, my eyes fill with tears. But with a quick, deep inhale, I keep them at bay.

"Anytime, Doodle-bug." The entire time we were tied up, I tried to keep her mind off the shitshow by testing out my best step-dad nicknames. She vetoed my best ones, and I'd Googled a whole fucking bunch these last few months. Precious, Nugget, and Bug were a no-go. Princess earned me a scowl and Kitten made her faux-vomit in her mouth.

"No." It's all she says and I sigh. I need a better strategy.

"Gumdrop?" She doesn't get a chance to answer because both Devon and Enzo shut that down immediately.

"No can do, mate. That's Tyler's nickname for Lina and you don't want to know what he does for—" Devon laughs when Marco whips around and nearly scorches him into a pile of ashes. "Right, then."

"Come on, Hals, let's get you to sleep. We've only got about forty-five minutes left before we get home." Hallie leaves with Marco, throwing a warm smile over her shoulder at her mother, then me—score—before disappearing down the hall.

"Doodle-bug? Really?" J snorts. "She's thirteen, not two."

"Well, she turned down my better options but I'm not giving up." With Ronan still stuck in lala land and Enzo and Devon furiously texting with the occasional conspiratory glance between them, I decide it's time to fulfill a lifetime dream while everyone else is busy doing shit.

Unbuckling my seat belt, I rise from my comfy chair—a dark coffee, not beige—and brace myself on either of J's arm rests, caging her in. My face is close enough to smell that unique blend of leather and arousal mixed with a pinch of citrus. At first, I had no idea why she always smelled that way, but then I saw her cleaning her leathers. The conditioner she uses on her hair is responsible for the orangey scent, and my presence for her arousal. Score for me.

"When I was a kid, I was the president of the math club at school." I wait because I know she has a smart ass remark to make.

"Is that supposed to be a turn on?"

My nose at the base of her neck, I inhale her all the way up to her ear. "It could, numbers are sexy. But do you know what's sexier?" My teeth bite into her earlobe and that tiny little moan that escapes her makes my dick hard in an instant.

"Your face between my legs eating my pussy?" There's no bite to her words, her body attuned to mine and her need for me growing by the second.

"That, but at fifty thousand feet in the air." When I pull back, I grin at her narrowed eyes.

"Hallie—"

"Is asleep." Cutting off her words is the only way to get one in with J.

Marco walked back into the main cabin a few seconds ago, his laptop open and his usual concentration firmly set on his work. Everyone else is either sleeping or, in Shoo's case, playing a game on his phone.

"Come on, let's see if that bathroom meets FAA regulations."

As soon as the door closes behind me, I turn my hungry gaze on J, my teeth sinking into my bottom lip and my groan too loud for this little tin can. But fuck me, it's impossible not to react when she immediately sheds her leathers, her panties, and jumps up on the small counter with her legs spread wide and feet planted on the wall opposite her.

No man could resist this sight. Okay, gay men probably could, but that's beside the point.

"Is this what you had in mind?" J's voice is all honey and spice with a touch of badassery that turns me on like nothing else.

Kneeling at her pussy as I unbutton my jeans and save my cock from getting strangled by my boxer briefs, I grin up at her. "Breakfast for this champion."

My lips brush against the folds of her pussy and my entire body relaxes. My arms wrap around her thighs and my mouth attacks her flesh like I haven't tasted her in years. Was it only this morning that I got my fill of her? It feels like a fucking eternity ago.

Squeezing her closer to me, I revel in the little groans and moans that she releases, probably despite her best judgment, but I love that I get to see her like this. Free and unburdened. Open and honest.

Mine in all the ways that count.

Lapping up her cum, I move my tongue to her clit and flick it a few times before going back in and fucking her cunt without an ounce of restraint. I lick and suck, the sounds of my mouth on her bouncing off the tiny box we're in. I can smell her need for me and it just makes me harder and harder until the need to fuck her takes over me completely.

"Get your dick inside me, D. Right fucking now!"

But I'm not done.

She'll get my cock when she comes, not a second before.

With two fingers at her entrance, I bite down on her swollen clit and push my digits in at the same time, curling them at the hilt and making sure I hit that perfect little spot deep inside her.

J's head bangs against the mirror, her moan tortured yet filled with pleasure when she tightens her thighs against the side of my head and fucks my mouth. Topping me. Taking from me. Owning every inch of me from my toes to my soul.

With her cum dripping from my fingers as her first orgasm subsides, I bring them to my mouth as I stand and face her. I love how relaxed she is right after I make her come. The one side of her that no one else gets to see.

My tongue licks one side of my index finger then the other before I bring them to her mouth and we lick together, our tongues meeting then retreating until I'm kissing her deeply, my hand cradling the back of her head and my cock slamming inside her tight little cunt.

We both groan, the weight of the day dissipating as her pussy stretches around my dick and pulses with her need for me to move.

And I do.

Slowly pulling out, I drive back inside her, careful not to hurt her, my hand serving as a buffer between her and the mirror.

J's ankles are wrapped around the small of my back as I ram in and out of her pussy, taking, taking, taking, until she gives me everything.

This time, when she comes again, I go off the cliff right along with her.

I'm hoping we were quiet enough to escape the inevitable comments once we walk back out but, to be honest, my ears are ringing too loudly with the pure pleasure that's running through my veins to know anything.

"Welcome to the mile-high club, hope you had a good flight." I kiss her again as she releases me, a rare grin on her gorgeous face.

"Ideal flying conditions."

Perfect, even.

By the time we make it back out into the cabin, we're put back together as well as possible. Contrary to my earlier worries, no one says a damn thing to us. Probably because they enjoy keeping their balls, but the knowing looks tell me they knew—or heard—exactly what was happening in that bathroom.

Meh, I can handle that. Now everyone knows she's mine. Neanderthal level achieved.

Just as we both sit back down, Hallie comes back to sit with us, flopping onto the seat next to her mother.

"The turbulence woke me up." She yawns, her head leaning on J's shoulder as I grin, looking out the window and feeling J's hot gaze burning the side of my face.

Turbulence, indeed.

"Hey, Guido! Get me some water, here."

It all happened so quickly.

Watching J rub circles on Hallie's back as she laid her head on her mother's shoulder, her gaze far away, probably processing this whole day or maybe her entire existence since her father died when the silence is interrupted.

Ronan's insulting words accompanied by his hostile, condescending tone puts every last occupant of the plane on high alert. Notably Marco and Enzo, whose Italian heritage is apparent in the dark of their hair and the hardness in their eyes.

Marco rises from his seat, his hands in the pockets of his slacks, wearing calm and collected like a blanket on his shoulders. Eyes locked on Ronan, he nods to Enzo, whose knee is bouncing up and down, then allows a slow, murderous grin to inch up across his mouth.

I'm a big believer that power isn't something you take, it's something born deep inside your DNA, and Marco Mancini has it in spades. Without speaking a single word, he can command an entire army and still be home for dinner.

As impressive as all that is, I'm content with commanding my little demon in the bedroom and also being home for dinner.

Enzo unfolds his thick body from the seat, turns to face Ronan, and takes two steps to him in the back row of the plane before he's stopped by a tentative voice.

"Wait." All eyes turn to Hallie as her head lifts from J's shoulder, but I don't miss the way her mother's fingers squeeze her upper arm, keeping her in place, protecting her...even if from herself. "I want to talk to him."

"No. Absolutely not, Kid. He's—"

"Evil, I know. But I have to say something to him. Please, Mom?" The conflict in J's eyes swims like a school of sharks, darkening the blue of her irises. "Please?" Hallie repeats, and if the way J struggles with releasing her is any indication, I know she's fighting against every cell in her body to keep Hallie away from Ronan.

"Five minutes." Hallie nods at Jordyn's low command and Enzo and Marco step aside, giving Hallie the space to stand in front of Ronan and the other dude sitting next to him.

"Ah, little girl, we had such high hopes for you." Ronan's words have me standing immediately, ready to pummel his face in like a punching bag, but I stop when Hallie looks at me; no fear in her eyes, no lack of confidence in her stance. Holy fuck. In this moment, she is the carbon copy of her mother, right down to her fisted hands at her sides.

"In just a few months, you ripped apart my entire world. You talk about the superiority of the Irish compared to the Italians, which, by the way, is ridiculous...I watched *Gangs of New York* and I'm still TeamMarco."

We all try to hush our chuckles, but damn, the king of the Irish mob just got schooled by a thirteen-year-old.

"But how can you say that when you're the reason my dad's gone? Because of you, he's dead and I'll never be able to tell him I love him again. Tell him that he was the best dad any daughter could dream of. You took him away from me. Away from everything I'll ever do in my life. I miss him." Her voice chokes on that last sentence and I'm fucking breaking inside because Hallie's pain is a living, breathing monster sitting on this plane with us.

"Because of you, I won't have my dad taking pictures of me graduating from high school or college. And he won't be there, hugging me when I get a doctorate degree or maybe cure cancer." Holy shit, this girl is aiming high and I'm here for it. On this day, I vow that I will make every one of those moments happen for her. It won't be her dad, but I'll take those pictures and I'll hug her and tell her how proud Murphy would be knowing his baby girl is going to change the world.

"He won't walk me down the aisle or hold my baby in his arms. And I'll never be able to hear someone call me Hals without feeling like my heart is being ripped out of my chest. You did this. You. Did. This." She then surprises the fuck out of me and spits on him. Right in his face.

"Okay, that's gross." Hallie frowns at the spittle dripping down Ronan's cheek, his glare on her deadly but harmless nonetheless. "Still, this is what I wanted to say…It won't break me. You hurt me but you can't break me. My dad is dead but he lives inside me. And you, sir, can go straight to Hell." With a nod like she's giving herself permission to walk away, she turns and runs straight back into J's welcoming arms.

Damn, I'm a little choked up knowing I've got the memory of a great man watching over us, making sure I don't fuck up in my quest to be the best step-dad in the history of step-dads.

"Here's your water." Enzo throws a plastic bottle of water at Ronan, hitting him square in the face, then turns to sit right back down just as Ronan starts to scream out profanities, waking up the pig-roast boy next to him.

Thankfully, the captain's voice telling us it's time to fasten up for our descent comes over the speakers just as Shoo shoves an old, recently worn sock in Ronan's mouth.

Then silence rains down over us and we don't speak until we land in The City, where two cars and a van wait for us.

Eddie stands there with his crew, pain mixed with hatred written all over his face as we load the two guys into the van and I watch as they truss them up on hooks and shit.

I mean, the mafia is no joke. Their organizational skills are legendary for a reason.

It takes us a little over thirty minutes to get from La Guardia to the docks where Marco's warehouse of torture sits, nondescript and completely normal, on a practically empty lot.

"Oh, I forgot to tell you," I whisper above Hallie's head to J as we pull up to the large open doors of the warehouse. Marco followed us here but he's taking Hallie to his Upper East Side mansion so she can eat, shower, then sleep. Apparently, there are only two people J trusts to take care of her baby girl and I'm not one of them...yet.

Jordyn's narrowed gaze bores into me.

"Yeah, yeah, you don't like surprises, but I promise...you'll love this one."

Quickly saying her goodbyes to Hallie as she switches cars and rides away with Marco, J turns to me and sighs.

"All right, let's see what's happening in there." I stop her as she takes her first step into the warehouse, my hand at the back of her neck and my lips so close I can taste her.

"Hey. She's going to be okay. We'll make sure of it." J's steely blue gaze searches my face like she's assessing and making sure I believe my words, that I'm not just saying what she needs to hear. "I promise."

With a nod that's more for her than it is for me, she tries to pull away but I'm not having that. My hand tightens around her neck and I pull her in those final inches it takes for me to kiss the breath from her lungs. The most amazing thing about this moment is that she lets me. She fucking lets me without fighting it, without simply relenting. She lets me because she, too, needs the touch of us.

"Now, let's see if my present works."

As we walk in, Shoo is circling the big barrel I had delivered, crouching and tapping the sides, using his nails to…I don't fucking know what he's trying to do but it's taking all of his concentration. To the side, Devon is whistling and testing his knots on the hooks that have been lowered from the ceiling. Meanwhile, on the far end of the huge open space, our two prisoners are tied to their chairs, duct tape firmly pressed against their mouths and eyes so wide I wonder if they'll pop out of their sockets. They look petrified and I can't feel an ounce of empathy for them.

"The only thing I need a barrel for is drinking, so I have no fucking clue what this is for, Boss." Tab is following Shoo around, his tall frame looking inside the plastic lined barrel, brows drawn together in confusion.

"Let me introduce you to the medieval techniques of long-term torture." My tone is light and airy like a salesman amped up about his new product. Giving Ronan my full attention, I wink. "That one's for you, big guy." The way he recoils makes my entire bloodstream sing with vengefulness.

"What do you mean by... 'long-term'?" It's J's turn to assess the big barrel, circling it and noticing how the top is made to open and close like a flower petal, allowing the head in the center to stand out. I had that custom made to limit the odors.

"Well, that's up to you. The human body can survive forty-three to fifty-seven days without eating but only five without drinking. How long these two pieces of shit live depends on your schedule. On a side note, the plastic is to limit the smells."

The hum that leaves J's lips is fucking delicious and I'm going to suck it out of her mouth as soon as I get her alone. The squeak, however, that comes from, I'm guessing, Petey just makes me laugh my ass off.

"You Yankees are fucking demented." Devon howls with laughter as he pulls on a rope to test it out.

"Says the Brit who's commonly known as 'The Butcher', which has nothing to do with ordering a slab of sirloin beef." How am I not supposed to be in love with this woman when her wit alone is sexy as fuck.

"Fair enough. I hear one of your capos is also The Butcher so I can't be all that bad." Devon chuckles, shaking his head before eyeing little Petey, who's about to shit his fucking pants. "Come on, now, boy. Let's see if you like a little bondage."

It takes about thirty minutes to get these two assholes set up, Devon leaving with Enzo as soon as they are. Petey is all roped up, looking like a scrawny sub who's forgotten his safe word, and Ronan is screaming behind his duct tape, eyes wide and body shaking with anger and fear and...is that snot coming out of his nose? Nasty.

We all step back, admiring the pretty picture of torture before us. If my parents were here, they'd wonder what happened to me. But here's the thing: these guys hurt my

Jordyn and they hurt her daughter. There's nothing more sacred than family and they didn't think twice about going after it.

Now, it's time to pay the bill.

"You know, I don't get it. I've tried for so long to wrap my head around everything you've done but I just...don't get it." J is slowly pacing in front of Ronan, his grandson crying with his head upside down and the blood making his normally pasty complexion turn a deep tomato color. Reaching out, she scratches at the corner of the duct tape then yanks it right off, making Ronan recoil.

"You fucking cunt, you won't get away with this. I'll make sure everything is—" J punches his face, his head bobbing back before he shakes it off and smirks at her, a drop of blood dripping from his lip. Oh, this guy doesn't get it. Yet.

"You should probably save your strength," I mock-whisper like it's a secret between us.

"And who the fuck are you?" Ronan spits my way, a blood vessel in his eye popping and turning the whites nice and red.

"I'm just trying to help, dude, but you do you." Pushing my hands in my pockets, I lean against the side wall and watch my girl do her thing.

"As I was saying." J sends a pointed glare my way but I just smile, proud to be here witnessing her badassery. "My parents weren't all that important in the grand scheme of things. Why did you have them killed?"

Ronan just rolls his eyes, scoffing. "You stupid girl, playing in a grown-up world not understanding the players."

My body twitches with the need to throat punch this asshole for disrespecting my woman but I force myself to stay put. This is her world, her moment. I'm just a spectator.

"The players..." J rolls the hilt of her knife around her fingers, the blade spinning then stopping when she continues speaking. "My parents, who stole a considerable sum of money from you." Ronan snarls. If his glare could shoot bullets at her she'd be dead. "Thank you for that, by the way. Helped to set me up when I ran away."

"You fucking thief! I fucking knew it!"

"Yeah yeah, let's call it severance pay for killing my only living relatives." At J's words, Ronan spits out insults and calls her every misogynistic slur in the book. I'd be impressed by his wide range of knowledge on the matter if I weren't completely pissed off about it too.

"You don't know fucking shit. I didn't order the hit on them. In fact, I didn't even know they'd stolen the money at first." Everyone freezes at this news. Wait, what?

When I look over to J, she's staring at Ronan, reading every single line on his face like I read code on a black screen.

"Who?" One word, that's all she asks.

Ronan just stares at her, silent.

Shoo walks over to him and punches him in the face. I'm a little jealous because I wish I could have done that. Didn't realize punching the dude was an option.

"Who?" The calm that rolls off her shoulders is the scariest thing I've ever felt in my life.

"Who do you think? Did you really believe you and the lad were going to run off into the sunset with a brand new baby and live happily ever after? Murphy was their prince and you were the peasant mistress. Stealing my money was just a convenient excuse to justify the hit."

I'm expecting J to leap and slice this guy's head right off his shoulders, but she does the one thing no one here expected.

She fucking laughs. Head thrown back, laughter loud, coming straight from her gut. I've never seen her more beautiful than she is now.

"Fucking crazy bitch."

Okay, that's it.

Pushing off the wall, I take the four steps I need to bring me face to face with this asshole. One hand at the back of his head and the other pummeling his temple until my knuckles start aching.

"You show her some fucking respect, you putrid shit stain." Turning, I give J a wink and a smirk then walk right back to my spot and watch.

"It's just so fucking ridiculous. My mother was raped trying to save me. Fucking raped, Ronan. Then she was shot. All that because I wasn't worthy of their son? It's pathetic." J shakes her head in disgust then stops as though another thought came to her. "Why did you go back to Florida? Cook said you were holed up in a bunker in Georgia. We only got to you because you showed your face in Florida."

At this point, Ronan's attention goes straight to Petey before he nods his chin in his direction. Kid's been quietly weeping up there. "Let him go and I'll tell you."

"How about this? You tell me and I'll make sure he eats and drinks." Tab brings J a chair and she sits, crossing her legs and watching Ronan weigh his choices.

"Give him water and I'll tell you." J nods to Shoo, her eyes fixed on Ronan. "Jonathan got greedy. Petey and Hallie—" J is up on her feet, her face so close to Ronan's I'm afraid he'll bite her nose off.

"Don't fucking say her name. Ever." Pointing her blade to Petey, I watch as Tab puts a gun to his forehead, making Ronan stiffen with fear.

"Their marriage would have been a strong message, an alliance of money and power. But Jonathan thought I was losing my edge and started demanding more." He pauses, leaning in and snarling. "I don't do renegotiations so I had to show them I wasn't cowering from you."

His confession brings silence to the room, except for Petey drinking his weight in water. Or trying to, but since he's upside down, it's proving a difficult feat.

"You're all fucking sick." With those words, J turns and heads to the entrance of the warehouse. "I'll be back tomorrow. Make sure they drink enough water to make their bodily fluids do their jobs."

Hmm, I think I'll run a bath for my girl then fuck that sadness right out of her.

Chapter Twenty-Two

J

Five days.

For five days, I've been waiting for shit to hit the fan while juggling torture time with Ronan and quality time with my girl. Waiting for something to go wrong...for Hallie to realize I'm a shit mom and for Dmitry to figure out he doesn't want to deal with my crap.

Being a mom is something I thought was lost to me, and now that I have it, I'm actually afraid that I'll do it wrong. There's only ever been myself to take care of, to keep safe, and being this kind of responsible for another human life is humbling in a way I never imagined.

My apartment isn't equipped for the kind of life I want to give my girl, so we've temporarily moved back into one of the wings in Marco's house by Central Park. The first night back in New York, Dmitry spent with Hallie and me. I stitched him up then spent the night on his lap in the corner of the guest room watching Hallie sleep—after soaking for about an hour in the bath he ran for me. It was everything, but I don't know if I can expect him to take on the both of us. With just me, it was a bit of fun, but now that I have my girl back there are more responsibilities. More than just myself to think about.

Dmitry has respected my request and stayed away since that first night, letting Hallie and me have some time to bond and grieve. Time we weren't given when her father was killed. I suspect it's only because of what Hallie's been through and the security at Marco's keeping him away. However, his regular texts have brought a smile to my face. Our little name change game has kept us both on our toes too, and I can't help laughing at them—with the added bonus that my laughing scares Shoo.

It's not that I don't want to be around him, because every ounce of my soul misses him when he's not around, force-feeding me kolache or challenging everything I do, but it's that very ache that makes this whole thing difficult for me. Guilt over the whole thing plagues me. Am I disrespecting Murphy by having these feelings for someone else? Is it too soon?

Fuck, I'm not this person. Love makes everything so much more complicated.

I pause outside the warehouse door, my palm on the handle...*fuck*. Love? Really? No...

"Hey, Little Demon, has my surprise been useful?" Dmitry's voice comes from behind me, followed by purposeful footsteps, and I close my eyes, trying not to smile.

"What're you doing here?" I turn to face him, hands on my hips, noting his new motorcycle parked on the curb further down the road. *I did that.* I turned him into a biker, well, as much as he's ever going to be.

He chuckles, narrowing his eyes and stalking toward me with that dangerous grin on his face. When he reaches me, he crowds my space, backing me into the metal door of the warehouse.

"Little Demon, don't mistake me staying away for a lack of feelings. Every second of every day, you are on my mind, sometimes you're running around naked and I'm powerless to stop you." He gives me that damn wink again and I put my palms against his chest to push him back—half-heartedly. He doesn't move an inch, continuing his little speech before I can speak. "The space you asked for...yeah, I'm done with that. So I'm here, to help, to watch, to be a pillar I know you don't need, but I'm staying anyway, and then I'm going to make my girls dinner." His lips press firmly against mine, his tongue quickly demanding entrance, and despite my reservations, my body gives in to him.

I meet his tongue stroke for stroke, our lips fused together and causing a fire to burn in my core, and even though it's only been a few days, I allow myself to remember how just being with Dmitry makes me feel. Fucking confused mainly, but relaxed and safe—two things I'm not particularly familiar with—are high on the list.

A low growl escapes from my throat as I claw at his biceps, the T-shirt he's wearing giving me perfect access to the bare, tattooed skin on his arms. Dmitry squeezes both my ass cheeks, lifting me, pressing my back against the door as I wrap my legs around his waist. His hard cock presses against my pussy, sending a buzz to the burning inferno already inside me before he pulls away, resting his forehead against mine.

"As much as I want to fuck you into oblivion, I believe we have someone waiting for us inside?" He pulls his head back and wags his brows, an excitement for torture hidden within the pale-green depths that I can totally get on board with.

Again and again, Dmitry surprises me. Not only is he not afraid of the life I lead, he encourages it.

With a deep breath, I snap my teeth at Dmitry and slap his arm to let me down. He responds with a chuckle as I slide down his body.

"You sure you wanna join me for this? It fucking stinks in there right now." My thoughts are rife with confusion when it comes to this man, but I have a job to do and I know Dmitry isn't going anywhere.

"Yup, thought it might. That's why I brought these." He reaches behind him and pulls out two neck tubes with skull designs on them. The kind that go over your head, sit around your neck, and can be pulled up and over your mouth and nose. They're pretty cool, actually—not that I'll ever admit it to him.

"You do know th—"

"Yeah, I know they won't actually block out the smell. The masks I ordered haven't arrived yet and I figured he doesn't have much time left. And to be honest, these are awesome." He shoves one over his head, pulling it up over his mouth and nose, and yeah, my libido is fighting for control.

The image of him in a black T-shirt, swirling tattoos snaking down his muscled arm, pale-green eyes peeking over the top of the material...I'm not sure I can let this man go.

"Fine." I roll my eyes, something that has become more frequent over the last five days. My daughter is a sassy little thing and she's teaching me bad habits.

I hold my hand out for the other neck tube, only for him to shove it over my head for me, positioning it in place so the bottom half of my face looks like a skull too. There's a heat in his gaze that tells me he likes this introduction to masks just as much as I do.

Shaking my head, I turn and push through the warehouse door with Dmitry hot on my tail. We walk through the corridor, past Marco's office—well, the office used by the head of whichever crew is using the space at the time. In this instance, it's me. As we walk through one more set of heavy metal doors, the stench hits me.

Ronan is in the corner of the room, tied up in a barrel full of his own shit, piss, and a fair amount of blood. I've been visiting daily since we finally caught him, gifting him with a few slices across his skin, asking a few more questions, then leaving him to watch his grandson, Petey, suffer within his intricate bindings where he dangles from the ceiling. Devon insisted on using his rope skills, and I've gotta say, they're impressive. Petey hasn't been able to move an inch in the five days he's been here.

I've been kind enough, allowing them both the occasional sip of water to keep them alive a little longer because I don't need them to die just yet. Ultimately, they're going to die, but Ronan put me through too much for this to be over quickly. Not to mention his admissions on day one left my nerves a little bare.

Medieval torture is something Dmitry discovered I have a not-so-secret passion for, which is why he bought me the barrel. It's the kind of thing that was often used for drunkards as a punishment, but they would only tend to spend up to twenty-four hours inside them, somewhere for the whole town to see to add to their shame. Well…Ronan's grandson just so happened to be lucky enough to not die at the Gallaghers', so we have our humiliating audience too.

The fact that Dmitry even thought to do this, in the middle of everything else going on, makes it obvious to me that I'm being a douche with all this confusion shit. I've realized I'm one of those people who thinks I need to push everyone away to keep them safe, and as of right now, I'm powerless to stop it.

Somehow, I don't think Dmitry will let me. I just kinda hope he sticks with me and doesn't get bored of me pushing him away. It's like a disease, I know it's happening, yet I can't control myself.

"By the way, thank you for the gift." I pause once we're inside the torture room, turning and inclining my head to Dmitry. I watch his eyes crinkle and I know beneath the mask, that dangerous smile that makes my knees buckle is hiding there.

"Welcome."

Both Petey and Ronan have their eyes closed, and for a brief second I think they might be dead, but thankfully, as we get closer, I can hear their ragged breaths as their bodies slowly fail on them. At this point, my Reapers have bets going on which one of the two will die first and when. I wasn't allowed to have a vote because I'm in control of their lives and Shoo didn't want me to cheat by killing one so I could win.

The unmistakable *woosh* of a knife sounds past my ear before it implants itself at the top of the barrel with a loud thud, making Ronan jump, groaning even in his weak state. Then another one flies past, landing perfectly centered in a piece of the rope tied around Petey's hanging body. He stirs, one eye opening slowly as he groans too.

"Woke them up for ya." He sounds so proud of himself and I can't help the smirk, thankfully hidden by the mask.

"Thanks, Dmitry." I almost want to say, 'Good boy,' but I refrain. Ronan doesn't deserve a show while he stews in his own crap.

"Good afternoon, Ronan. How are you today?" I take out a dagger and slowly drag it across his forehead. Immediately, blood begins dripping down his face and into his eyes, causing him to scrunch them closed before he attempts to spit at me.

It doesn't work. He's too dehydrated to produce enough saliva, and I let out a short, sharp, laugh at his pathetic effort.

"Kill...me." It's all Ronan's said for the last two days, with the flies buzzing around him, walking over his fresh and old cuts, eating the shit he's sitting in. There are even maggots that are beginning to chew at his flesh.

To be honest, I know he won't last much longer. His words are breathy when he manages them, and he had a seizure when I came to see him yesterday. Thankfully, I got answers to most of my questions in the first couple of days.

The greedy bastard actually thought I'd keep him alive if he told me everything, which just proves how disloyal this cunt is. Therefore, giving me more reason to make sure he doesn't walk this Earth anymore.

N.O. ONE

I know Murphy's parents were responsible for what happened to my own parents all those years ago. They didn't want their son having a baby with the spawn of mob scum, so they orchestrated the whole goddamn thing. My parents hadn't just stolen that money I found, the money I believed for all these years was the reason they died, no. The Gallaghers planned everything down to the last detail. Well, except for the whole me getting away thing. But this is why they told Murphy I was dead. Why every record that exists for Jordyn O'Neill says I'm dead.

Then, when they found out I was back on the scene, they paid the Irish an obscene amount of money to try again. Murphy was never supposed to die, I was. Found that out two days ago. Ronan Callaghan, the canary that just keeps on singing.

Hearing that pissed me right off, but I've spent so long being angry, looking for revenge, coming up with reasons that I can't have or do what I want, so I'm glad the Gallaghers died quickly.

I've taken a page from Fizz's book and decided it was for the best. I'm not going to let their quick deaths bother me. Those people didn't deserve to spend another second in my presence, in my daughter's presence.

All this means I'm going to need to get creative to legally keep Hallie, but Glitch and Dmitry said they're working on it so I'm trusting them to have my back—another reason I feel like a douche for doubting what's going on with me and Dmitry.

The speaker in the corner of the room continues to play white noise, the last sound this pair of fucknuts will ever hear.

Petey admitted to helping Cook take out our mafia soldiers, squealing like the little pig he is in hopes of getting off lightly. But he and Cook took out at least twelve of our men, so there was never a "getting off lightly" option for him. What he and Cook hadn't accounted for was me being friendly with Zavier. The fact that I had met and assessed this man myself before any of this even happened meant I could easily get a read on him, and a murderer he is not.

"Wanna play?" I pose my question to Dmitry, unsheathing one of my knives and holding it up.

"Always. Terms?" He's quick to respond, bouncing on his heels in anticipation.

"Hit each target I name without killing them." I shrug.

"What're we playing for?" His question is full of promises only he can make.

"For each target I hit, you owe me an orgasm?" I laugh a little, because that is not usually something I'd come out with, but fuck it, I'm letting my cunt speak for my brain for once.

"Deal. And for every target I hit, I get to give you an orgasm?" He wags his brows, and wow, I foresee a blackout number of orgasms in my future.

"Done. First target, the rope around Petey's right wrist." The trick is to not throw it so hard that it pierces his skin, but hard enough to stick into the thick rope without it falling.

Lining up my first knife, I hold it by the tip before throwing it, watching it spin like a dancer as it flies through the air, perfectly landing in the target rope. There are several ropes intricately holding his body suspended from the ceiling, and I'm making sure to pick targets that won't fuck it up by loosening him completely.

Although, if he falls from that height, in the state he's in, he's a dead man anyway.

Dmitry follows suit, throwing a knife at the target, his blade sitting beautifully next to mine.

"Left Knee." Again, I line up my shot and throw. Perfect. Petey yelps, but it's so faint, so without effort, and

I know that means my knife split skin. The blood now dripping from beneath the rope confirms my suspicions.

"*Tut tut.* Does that make it a fail? Because I'll let you off, Little Demon. You can still have that orgasm." He throws his next blade, and it glides through the air, again, landing perfectly next to mine.

I choose to not comment on my mistake, opting for aiming at Ronan's torture device instead. "Tip of the barrel."

We do this for ten minutes, having to retrieve our daggers a couple of times to keep playing. I'm on for at least thirty orgasms, and as much as I hate to even think it, I hope he doesn't try and fulfill them all at once.

Petey's breathing becomes more ragged than usual, which I know means his death is imminent. This is one of the final stages of starvation and dehydration, along with dizziness and severe muscle loss. It's surprising how little time it takes for a human body to decline when it's not getting the fuel it needs.

Ronan must hear it and he slowly moves his eyes upward to look at his suspended grandson—because, of course I made sure Ronan has a good view of his kin's slow death.

Torture upon torture for this man; I feel like I've truly outdone myself with this one.

"N-no! L-let h-h-him go." Ronan sounds pathetic, his rough, barely-there, breathy voice sounding about as powerful as the flies crawling all over him.

"I had to watch Murphy die. I'm just reciprocating." I laugh, having too much fun watching him suffer.

It would be so easy to kill them now, to end their miserable lives, but I think I can let this drag out for a few more days. Ronan gets to watch Petey die, because he is definitely going first if his erratic breathing is anything to go by.

"I'm bored, wanna come play again tomorrow?" I direct my question to Dmitry and he nods eagerly as I walk over to Ronan with a bottle of water.

Pouring it over his head, I make him work to get any down his throat, allowing the rest to run down his tied-up, fully-clothed body and into the mess building up in the bottom of the barrel.

I don't bother with Petey, he won't last the night, but I'm going to leave him hanging there for Ronan's pleasure.

"See ya in the morning, Ro-Ro. If you can last that long." It's possible that heart failure could take either one of them at any moment, I would just like to be here when the light finally leaves Ronan's eyes.

ONE LOVE

We leave the room and I'm horny as fuck—despite the disgusting smells that have assaulted my senses since we walked in there—but I also want to get back to Hallie. She's spent the day with River, and I don't doubt she's had fun, but I'm conflicted yet again.

Spending time in the torture room with Dmitry has been fun, and I'll forever believe the skull mask over half his face is one of the sexiest things I've ever seen, I just need to do the whole priorities thing. Priorities means I can't get fucked just because I'm horny when I should be spending time with my daughter.

Motherhood is difficult.

"I need to get back to Hallie. Same time tomorrow?" There, I can do that, I'm coming back anyway.

Now outside, Dmitry rushes at me, bending just in front of me and pushing my stomach onto his shoulder, and lifts me like a fucking caveman.

"No more space, Little Demon. Told you I was making dinner for my girls, and Stefano arranged all the ingredients I'll need already." Stefano is Marco and River's house manager, but really, he's more than that. He's a very close family friend and used to be the underboss to Marco's father back in the day. For a man of his distinction, he's a fucking ninja with the ability to appear out of nowhere.

"Now, you, ride that beautiful ass back to Marco's place. I'll see you there." He offloads me onto my Harley, lifting my helmet from where it sits on the tank and sliding it over my head. Then he opens the visor and awkwardly kisses my nose before slamming it shut again.

My muffled response of protest goes unheard as he begins humming to himself and walking to his own motorcycle, picking up his helmet and sliding it on. Damn, he looks sexy with a helmet on. I wonder if he'd keep it on to fuck me sometime?

It's just as well he doesn't hear my protests, because I know he wouldn't pay attention anyway. Here he goes again...pushing me. Challenging me.

And I hate myself for loving it so damn much.

The warehouse is cold this morning, a chill in the air as I walk into the torture room alone while Dmitry has gone to get breakfast kolache. I'm fucking addicted to the pastry.

Petey is dead, his limbs limper than usual, his skin so pale it's almost see-through, and I slide my gaze over to Ronan.

He's so close to death it's not even fun anymore. I don't want him to pass peacefully in his sleep.

"Wake up!" My yell echoes around the room, stirring Ronan, and his eyes slowly open into dark slits.

His mouth is so dry and cracked he can barely move it, so I pick up one of the water bottles from the cabinet in the corner of the room. I do the usual, pouring it over his head, watching his tongue poke out and his mouth open as he tries to get as much of it down his throat as possible—it's not a lot. He's so fucking pathetic. I'm done with spending my time making sure he's suffering. I'd rather be spending it with Hallie. As much as she loves spending time with River and Polo while I'm working, I control my own hours. Which is just another reason I should just fucking end this douche now.

"Wh...B-b-b-itch..."

"Yes, I am." I laugh, a dark lilt to the tone, pulling a knife from my hip and oh-so-slowly dragging the blade across Ronan's throat. I don't go deep enough to make his death quick, enjoying watching him struggle, moving his head from side to side, gurgling incoherent noises. Blood falls from the wound, covering his throat and his already-dirty white shirt, dripping down into the cesspit of his waste.

It takes about two minutes for the light to finally leave his eyes, and the satisfaction of how much he's suffered over the last six days makes me happy that Dmitry is on his way with food...and his cock.

Chapter Twenty-Three

D

"Wait, that makes no sense," Hallie says as she lays out the oversized blanket on the recently-cut grass in Central Park. I demanded—that's right, I demanded and survived—that J let Hallie spend some quality time with her newly found step-dad. She may have growled and threatened my balls on a few occasions if I dared say those words to her daughter. Apparently, I'm the only one ready for a family around here. That's okay, it's only been a month since this little teenage hellion has returned and I don't think I've ever been happier. Now, July in The City? That's a whole other beast.

"It's marketing genius all the way back to nineteen seventy-nine. An epic space opera. Focus on the 'epic'." I flop down onto the blanket after placing the bag full of munchies Stefano prepared for us. That man is a godsend. A little creepy with his sudden appearances, and I'm convinced at this point that there are secret passages all around the Mancini mansion, but I may try to bribe him to come live with us. Although, our kolache breakfast tradition will stay exactly as it is.

"But why didn't they just make the first movie and then move on from there? All this does is confuse people."

Clearly, I need to be more convincing with my explanations.

As people begin to gather around, taking up more and more space around us, I turn to Hallie and put on my serious face, ignoring the recoils of the good folk of New York when they see my scar. I'm used to it but I don't want it to be a problem for my step-daughter. Fuck, I love the sound of that. Okay, one thing at a time.

"Episodes one, two, and three were filmed and put out after episodes four, five and six. Chronologically, the story doesn't match the real-time filming. I'm guessing it has to do with not anticipating the absolute masterpieces they were making."

Hallie rolls her eyes and bites into an apple. I frown.

"Please tell me he's put unhealthy snacks in there." Rummaging through the bag, I find fruit, nuts, and...are those raisins? I shudder.

"Nope. Stefano doesn't believe in unhealthy snacks."

My expression must be hilarious because Hallie starts giggling around a mouthful of apple. I'm not joking. Stefano's invitation is officially revoked.

No unhealthy snacks. What is this? We're in America, dammit. Snacking is our God-given right.

Reaching into my private emergency stash, I pull out a jumbo-sized pack of Twizzlers and grin. "Good thing I'm always prepared." We smile at each other and, in that moment, a little thread of gold is weaved between us, creating our own little bond.

"To be honest, I'm more of a *Star Trek* fan. Chris Pine is so hot."

My head snaps to the side as I stare, dumbfounded, at her.

"You can't...he's not...That's not how this works, Hallie. You can't just choose a side based on an actor's looks. There's a philosophy to it all, a conscious choice to stand with the rebels and fight dictatorships all across the universe." Okay, I may be getting a little animated here, my hands moving like I'm suddenly one hundred percent Italian and my voice rising to an octave from the time before my balls dropped. "And to be clear, Harrison Ford was also hot." I think?

"Eww, he's old." A string of Twizzler is getting chomped by her front teeth as she speaks like she isn't destroying my soul.

"No, Hallie. He's...timeless." I may have to revisit this whole step-dad thing. There's a chance I'm awful at it.

When Hallie bursts out laughing, her finger pointing at me like she's just made the greatest joke in the world, I start to understand the trap.

"Hmm, she put you up to this, didn't she?" Dammit, I knew I shouldn't have explained the whole debacle to J, she loves to see me suffer.

"Oh my God, you should have seen your face. She was right though. You get all tense and red and your eyes look like they're about to bulge out. You must really love Chewbacca."

I narrow my eyes at her. "He's the secret weapon. Always." My words are muffled around a Twizzler.

"Kinda like you, huh?" I freeze at her words. My entire existence is suspended in mid-air whereas she's just staring at the giant screen they've set up on the landscape right off Sheep Meadow and the Seventy-second Street Cross Drive.

Those words mean something to me. It feels like an acceptance, a hand held out for me.

"Is it too soon to say I want to be your step-dad?" Fuck me, I pinky promised J I wouldn't. Goodbye balls and any hope of having more children.

Hallie turns to look at me, mid-bite, then faces the screen once again.

"Too soon." My bravado deflates a little at her admission. Oh, hope, you heartless wench. Then again, she's probably right…way too fucking soon. "Ask me again after I visit my dad."

Instead of ruining the moment with words, I'm saved by the projection as the signature opening crawl of the movie starts running across the screen, giving the run-down of the galaxy and just how far away it is.

Not twenty seconds later, the warm, familiar, smell of leather hits my nostrils at the same time as a rare July breeze coasts across my face. My Little Demon is somewhere around here. Before I have the chance to do a quick scan of the lawn, I hear a deep voice calling out. "Watch it! You're in the way."

I tense, checking on Hallie first, but she's just whipped her head around and I swear to fuck that tiny scowl on her face is a Jordyn trademark.

"He's talking to your mom, huh?"

"Yup."

"Did she freeze in her tracks?" Please say no. Pleeeease just say she's headed straight for us.

"Yup." I sigh. Someone's about to lose a body part.

Twisting back in the direction of the voice, I first grin at how fucking hot my woman is, then I stand to make sure she knows I've got her back. Not that she needs it.

"Whattaya lookin' at, lady?" the guy says as J visibly tries to hold herself back. I get it now, I really do. When she'd told me she didn't "do people", I thought maybe she just needed to get used to the idea. Nope, her trigger finger is way too itchy for her to be out in public with drunk idiots. Too many fucking witnesses with an impossible clean-up job.

"Is there a problem?" I take a step forward, my voice strong, and I can see we're gathering the attention of...oh, I don't know, about a hundred people around us? Fucking awesome. Worse, though, is J's scowl aimed at me.

Pointing to my chest in surprised innocence, I mouth, "What?" I know what. Nobody needs to come to J's rescue, but come on, now I wanna have some fun too.

"Yeah, you need to keep your gal in check there, buddy. She's ruining everyone's night." At this idiot's words, we both turn, oh so slowly, to look at him, and I'm pretty sure I hear him tinkle in his man panties.

Jordyn takes one step toward him when Hallie's voice rings out. "Mom! I'm bored." Oh, you little genius. Also, not fucking cool. There's nothing boring about *Star Wars*, but I get it, I get it. Chewbacca takes one for the team.

With a snarl aimed his way, we return to our blanket, gather our shit, and walk away from my favorite marathon in the world. The kind that doesn't involve running, 'cause that shit's for masochists.

One arm around Hallie's shoulder, J walks past the dude without giving him a second look. The moment's passed and her priority is now her daughter. Me, on the other hand, I don't have that kind of distraction but I can be the better man.

"Little bitch." His low murmur hits me just as I'm passing him so I do the only logical thing.

The heel of my boot presses just enough on his balls to get his undivided attention.

"What was that?" I ask, my hand on my ear as if to amplify the sound.

"What the fuck?"

"Nah, I don't think that's what you said." I press a little harder.

"Nothing, man. Fuck."

"Is this your man?" I look over at the tiny little woman whose eyes are bulging right out of her head in shock and fear. She nods.

"Do you have children?" She shakes her head.

"Do you want children?" There goes the nodding again.

"Hmm, I'm a generous guy. Next time you want to insult a lady, think about your future children and the fact that you may have lost them today." Pressing just a little to make my point, I grin, wink, then step away under the moans and curses of half the nearby spectators. There are phones pointed our way, no doubt about to go viral, but I'm careful to hide my face enough not to get caught full on.

When we reach J's bike, Hallie grabs the helmet we bought for her a few weeks ago from the top case. It took me two hours to convince J to buy it using the argument that Hallie's safety was more important than the aesthetic of the bike. I may have insulted her, but before she could maim me, I kissed the fuck right out of her and she forgot to be pissed.

"Meet me back at my place? I wanna show you something." With my hands shoved deep inside my jeans pockets, I'm suddenly nervous, worried this will all backfire on me.

J looks at Hallie who shrugs. Fucking teenagers and their ability to say a thousand words with one gesture. Problem is, depending on their moods, those words could be a million different things, which means the probability of getting it right is next to nothing.

"Hey, Kid, I don't speak teen yet. Is that a yes or a no?" Fuck, I love this woman.

"Sure. Least we could do after ruining his night out." Hallie beams at me, teeth and all. "Sorry about that but we didn't need to have a live action show play out in front of fifty phones over there."

"Hallie to the rescue. You are your mother's daughter...Sugar Booger?" I'm still trying out new nicknames. Fuck, this is hard, man.

"If you EVER say that to me again, I'll knee you in the man-parts."

I cringe. Definitely her mother's daughter.

"So that's a no, then."

J shakes her head and pats the seat behind her. "Still want the package deal, Stalker?"

I grin. "More than ever. Okay, just sent you the pin to my house. You'll get there before me but...don't freak out, okay?" Angling her helmet to the side, I place a soft kiss on her neck, ignoring her tiny growl-turned-moan, then step back as Hallie gets on the bike, holding out her hand. I kiss the back of it and wink at her.

"See you soon, drive safe."

By the time I make it to my truck and battle through New York traffic, it takes me almost an hour and fifteen minutes to get to my place. Before now, going home was just a pitstop to more important things, but everything's changed these last six or so months.

I met the love of my life. Stalked the love of my life. Fucked the love of my life senseless on many different surfaces. Met the love of my life's daughter and fell in love with her too.

Having a home seems like the next step but I'm an eager man with the patience of a two-year-old and J's more of a dinosaur with the skittish tendencies of an alley cat. Okay, that analogy just escaped me but my point is…I can't fuck this up. It has to be perfect and I know for a fact that the only way to make my kitty happy is get the mouse on board.

My cute little mouse with the perfected eye-roll.

ONE LOVE

To be fair, I may have gone overboard when I decided we'd need a family home. It's not like I don't have the money, and my primary goal was to get Hallie to do the job of convincing her mother for me. I'm pretty sure the pool and fully-furnished basement, or Play Cave as it shall be named, will do the trick nicely.

Just as I pull up to the house, I push the remote for the garage and signal J so she can pull in beside me. Okay, so, she's not gone yet, this is promising.

"Are you fucking serious right now?"

The sigh that escapes my mouth isn't one of surprise or disappointment because I knew this was coming. But hope perked up there for a second.

"Oh my God! This is soooo cool." Oh, Hallie, you are so getting spoiled for Christmas.

"I did say, 'Don't freak out' and it looks like you're freaking out." I high five Hallie, who's practically bouncing on the balls of her feet waiting for me to open the side gate. We could go in through the garage and into the kitchen via the mudroom—of course—but I want to give them the full effect.

"I think this is bigger than the Mancini house," Hallie whispers, her eyes darting all around, taking in the scene, the neighborhood, and the house itself.

"Nah, nothing's bigger than that palace," I say, looking over my shoulder and grinning. "You ready?"

"Yes!"

"Hell no."

Good enough for me.

Walking in through a canopy of trees, we are met with the Belt Parkway lighting up the Mill Basin water. It still takes my breath away, if I'm honest. Nothing wrong with a little quiet and beautiful view.

"Millionaire's Row? Really? I thought you lived closer to the casino in some apartment?"

How do I say this?

"I did but it wasn't family friendly." There, I put it all out there.

"This is definitely better than an apartment." Hallie's jumping around, touching everything from the outdoor oven to the chairs and umbrellas, even dipping her toe in the salt-water pool.

"You know, bribing Hallie to get to me isn't going to work."

"Oh, it might work, Mom. Seriously. I could live here alllllllll day."

Is it possible to do a Christmas in July just for Hallie?

"This is going to be my Hell for all the wrongs I've done, isn't it?"

Hallie and I both roll our eyes in the most dramatic way possible and, just like that, we're allies and my next surprise suddenly doesn't seem so scary.

By the time we visit six of the seven—yes, seven, and I'm not even ashamed—bedrooms, the huge motherfucking kitchen where I plan to spread J out like a fucking feast for my mouth, and the ridiculous amount of bathrooms in this place, we finally come to the pièce de resistance.

"Ta da!" Making a grand gesture of opening the last bedroom door is met with the most satisfying gasp I've ever heard that didn't have anything to do with Jordyn's thighs or tits or ass or...fuck, focus, man.

"This is for me?" Hallie walks in, her bed in a sort of mezzanine with every wall below covered in built-in bookshelves.

"Yes, *Myška*, it's all for you." I didn't even need to search out that little gem of a nickname. It came so naturally that I know it's perfect.

"What is that?" Hallie pulls back, eyes darting from my scarred eye to the other, curiosity etched all over her features.

"My little Myška, my little mouse." Okay, so now I'm nervous.

"My little mouse…Meee-sh-ka." Hallie reproduces my Czech accent almost perfectly. Fuck, my chest burns with pride and love for this kid. "Yeah, I like that one. Thank you for all this, D. It means so much."

Before J sold Murphy's house, I made sure we got all of her books to safety. And by safety, I mean here, in her new bedroom. Although the setup isn't exactly the way Murphy had built it with two bedrooms meshed into one, this one is one giant space that she can decorate herself, but at least her books are already there. Her other personal belongings, she already has at Marco's place. When I said I didn't want to replace her father, I wasn't lying. No one could, he was an incredible man who didn't deserve his fate, but I will honor his memory by caring for her as though she were mine. I may not have known him but I'm pretty sure he'd be okay with that.

With tears gleaming in her pretty hazel eyes, Hallie throws herself at me and hugs me so tightly I almost lose my breath. My tatted arms look so strange next to her pale, flawless skin that I'm reminded of how precious she is, how vulnerable. Life hasn't finished throwing her curve balls, but that's okay, we'll be here to teach her how to hit those motherfuckers and turn them into a homerun.

Together, like a real family, we make some popcorn before I lead them to the basement where the Play Cave is set up, giant screen and all, and we're finally ready to start the *Star Wars* marathon. I'm many things, but a quitter, I am not.

An hour and a half later, Hallie's asleep, her light snores a testament to how conked out she is.

"I'll take her to bed, wait for me in the bedroom?" Leaning forward, I curl my fingers in J's hair, pulling her toward me just as the droid army is completely shut down. Our kiss is lit up by the LED of the television, our mouths sliding smoothly together, tongues dancing without an ounce of pressure or danger or darkness.

No, tonight we taste normality and I can't wait to bury myself so deep inside her that when I pull out, a fraction of her soul stays with me.

Following J as she helps Hallie up the stairs, my mind begins wandering about, planning and plotting, contemplating how many times I can make her come before she passes out from pure exhaustion.

From this vantage point, my shoulder propped up on the door jamb with the entire view of the bedroom available to me, I'm not ashamed of my stalkerish tendencies. Seeing J embrace her role as a mother is a beautiful thing, a pure and unfiltered side of her that she didn't even know she possessed.

Hallie had brought her backpack with her, all her sleepover necessities included just in case they didn't like the house and we'd have to return to Marco's and buy another one in the morning. To be fair, I'm glad they—well, Hallie—loves the house because turning it over now would probably cost me a pretty penny.

Just as she places her things on the dresser, I step away and close the door behind me, offering them their privacy as I make my way to our bedroom.

Minutes later, with my hands flat against the off-white tiles and my head hanging between my arms, I revel in the perfection of this water pressure washing off the hot, humid stench of the New York minute. That's when I feel, more than see, my little demon step into the large Italian shower and wrap her long, strong arms around my torso, pressing her entire front against my soaked back.

"Hmm, nothing better than feeling you skin on skin." She squeezes me just a little tighter before she finally speaks.

"I know I'm not the most emotionally open person out there—" I snort at her assessment then yelp when she pinches my nipple. To be clear, the jury is still out on whether or not I hated that. "As I was saying, I don't always get flowery with my words but I do know this and I need you to know it too. I appreciate you, Dmitry." Oh, fuck. I'm not talking or interrupting or, hell, I'm not breathing for fear she'll stop. "I appreciate your creepy tenacity because it means I don't have to ever ask, you just...get it." I lean on one arm, my free hand clasping hers under the heavy fall of the multiple shower heads so I can lift it up to the middle of my chest and press hard against my sternum. Still, I don't speak. "I appreciate that you never forget that we are two, a package deal, suffering from similar wounds that may or may not ever heal." Fuck, my heart is beating so fucking hard I'm worried it'll just take off and do a loop around Mars just for shits and giggles. "But mostly, I appreciate you for giving me all of you. No lies, no secrets, no ulterior motives. Just...you."

At this, I turn around, both of my hands now firmly on her wet cheeks, not sure whether it's from the water or from tears. Hell, maybe both. Tilting her head up so she can't miss the intent in my gaze, I notice for the first time in probably ever, the finite part of her that isn't strong. I see the teenage girl inside who suffered, the grown woman who lost deep, the mother who is scared of fucking up. I see the questions and the fears, the relief, too. Because for the first time, in this cocoon where nobody else exists, she can drop her walls and show me the real Jordyn O'Neill and, by fucking God, she's nothing less than breathtaking.

"Hey, listen to me. You and me? We're not perfect. We're a little crazy and a little unstable with a small dose of coo-coo, but we are whole. Our imperfections, when you put them together, create the image of happiness. That's all we can ever wish for, right?"

"Right." Our mouths crash together under the rain of the shower and all thoughts of thank you and all that shit fly out the proverbial window. Pushing her back against the opposite tile wall, it's my turn to press against her skin. To rub my front against her front. To push my cock between her legs and swallow her gasp as though it were my own.

No more witty one-liners, no more smart-ass remarks. Right now it's about us, about this moment where our lives finally converge into one unit. One family. One love.

Falling to my knees, I take one leg and hitch it up over my shoulder as my mouth takes a moment to worship her pussy, all pretty and pink and so fucking eager for my tongue. Even in the steam and rain, I can see her cum seeping down the inside of her thighs and the sight does something primal to me. It awakens that deep, animalistic, part of me that likes to watch her be herself. Her true, violent, and hardcore self. The part of me that knows I'm in love with a woman who has too many facets to count and that's okay. I'll spend the rest of my life getting to know every one of her nooks and crannies.

But first, I'm going to start right here and make sure she knows I'm addicted to her taste and a goner for her pussy.

As my lips suck hard, my tongue lapping up every drop of her, she fists my wet hair and starts riding my face like a fucking cowgirl on speed and it's glorious. The house is huge so she doesn't even bother trying to be quiet, which means the tiled room is amplifying her moans and when they reach my ears they just turn me on tenfold.

When she comes, she comes with her entire body. Shaking and groaning, her fingers nearly ripping my hair from my scalp. Do I care? Fuck no. Not when J is nothing less than open to me.

As she lifts her leg from my shoulder, I get back up, facing her, and grin.

"Wanna share my meal?" I don't wait for an answer and let our lips and tongues do all the communicating. "Turn around, Little Demon, my dick's begging to get inside."

Not a second's hesitation from J. She turns, spreads her legs, and arches her back like a good girl about to get filled up like a bad girl. After all of the emotional unpacking from mere minutes ago, we're both ready to just fuck it all out. This is one of our love languages and her consent is as beautiful as any *I love you* she could ever speak aloud.

This round is hard and fast, her pussy taking me deep, squeezing my cock like it wants to choke it dry, and I just might let her. Wrapping one hand around her wet braids, I pull her head back while gripping her hip with my other fingers. It's a bruising fuck, a fuck that owns and takes and delivers a million promises of darkness and lust. A fuck that comforts her shadows and heals her wounds.

And I'm the one who can give her all that. Me.

"I need you to come all over my dick, Little Demon. Show me that you're having the time of your fucking life. Pun. Intended." My hips are slamming into her ass, the *slap, slap, slap,* of skin on skin is the most erotic thing I've ever heard with the water making the sound louder and louder.

"Fuck, Dmitry, fuck!" And there it is, her entire body tensing, shaking, then releasing with an audible hitch to her breath that transforms into a long, howling plea for more or stop or I don't fucking know because I'm coming completely undone. I think I growl, an actual animalistic sound that's somewhere between a hungry beast and whimpering puppy. Jesus fucking Christ, I will never take a normal shower again.

"Fuck, baby. Can you promise me that every time we shower, we get complementary orgasms?" Then she does something so rare it stuns me silent.

Jordyn laughs. A laugh so carefree and natural and young that it takes me aback. It shocks me into some kind of alternate world where the mafia and the killings and the...fun...doesn't exist.

"Yeah, Stalker Boy. Showers and orgasms are on the daily menu." I grin when she turns back around and bites my lower lip.

"Let's dry off and do that all over again. Except this time I want to tie you up and—" She places her thumb and fingers on either side of my mouth, giving me a fish face before she speaks. I love her playful, it makes my dick hard.

Okay, everything she does makes my dick hard but that's beside the point.

"If anyone's getting tied up, *baby*, it's you." Well, fuck. Okay. I'm down with that.

By the time we'd dried off and jumped on the bed, my dick was already eager for round two. For the first time, the foreplay comes only from her and it's fucking amazing.

True to her word, my little demon ties me down like a pro. Between the belts and the scarves, she ties my wrists to the headboard and my ankles together as she kisses and licks and bites every available inch of me, before bringing her mouth to my dick and sucks any remaining cum she can find.

Then she does some crazy fucking trick with her tongue on my little cum slit and my dick goes full mast ahead, sailing like Jack Sparrow chasing his rum. Better than anything is my little demon swallowing every fucking drop of it.

As soon as she releases my bindings, I flip us over until I'm propped up on my elbows and looking down on her. "You're really good at that, Little Demon. But I think you need more practice. Same time, same place tomorrow?" We chuckle at that as I bring my mouth to hers and it's my turn to taste myself on her lips. And we taste fucking fantastic if I say so myself.

As my entire body lies on top of Jordyn, my cock slipping inside her wet and tight little cunt, I search her blue eyes for something, anything, that would give me more hope than just fucking. Like a small flicker of blue light, she gives me exactly what I need in a way that is purely Jordyn O'Neill.

"You can stop looking at me like that. Yes, I love you. Whatever, get over it. And I need to pee." Fuck, I love this woman.

"I don't know what you're talking about. I already knew that the first time I fed you kolache. It's my secret weapon." My wet, spent cock pulls out of her warm, tight little pussy as I roll over to allow her access to the bathroom, watching her ass bounce from one side to the other with every step she takes.

"Stop creeping on me." I laugh just as her phone starts ringing. "Can you see who it is, please?"

My entire body is like jelly but I'm quick enough to reach it before the last ring.

"It's Crank." But just as I answer, the phone stops ringing.

Then starts up again.

Guess duty calls for my pretty little Reaper. Fuck.

"Answer it, I'll be there in a sec." I can hear the toilet flush and by the time I press the green call button, the sink water is running.

"What's up, Crank?" There's a second's pause, probably the time it takes him to realize I'm not J and what exactly he can and cannot tell me.

"I...is J there?" Fuck, I do not like the sound of his voice. Not one fucking bit. Raw and gravelly, like he's been eating hot peppers for the last two decades.

"Yeah, man, hold on." Just as I answer him, J's grabbing her phone, and without any finesse, she dives in.

"What's going on? I thought we had the night off." Naked and fucking gorgeous, she stands at the foot of our bed, probably debating on whether or not to get back into bed or get dressed.

"Fuck." And now I don't like the sound of *her* voice. "What happened?" Taking the two steps that separate her from the mattress, she sinks onto it, her back to me.

In a flash, I'm there, my legs on either side of hers, my ear listening in on the conversation.

"She's gone. Just...gone. I thought she was asleep, you know? She's a napper." J's nodding her head, even though he can't hear her response, but I don't think she wants to interrupt him. "What am I supposed to do now?"

Pulling away, our eyes meet, my confused greens to her watery blues.

Then she mouths one word and I know this is going to hurt her...again.

"Fizz."

Chapter Twenty-Four

J

Physical pain is something I've become accustomed to, but the pain that comes from losing someone you love is excruciating. There are people who have survived more death than me, yes, and I commend each and every one of them who are still standing, breathing, living, because this shit is hard. My stomach revolts, rolling in on itself, and I sip on my water to keep the sick feeling at bay.

I was relatively young when I lost my parents, when I thought I'd lost my daughter and left the love of my life behind, and I used that pain to fuel me. Death became the norm, my world, and I created a whole new family for myself. Then Murphy came back, only to be ripped away from me within weeks of reuniting, but my daughter came back too. This ray of sunshine in a cloudy sky. Again, I let my anger and pain fuel me into making things right, and now...Fizz.

Two weeks ago, she died in her sleep, something about a brain aneurysm that was impossible to detect, and I have nowhere to focus this pain. No way of punishing those responsible. The only silver lining to losing one of the kindest women I've ever known, who looked after everyone before herself, is that she didn't die in pain.

Hallie, Dmitry, and I are at the Reaper clubhouse. After the funeral last week, we decided to have our own private wake for our Fizz. Fiona. We're all sitting around the large table where we have our "family" dinners that Fizz used to prepare, with several containers of various take-out foods strewn about. Our plates are half full, our drinks are almost empty, and conversation is flowing.

"Do you remember the time she walked in on Shoo *jacking off* in the shower upstairs?" Flower mouths the words "jacking off", the way you do when you're trying to say a word you don't want little ears to hear. There are nods and smiles all around as we listen to her reminisce. "She told him that if she caught him holding his sausage hostage in the communal shower again, she'd chop it off and cook it for his next dinner." We all laugh at the memory.

"She would've done it too!" Shoo fake-shudders, sending more chuckles rolling over the table.

Fizz was a formidable woman. She was soft and loving, caring and kind, loyal to her very core, but she was also a force to be reckoned with when it came to getting shit done.

"Her blueberry pie was pure chef's kiss." Binx rubs his stomach at the thought, his eyes closed and a small smile on his face at the memory.

"Yeah, and the raspberry tarts were the fuc—" Tab stops mid-sentence, glancing to Hallie, then me, before grinning with a small shrug. "Her raspberry tarts were the bomb."

I raise a brow in response and subtly shake my head, rolling my eyes a little. The fact that my crew are adapting to this whole having a thirteen-year-old kid around so well only makes it hurt a little more that Fizz isn't here. She'd have fucking loved Hallie.

Though my initial thoughts were to keep Hallie away from the clubhouse, I have since realized there isn't a safer place she can be.

The crew continues to share stories and my girl listens, enraptured by the tales, a huge smile on her face. That smile is everything to me, especially considering what this little girl has been through. She's grown up so much in the short space of time I've known her, and I hate that part of her childhood has been marred by so much pain and suffering. This is why I'm going to continue to do everything I possibly can to make sure she has what she needs. It doesn't mean she'll always be this happy, but she'll always be safe and loved.

Dmitry listens intently to the conversations too. He only met Fizz a few times and they shared some recipes at a family dinner, but his focus is mostly on me. I can feel his gaze burning holes into the side of my head and I turn to him, raising my brows in a silent question.

He grins, that dangerous grin I fucking love, and that's all he needs to do to have my heart beating heavily in my chest. I've been so close to running, to packing Hallie up and escaping from my pain…just to do something, but I know Dmitry would follow me to the ends of the Earth. It's bad enough that I have to bring Hallie into my world, but to bring him into it too feels cruel on my part.

He's been through his own shit and he's come out of the other side of it a relentless, determined, and all-around great man. I just don't know if putting him through my shit is going to be too much. But time and time again, he has proven that these kinds of thoughts are completely unfounded. Without hesitation, he has been here the last few months, for literally anything. He even bought me a special torture device—well, a barrel, but I'm not splitting hairs.

It's these confusing thoughts that had me ready to leave him behind before Fizz died. But if I had done that, I know I would've regretted it. I don't want to be that person who runs away from what could potentially be a lifetime of happiness because I'm trying to protect him. This random tragedy, losing Fizz, has only cemented the fact that death can happen anywhere, at any time. Staying away from Dmitry won't secure his safety. But if the three of us stick together, we can do fucking anything. I know it.

It feels selfish to love him this much. I never thought it would be possible for me to love someone else after Murphy, especially not so soon. Murphy still does and always will hold a piece of my heart, but Dmitry has helped to glue it back together, piece by gruesome piece, and his hold on it is solid, unwavering.

My baby girl could have kicked up a fuss about Dmitry, could have wanted nothing to do with him, and I would have totally understood her position, but the fact that she's strong enough to accept such change after losing everything she ever knew is a testament to how her dad raised her.

As Binx recounts a story about Fizz trying to teach him to bake, I glance over at Crank next to me. We all suspected something had been going on with them for a while so I know he has to be struggling. His facial features are downturned, his dark hair is a mess, and the bags under his eyes could hold Tab inside.

I nudge Crank to get his attention, because it certainly isn't on the story Binx is telling. He lifts his eyes and looks at me, sadness swirling far into the depths. Not having anyone to put in our crosshairs for this is hard on all of us, but I suspect it's hitting Crank the hardest.

"Come help me make some coffee." I practically whisper the words. The drinks are almost empty and everyone will be driving or riding home soon, so it's a good chance to chat. See where his head's at. He nods, just the once, and we both stand. "Going to get the coffee on, back in a sec." I look at Hallie next. "Hot chocolate?"

"Yes, please." She grins wider than before, nodding, and the warmth I get from that is fucking surreal.

Fizz was the emotional support in our group, and while none of us are really talkers, she still always listened. Personally, I feel uncomfortable as shit as Crank follows me through to the kitchen. Cue the most awkward conversation in the world.

"How are you doing?" I keep my back to him, setting up the coffee machine and pulling mugs out of the cupboard.

He sighs heavily behind me. "Yeah, good."

I turn then, facing him, watching him solemnly leaning back against the kitchen worktop.

"Bullshit. One thing we don't do, Crank, is lie to each other. We may omit information from time to time, but we never lie." We also don't really do emotions and all that comes along with it, but I'm a responsible capo and these people are my family.

Crank lowers his eyes to the floor, shaking his head, and huffs. "What do you want me to say, J? That she was my everything? I loved her? And now I'm breaking inside. My heart physically hurts, J. So much that I can barely breathe. Every time I close my eyes, she's there, lying next to me, her dark curls tickling my nose when I wrap my arms around her. I can't fucking live without her, J." His voice is raspy, but it's full of anger, and I get it. I really do. I have felt all of those things, been where he is. He just needs something to focus this pain on rather than himself, because I am not losing anyone else any time soon.

"You *can* live without her. You're doing it right now. It's hard as fuck, but you're strong as fuck." I'm not exactly eloquent or full of wisdom, but he's listening, because he huffs a laugh and shakes his head again, lifting his eyes to meet mine.

"Fizz used to say that I was strong as fuck too." A small smile ghosts his lips.

"Well, there you go then. You wouldn't wanna make her a liar, would you?" I pour the coffees and prepare the hot chocolate, my tone firm. I think someone has bought a new variety of coffee beans because this smells a lot different than our usual brand.

"You know you're shit at this whole talking thing, right?" Crank laughs. It's low and light, but it's there.

"Yeah, but you're smiling, so I'll take it as a win." I shrug, placing the now-full coffee cups on Fizz's favorite serving tray, tilting my head toward the door for him to follow me out. "Meet me at the cage tomorrow, bring your gloves," I call back.

Dmitry grips my wrist once I put the cups down, pulling me onto his lap and wrapping his arms around my waist, squeezing me tightly. I smack his arm in jest before my stomach really turns and I have to excuse myself, almost leaping from his knees for the bathroom.

"Stay there, my little Myška, I'll make sure Mom's okay." Dmitry's voice is strong and soft all at once as he speaks to Hallie before following close behind me.

He's quick to keep up with me, holding the bathroom door open as I rush in and fall to my knees in front of the toilet. My hair is already pulled back from my face in my regular French braid, but that doesn't stop Dmitry from holding the end so it doesn't flip over my shoulder. He rubs my back as the contents of my stomach erupt from my throat, giving me zero space, and I don't hate it.

The Chinese food I forced myself to eat earlier clearly hasn't agreed with me, but I haven't been sick like this since forever.

Since...

Oh, fuck no.

Epilogue

D

Nine Months Later

"Holy shit, baby, I can see the top of its head!"

"Sir, we're going to need you to step away now."

My head snaps up from the captivating view of my kid being born long enough to narrow my eyes at this dude who clearly attended the University of Dipshit, in NoBedsideMannersLand.

Jordyn's got a death grip on my hand, and by death grip, I mean I'm pretty sure she's actively trying to sever every one of my nerve endings with her claws. I'm not kidding, pregnancy made her nails grow like they had one fucking mission…dismember me right here, right now.

But that's okay. I'll fucking take it and more.

Back to this so-called doctor.

"That's my baby trying to push its melon-sized head through my wife's vagina—"

"Not your fucking wife." I ignore Jordyn's love language, giving her a tiny squeeze since it's all I'm capable of doing at this point.

"Tomayto, baby. Toe-May-Toe."

"Yes, I understand that but I need to get between your wife's legs—" Oh the motherfucker did NOT just tell me that.

"Not his fucking wife."

"Not for lack of trying!" I throw back at her, my death glare firmly fixed on this nutwit.

"Sir?" A tall nurse with eyes like a doe, kind and patient, pats me on the shoulder and leans in.

"Yes?" I answer, moving back an inch.

"Jordyn needs your full attention right now, okay? Baby Novák is in good hands and you can cut the umbilical cord when the time comes, okay?"

I nod because I can't take my eyes away from my incredible little demon who's about to push an entire fucking baby out of her...but how? How does she not pass out from this pain? By the time we made it to the hospital, because Jordyn's pain threshold is a little superior to most humans, it was too late for the epidural, so she's going full Rambo on this one. Hell, I'm sure she would have laughed at my ass for even suggesting it.

"Okay, Jordyn, I need you to hold it...breathe, breathe, breathe. Now...push hard and long." Jesus fucking Christ, hard and long? I do NOT need this dude using that kind of language while he's got his face all up in J's hoohah.

But then Jordyn reaches behind her head, fingers wrapping around the metal board while the other hand almost rips mine from my wrist. Just then she breathes, breathes, breathes and with the force of a fucking lion, she takes in a final deep breath, screaming long and loud and hard and holy fucking mother of my child, her scream is replaced by the most beautiful, most amazing sound I've ever fucking heard.

We lock eyes, Jordyn and I, a tiny moment for just the two of us before our entire world swells with more love than we could ever imagine.

"It's a girl! Welcome to the world baby Novák!" I see the moment a tear falls from J's left eye and it's the exact same moment one falls from mine.

"Nováková," I say, a little dazed, as the nurse brings the baby to J, all gooey and bloody and wet and holy shit, she has the lungs of an Olympian swimmer. Usually, last names in the Czech Republic, like most other Eastern European countries, would change according to sex. J and I decided not to follow that tradition but I wanted to honor my roots for just that moment in time. My parents will be proud and are eager to meet my girls. In fact, they should be landing from San Francisco in about three hours.

"Oh, I'm sorry, I thought it was..."

"It is, it is." I lean in, the confused nurse and the rest of the world ignored, kissing my woman's sweaty brow, then whisper, "Thank you, you were awe-inspiring. You gave us a baby. A baby girl."

Forehead to forehead, we both close our eyes before I back up and we stare at our perfect creation. She's tiny and completely fucking bald and I wonder if she'll stay like that. Until she opens her eyes and all I see is blue, blue, blue.

And for the third time in my life I fall completely and utterly in love.

"Welcome to the world, Kiara O'Neill Novák."

Six Months Later

When Jordyn works all night on a clean up with her crew, I make sure the kolache is fresh for when she walks in the door. Kiara is in a baby sling wrapped around my chest as I move around the kitchen, turning on the coffee pot at the sound of J's Harley out front.

"Mom's home!" Hallie skips into the kitchen, practically skidding to a stop beside me to kiss her baby sister on the forehead. "Any apricot, D?" She peeks around to the pastries on the counter and I grin, passing her the apricot one.

"I made this one especially for you, my little Myška. Wanna lose at COD when Kiki goes down for her nap?" I ruffle her blonde hair, careful not to jostle Kiara while I pour myself and J a fresh coffee.

"You wish. I'm gonna kick your ass." Her voice is strong, determined, and full of laughter, which is abruptly paused when J walks into the kitchen.

"You're going to what now?" J's brows are raised, her hands on her hips, her stern face with the hint of a smile staring directly at Hallie.

"Sorry, Mom." Hallie sighs, still grinning as she turns to me again. "I'm gonna castrate you." She laughs again, skipping back out of the kitchen and high-fiving her mom on the way out.

That's when I spot a dark fleck on J's cheek, just below her left eye. "Come here, Little Demon."

"Why? You gonna spank me again? You really should wait until the kids are asleep." She smiles, sauntering over to me with a swing to her hips that can make a man drool.

She looks tired, but happy, and as I stand directly in front of her, Kiara between us, I cover Kiara's curious gaze with my left palm, licking the pad of my thumb before wiping away the small drop of blood on J's face.

"There." I lean down slightly, kissing her softly because anything more with a baby between us is impossible.

"Thanks." She smiles up at me before putting all her attention on Kiara. "And how's my tiny baby this morning? Come to Mommy."

I help J unwrap Kiara from her sling, watching as she snuggles our baby girl into her chest, sniffing up the baby smell that still lingers.

I'm not sure how I managed to get so lucky with three beautiful girls to love, but I do know I'm never letting them go. Which is exactly why I have a plan today.

"Here, eat this and go shower, Little Demon." I shove the lemon curd kolache into her now-open mouth, smiling as she shakes her head in disbelief.

"I'm going, I'm going." Her words are mumbled around the pastry and she passes Kiara back to me, kissing us both on the cheek before leaving the room.

"Okay, tiny one, time for Plan Get Mommy To Not Kill Daddy," I whisper to Kiara, holding her high in the air, and she giggles. One of the sweetest sounds known to man.

Picking up my phone, I send a text to River to let her know J is home and we're ready. The reply is instant and I head to put Kiara down in her bouncy chair in the game room where Hallie is waiting for me. The game system is all set up and I drop into one of the gaming chairs, picking up a controller.

"Ready to lose?" Hallie looks to me and grins.

We play for ten minutes before J rushes in to whisper in my ear, "I need to go and meet Marco for something. I'll be back in about an hour." Then she kisses me on the corner of my mouth, moving to Hallie next, finishing with Kiara.

"See you soon, Little Demon."

"See you soon, Mom."

Hallie and I feign interest in the game, as though we're too engrossed to offer her a proper goodbye, both of us barely glancing in her direction.

As soon as the front door clicks closed, we turn the game off, put the controllers down, and grin at each other. It's go time.

"Come on, my little Myška, to the Batmobile!" I stand with one hand on my hip, pointing my other hand toward the sky, and Hallie laughs, stripping off the bathrobe she's been wearing to reveal her pale-green dress underneath.

The color choice was her own, as was the dress itself, with the tulle falling to just below her knees.

After strapping Kiara into her car seat, I climb into the driver's side of my car and nod at Hallie in the passenger seat before starting the engine.

It takes thirty minutes to get to Worth Street, another ten to find somewhere to park, and finally, we're walking up the white steps toward the entrance of the Office of the City Clerk. River is waiting at the entrance for us with a double stroller with a beautiful sleeping girl in a green dress matching Kiara's on one side, and she immediately holds out her arms for my baby girl.

"Thank you for this, River." I pass over Kiara and take a deep breath. It's finally happening.

"No problem, D. You know that Marco and I consider J family. That makes you family too now. Does she still not know?" River cuddles into Kiara before carefully strapping her into the spare seat of the stroller.

"Nope." I grin again.

"She's gonna have your balls for this." She laughs, smoothing down the sleek red pencil dress she's wearing.

"Hopefully." I wag my brows and lead the way to our reserved room.

"Do you think she's figured it out?" Hallie asks as we stand, waiting for my little demon after Marco sent her on a little wild goose chase.

I don't have time to answer as the doors open to reveal a vision in black and white standing next to Marco. Holy motherfucking shit, she's stunning. And she has answered Hallie's question all by herself. *She figured it out.*

It's no surprise, my wife-to-be is one of the most intelligent women in the world.

She smirks and raises a brow at me, linking with Marco when he offers his elbow. This bit wasn't planned. I had assumed he'd bring her here and she'd walk through those doors on her own. I also thought she'd be wearing the bike leathers she'd left the house in because a fussy dress isn't usually her style.

But this...this is more than I ever dreamed of. She figured out what was happening and still came. In a fucking beautiful dress.

Now I feel a little underdressed with my faux-tux T-shirt and black jeans.

The world around us falls away and I consider myself the luckiest man on Earth to be watching this woman walking toward me, to marry me. The dress is floor length, hugging every curve on her hour-glass figure and loose around her feet. It's mostly black lace, with a few patches of white sneaking through on the skirt and bustier-style bodice. There has never been a more perfect dress for my wife-to-be.

The Imperial March from *Star Wars* begins playing through the speakers as Marco and J walk toward me, Hallie, Kiara, River, and Aria—Marco and River's new baby girl. I figured this was our song since she never changed her ringtone after I did it for her.

Now standing in front of me, I grip her hands in mine, smiling at her in the way I know makes her knees weak.

"I love you, Little Demon." It's all I can think of to say; she's so fucking stunning it's almost surreal. Knowing she's about to become my wife only makes me want her more.

"I love you too, Stalker." She kisses me, hard and fast, before we finally get married.

After the ceremony, River and Marco acting as our witnesses, Kiara chooses that moment to need attention. I pull her out of the double stroller from next to Aria, resting her on my hip, holding out my other hand for my new wife. She takes it readily and Hallie walks beside us as we leave the room. The next room we enter is the one where we'll be signing Hallie's adoption papers.

While Murphy will always be her dad, this lucky little girl gets the pleasure of having two.

"Congratulations!"

"Holy shit, you're wearing a dress!"

Flower and Shoo's greetings as the doors to the room open are the first thing we encounter, followed by the rest of J's Reapers. I know my little demon will hate the attention on her, but all these people love her so much, it felt wrong to keep them out of such a big moment.

"I'm gonna stab you a little for this later," J whispers into my ear, amusement clear in her tone.

I chuckle, and Kiara gargles something incoherent, reaching out for her mommy. I pass her over and lean into my wife, bring my lips to her ear, and whisper something of my own. "Are you ready for another one yet?"

Her response is immediate and makes my grin widen.

"Fuck off."

If you have read The Escort Series and KOK already... you should read Psycho Hate next!

Remember Aleko Kastellanos...? ;)

https://geni.us/PsychoHate

The Blonde One

Argh! Every time we write a new man, he becomes my new favourite. That being said, I am a total book boyfriend whore, so... ;)

This one took everything we had and some more to make it perfect. We had to do Murphy justice, we had to keep his memory alive, but we also needed y'all to understand he just wasn't right for J.

Dmitry though... *swoons*

After a tough old year, we did it. We finished another series together, and don't worry... we have sooo many more planned for the future. Brunette is not getting rid of me anytime soon. 2024 is going to be a hell of a year for us and releases. So please show all the support you can by checking them out, pre ordering, leaving reviews, and all those things. We'll be forever grateful!

Thank you to all of our readers, each and every one of you, for picking up our stories, for getting involved in our world. It's amazing that even one person did, and we're overwhelmed by the responses we've been getting—in a good way!

Sarah, Hilary, Zoe, you're all bloody troopers! Taking the time to read our words, give us your feedback, and every piece of it was invaluable. However... Imagining Shoo hoovering in a maid's uniform will be an image that follows me around forever! Thanks, Zoe...

David!! (In my head, I always say that like Alexa from Schitt's Creek.) As usual, you're a friggin' superstar. Thank you for making our words shine. We'll buy you a nice new cattle prod next Christmas as your current one must be worn out by now ;) Thanks for not quitting this time! We love yooooou.

To our families... the husbands, the kids, the folk that drive us crazy, but understand it's book-wifey time when Brunette and I are on a video call—which is often!

And to my Brunette, I fucking love you, woman.

THE BRUNETTE ONE

Damn it, Blondie. You've said it all and now I'm just gonna sound repetitive and we all know I hate repetitions! Also, I'm not judging your book boyfriend whorey ways, I approve and predict our next series will be another notch on your fictional headboard.

So, yes, this duet took a lot from us. It was an emotional ride right from the start because we knew before even writing the first sentence how book one was going to end. That anticipation was hell and WE TRIED...WE TRIED SO HARD...to keep Murphy alive but, here's the thing; Murphy was perfect but he wasn't perfect for J. That was the bottom line and we refused to give J anything less than what she deserves.

I know Blondie has thanked our team but I'd like to reiterate and add on...

Hilary, Sarah, and Zoey you have no idea how important your suggestions are for us and we appreciate you to the moon and back.

Daviiiiiiiiiid- To answer your question of "Why are you like this?" I say...because it makes you snort/laugh/wheeze/threaten/scream/choke and we can't get enough of it.

Candi PR- A huge thank you for your professionalism and hard work getting our books out there! You're amazing!

Sam O'Neill- Girl...where would we be without you? In the basement curled up in a fetal position, probably. Thank you for EVERY thing you do. You're the best!

To all of the members in our FB Bada$$ group, y'all are life for us and we appreciate you every single day. Thank you for your support, your love and your outraged messages in our inbox!

Also by N.O. One

Dark Romance

The Escort Series (MF)

The Rich One ~ https://geni.us/TheRichOne

The Kinky One ~ https://geni.us/TheKinkyOne

The Filthy One ~ https://geni.us/TheFilthyOne

The Broken One ~ https://geni.us/TheBrokenOne

The Almost One ~ https://geni.us/TheAlmostOne

The Forever One ~ https://geni.us/TheForeverOne

KOK (RH)

Kings of Kink ~ https://geni.us/KingsOfKink

The Reapers Mafia Crew Duet (MF)

One Kill ~ https://geni.us/TheReapers1

One Love ~ https://geni.us/TheReapers2

The Psycho Trilogy – Sons of Khaos (MF)
Psycho Hate ~ https://geni.us/PsychoHate
Psycho Love ~ https://geni.us/PsychoLove
Psycho Reign ~ https://geni.us/PsychoReign

A Night To Remember - Shared World (MF)
Once Upon A Sale ~ https://geni.us/OnceUponASale
Whole Series ~ https://www.amazon.com/dp/B0CLKVXLXJ

STALK US

Website & Newsletter: www.author-no-one.com

Facebook: https://geni.us/Facebookauthor

Facebook Group: https://geni.us/FierceReaders

Instagram: https://geni.us/Instagramauthor

Goodreads: https://geni.us/Goodreadsauthor

Bookbub: https://www.bookbub.com/profile/n-o-one

Linkedtree https://linktr.ee/n.o.one

BOOKS WE THINK YOU SHOULD READ

Dark Romance

DATE WITH THE DEVIL (MF) ~
HTTPS://GENI.US/DWTD

Contemporary

THE UCC SAGA
DISHEVELED ~ HTTP://AMZN.TO/2ARPBXP
DISARMED ~ HTTP://AMZN.TO/2MYVXNN
DISCARDED ~ HTTPS://AMZN.TO/2VWTRPF
UCC BOXSET ~ HTTPS://AMZN.TO/3LJVEPE

STANDALONE
THE WISH ~ HTTPS://AMZN.TO/2FTIKQB

Rom-Com

THE WOOLF FAMILY SERIES
SCREWED ~ HTTPS://GENI.US/SCREWED
SCREWED UP ~ HTTPS://BIT.LY/3IBFWKB
SCREWED OVER (COMING SOON)

Supernatural

SOUL GUARDIANS SERIES
REPRISE ~ HTTPS://BIT.LY/3CT9NPE

Eva LeNoir
Fun Flirty Romance

OTHER HUDSON INDIE INK AUTHORS

Paranormal Romance/Urban Fantasy

Stephanie Hudson

Xen Randell

Sorcha Dawn

Georgia Seren Mills

Crime/Action

Blake Hudson

Jack Walker

Contemporary Romance

Gemma Weir

Nikki Ashton

Nicky Priest

Jax Knight

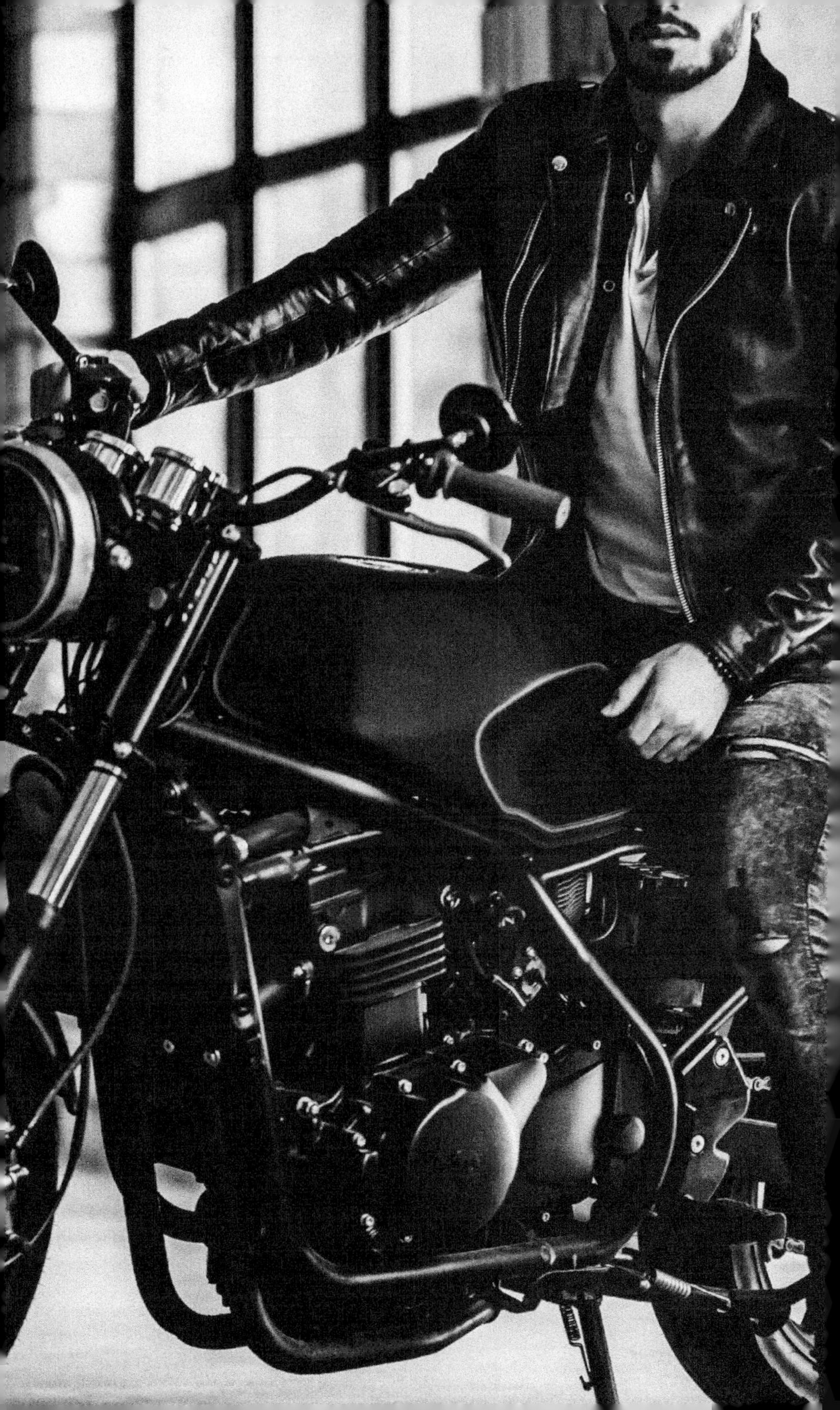

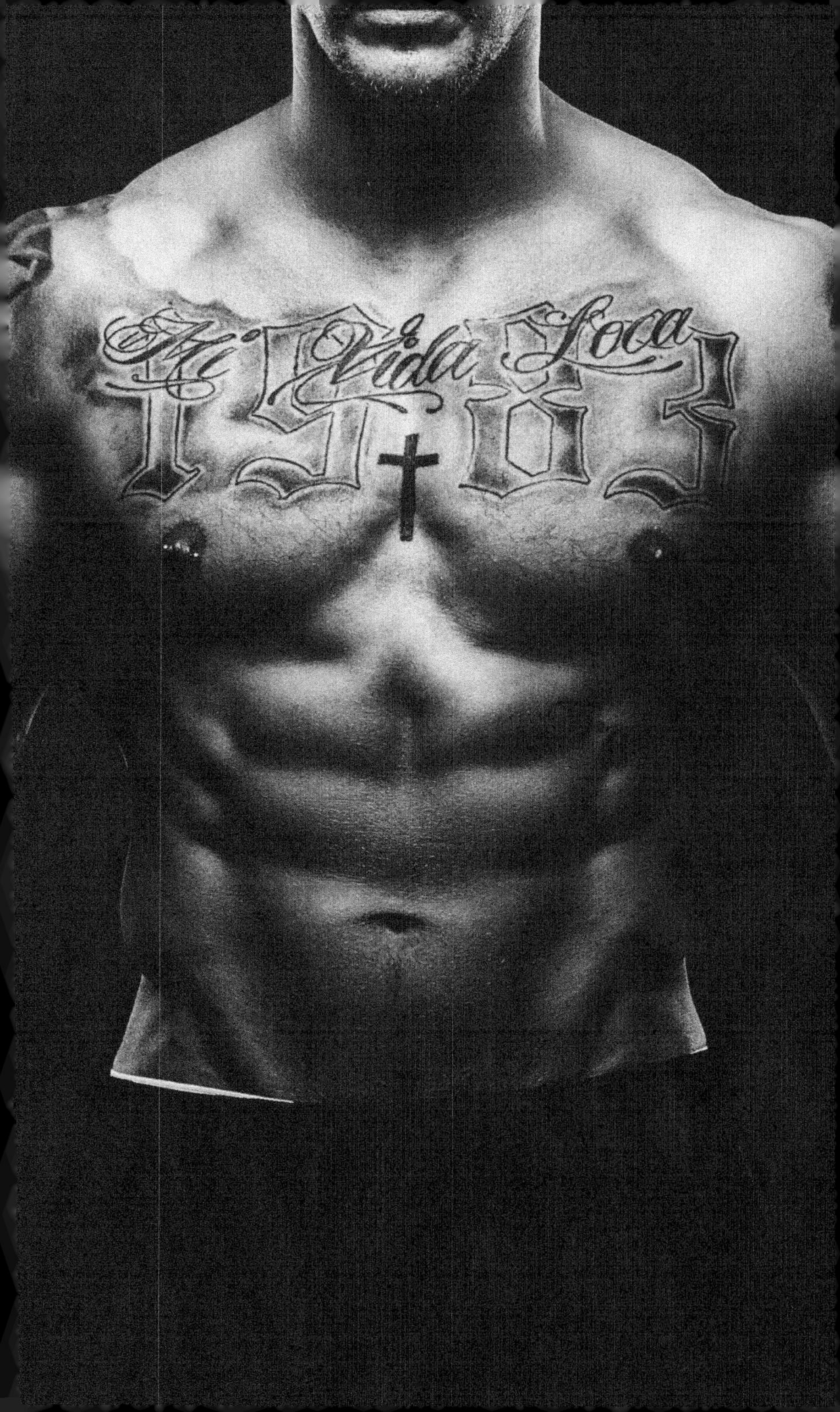
Mi Vida Loca

Printed in Great Britain
by Amazon